BURIED
UNDER
ICE

New York Times & *USA Today* Bestselling Author

CYNTHIA EDEN

PROLOGUE

He was perfect.

Until three months ago, Lark Lawson would have sworn that she'd never fall in love. She'd avoided the situation for twenty-eight years, after all. She'd never *clicked* with anyone. Hadn't felt the insane attraction that was supposed to exist in books. She'd never looked at someone and thought...*I want to spend forever with you.*

All of that had changed when she met Oliver Foxx. FBI Special Agent Oliver Foxx. Smart, loyal, dedicated...and sexy as hell. Oliver had rolled into her florist shop one day and from that first moment when he'd confessed his confusion at picking out flowers for his mother...

She'd started to fall.

The candlelight flickered from the middle of their table. They were currently at a posh restaurant in Vegas. Expensive food. Stunning service. Not that she cared about any of that. But...

This is one of those places where proposals happen. And Oliver had definitely been hinting that he had something major to tell her. Was three months too soon for a marriage proposal?

Maybe but...

But last night, Oliver had finally lost that iron-clad self-control of his. They'd given in to the desire that seemed to pulse beneath the surface whenever they were together. Their passionate kisses hadn't been enough last night. Not for her. Not for him.

And the sex that had followed...

Oh. My. God. She crossed her legs, aware of an ache in her core because...*I want more.* So much more. She'd raked her nails down his back last night. Come for him over and over. And...

I love him. She wanted to tell him that news right then and there. The way she felt wasn't just about the phenomenal sex they'd shared. She loved him.

But the friendly waiter was talking about wine. Her gaze darted from the waiter back to Oliver. She found Oliver's dark, intense gaze locked right on her. For a moment, his handsome face seemed almost...angry, and she tensed. Automatically, she reached out and curled her fingers around his hand as it pressed to the top of the table. Or, rather, as his hand pressed to the white cloth on top of their table. "Oliver?"

He sent her a smile. A tight one that didn't reach his eyes. His head turned toward the waiter. "Just bring us your best bottle of wine, would you? Thanks."

The waiter hurried away.

She kept her hand on top of Oliver's. "Is something wrong?"

A muscle jerked along his jaw as he focused on her once again. "The case I'm working..." His voice came out gruff. "It's been...real brutal."

Her stomach knotted. Oliver worked Violent Crimes at the FBI, and he rarely talked about his work with her. Not that she *didn't* want him to talk about it. She did, but the job required him to keep things confidential. But she knew about the case he was currently investigating. It would be impossible *not* to know. The stories about the attacks had been on the news for months.

Someone had been abducting and murdering women in Vegas. The women—all with dark hair and in their twenties—were later found, strangled, with a coil of white rope still around their necks. And in their hands? A bouquet of white flowers. Mostly roses, but also carnations, peonies, and even hydrangeas. Because flowers were such a big part of her life, she'd zeroed in on the images that had been posted in the media. She'd even thought that maybe she could help Oliver with his case.

But...

During their time together, he'd never asked for her expertise. And, really, what was she going to do in a murder case? A case with an actual serial killer?

The thought of a serial killer hunting in her city had goose bumps rising on her arms. "I know you want to catch him."

Oliver's lashes flickered. If possible, his square jaw hardened even more.

Right. Of course, he wanted to catch the killer. What a silly thing for her to say. Oliver had to deal with the victims' families. He had to see the dead bodies. Lark had no idea how he did the job day in and day out. When you fought monsters all the time, didn't it take a toll on you?

Her gaze darted around the restaurant. Dimly lit. Soft music playing in the background. Couples huddled close together. A romantic night for so many. Only now it seemed...wrong. Wrong when Oliver was surrounded by so much death. She squeezed his hand. "We don't have to be here. Why don't we go to your place and relax in private? Whatever you have to tell me..." Lark licked her lips. "We can do it there."

He glanced down at his watch, then back up at her. "Not time to leave yet."

She blinked. That was an odd thing to say.

He cleared his throat. "I mean, you haven't even had a drink, much less dinner. Besides, I need to be here with you tonight."

I need to be here with you tonight. The words chased some of the chill from her body just as the waiter arrived and opened the wine. He poured with a flourish for them. Normally on their dates, Oliver usually did the whole wine tasting routine. Tonight, he didn't. He didn't even touch the wine that had been poured for him.

She did. She grabbed her wine with her left hand and took a big, fortifying sip. *This is it. You go first. Don't be scared.* Only she'd never actually said these words to a man before...

I love you.

Sure, she loved her twin brother Lane. Absolutely adored him. He'd been her rock for most of her life. When her parents had died, she and Lane had just been teenagers. Thirteen years old. There had been no other close family. Just the two of them. They'd gotten shuttled from foster home to foster home.

They'd been desperate to reach adulthood. To escape that life. To start over.

They had.

Maybe she had trust issues. Maybe she distanced herself from people because she expected no relationship to last. Or at least, that was what a therapist had told her once. Back when she'd been a teen, she remembered overhearing one social worker say that Lark had attachment issues.

And the things the social worker had said about Lane...

No, no, stop it. All of that is over.

She took another sip of wine. Her fingers trembled as she put the glass back down. "I know you asked me here tonight because you had something important to tell me."

His head tilted to the right. The candlelight sent shadows chasing over the hard planes of his face. He really was incredibly attractive. Almost movie-star perfect. The kind of gorgeous you don't see in real life. The kind that caught you off guard and made you do a double—or triple—take.

Tall, well over six feet, with broad shoulders that stretched the black blazer he wore. His dark hair brushed over the back of the blazer, and a lock of hair tumbled charmingly over his forehead. A strong jaw, high cheekbones, and eyes that smoldered. Oliver sort of burned with a barely leashed sexuality.

Or at least, he did to her.

Because whenever she was around him, she felt edgy. On the verge of losing her control. And she valued control above all things. She created schedules. She made daily to-do lists. Her life always followed a plan.

But meeting Oliver had changed all of her plans.

His hand turned beneath hers so that he was now holding her fingers. The light calluses on his fingers slid against her skin.

Heat surged through her. It always did when they touched. "Oliver..."

His gaze met hers. His left hand pressed to the top of the table. His right hand went right on holding hers.

"I love you," Lark confessed. Breathless. Soft. Done.

She smiled as the tension poured from her. That admission really hadn't been nearly as hard as she'd thought. The words had just come out. If you were going to take a leap, why not dive right in?

He didn't smile back at her.

Didn't say the words back, either. And it took a moment for the heavy silence to register.

"I-I just wanted to tell you," she stammered quickly. A stammer that she'd worked hard to overcome. It only slipped out now when she was very nervous or very stressed. "These last few months with you have been wonderful, and I wanted you to know how I felt." Her phone beeped as a text came through. She'd hung her purse over the back of the chair, and the beeping and vibration of the phone made the purse seem to softly pulse.

She ignored the pulsing and the text. This moment with Oliver was more important than anything else.

"I didn't expect you," he said. His voice was rough. Angry? No, surely not. "Never counted on you at all."

That seemed like a strange thing to say. Not incredibly romantic but...

"We need to talk, Lark." Gruff.

She nodded. "That's why we're here, isn't it? You said you had something important to tell me." She smiled at him. "I had something important to tell you, too." And she had told him. *I love you.* After last night, she'd known that holding back with him wasn't an option.

I have never wanted anyone more than I want him. She'd never been so free during sex. Never just let go and let the passion take her.

With Oliver, she didn't hold back. She didn't *want* to hold back. She wanted him. *So say the words.* "I want to go home with you, Oliver. I want to stay with you all night long."

A flash of pure lust filled his eyes. There was no mistaking his need.

Her shoulders straightened as some of her confidence returned. She smiled at him once more. "Now, what did you want to tell me? Or...ask me?"

It's probably not a proposal. Settle down. It's been three months. It's probably not—

But, hell, a girl could dream, right?

Her phone chimed again. And, again, she ignored the text and stared expectantly at Oliver.

"We're closing in on our killer," he rumbled.

Um... "That's wonderful." It was. "I know everyone will feel better when he's locked away."

The killer was a male. At least, according to the profile that had been released to the media, he was. The suspect was most likely a white male, mid-to-late twenties, physically fit, and living in Vegas.

Of course, that profile had matched *thousands* of men in Vegas.

"Most people will feel better." His hand pulled from hers.

Her phone chimed again.

Then immediately...again.

"But there will be some people who are...upset."

Her brows shot up. "Upset that a killer is behind bars and the streets are safe?" A nervous laugh came from her. "I can't imagine anyone feeling that way."

Oliver grimaced. "Don't be too sure," he muttered.

Her phone chimed again.

Unease slid through her. Someone really wanted to reach her. She grabbed her phone out of her bag.

The texts were from her brother.

Lark, I need you at the house.

Emergency.

I need you.

"I'm so sorry," she told Oliver as she swiped her finger over the screen to call her brother. "I have to talk with Lane."

But when she tried to reach him, the phone just rang and rang.

Then voicemail kicked in.

"What's happening?" Oliver asked her.

The waiter edged toward their table. "Would either of you be interested in an appetizer?"

She called her brother again. No answer. Voicemail. "I have to go," she blurted.

The waiter and Oliver both glanced her way.

"My brother—he said there's an emergency at the house. I have to go." She rose. "I'm so sorry. I can find a cab and get home. Eat your dinner. We'll catch up later—"

But Oliver had already stood, too. He tossed some cash onto the table. "Of course, I'm coming with you."

Because that was Oliver. Always ready to help.

One of the many reasons she'd fallen so hard for him.

He'd helped her over and over. Helped clear out old boxes from the house she shared with her brother. Helped to organize items in the basement. He'd even befriended her brother, and Lane was notoriously difficult to approach.

They didn't speak again until they were in Oliver's sleek ride and heading down the wet streets. The rainstorm from earlier had passed, but the dark roads seemed to gleam with a shine from the water.

She tried reaching her brother again. He didn't answer. She fired off a text. *What is happening? Are you hurt?*

Her greatest fear. That her brother would be hurt. He was her only family. They'd looked out for each other for so long.

"I...I didn't get to tell you..." Oliver's voice came slowly. "I *need* to tell you..."

Her left hand curled around his fingers as he gripped the steering wheel.

He braked at a light, and his head turned her way. "I didn't expect you."

Her phone dinged. She'd kept it gripped in her right hand. Automatically, she looked down.

Being arrested. Get to the house. Hurry.

What? *What?* Her breath choked out. "My brother is being arrested! We have to get to the house, now!"

The light changed.

But Oliver didn't move.

He kept staring right at her.

"Oliver?" Lark prompted. "I need to get to my house. Hurry!"

He looked down at her hand as her fingers covered his. "I'm sorry." Low.

So low that maybe she hadn't heard him correctly. "What?"

"I'm so fucking sorry." Then he focused on the road, and he drove them forward.

***

Chaos.

That was what she found when Oliver braked in front of her home on the normally quiet suburban street. Police lights flashed. There was even a big, black SWAT van to the right. Cops were running everywhere.

And...was that a news crew? Stationed at her neighbor's house and filming everything?

She shoved open her door and tried to lunge out of Oliver's vehicle.

But Oliver grabbed her hand. "You don't want to go in there. Just...stay here. They'll be bringing your brother out soon."

She twisted her hand and jerked free of his hold. "What are you talking about?" He *hadn't* talked on the ride over. Not since he'd gritted out that he was "so fucking sorry." Her stomach twisted and heaved, and terror clawed at her. "Who will be bringing him out?"

"My team."

Ice seemed to coat her skin, starting with her face and working to encase her entire body.

Without another word, she jumped out. Then, frantic, she ran for her house.

Only to find uniformed cops blocking her path. One blasted, "This is a crime scene! Stay back! Go with the others!" He pointed to the right.

To the right...where her neighbors stood. Gaping. Recording with their phones. Watching her.

"This is my home!" Lark cried. "Not a crime scene. I want inside. My brother is in there."

"Your brother?" The swirling lights hit the cop's face. "That piece of shit is your brother?"

Her heart slammed into her ribs.

Hands curled around her shoulders, and she flinched in surprise. Automatically, Lark whirled.

But it was just Oliver. "I didn't want you here for this," he said. A stoic mask covered his face. "I tried to keep you away. That's why we were at the restaurant. So you didn't have to see..."

"*Lark!*" Her brother's yell penetrated through the chaos and had her spinning right back around.

Two men in dark suits pushed her brother from the house. Her *cuffed* brother. His hands were behind his back.

She sprang toward him, only to have Oliver lock his arms around her waist and pull her back against him.

"Baby, no," he rasped against her ear. "You can't stop this. You don't know what he's done."

She elbowed Oliver as hard as she could and lunged for her brother. "What is happening?"

A cop grabbed her before she could reach Lane. A much rougher hold than Oliver had used, and he shoved her back. She slipped and fell to the ground.

"*Watch your fucking self!*" Oliver shouted at the cop. "She's not part of this!" He reached for her. Lifted her up. Swept his hands over her as if he was looking for injuries.

She pushed his hands away.

The two men in dark suits—they were hauling her brother toward a patrol car.

"Stop!" Lark yelled.

They didn't.

Her brother craned his head and looked back at her. "Call a lawyer! I tried to tell them they were wrong—I would *never*—they wouldn't listen! I had to sneak and contact you—*they won't listen!*"

The drumming of her heartbeat filled her ears.

One of the men opened the rear door of the patrol car. He put a hand on Lane's head and thrust her brother into the interior of the car.

"I didn't do it, Lark!" Lane shouted. "I swear, I didn't kill those women!"

Those women...

The door slammed. The man who'd put her brother in the vehicle slapped his hand on top of the patrol car. As if he'd been waiting for the signal, the uniformed driver sounded his siren and drove forward.

While her brother, trapped in the back of that car, stared desperately back at her.

The drumming of her heartbeat grew louder and louder. Not just a pounding now. More like constant thunder blasting in her head.

Eyes were on her. She could feel them. Her neighbors. The cops. The reporters.

Oliver.

The two men in dark suits marched toward her. She stiffened as they approached.

"Agent Foxx, we didn't think you'd be at the scene tonight," the taller one said. Tall but lean, with a closely trimmed beard on his face.

"Change of plans," Oliver snapped back. "Especially since you let the bastard *text* his sister. What the fuck?"

The other man—the other agent—grimaced. "We were questioning him. Fool was talking freely, and we didn't realize that he was sending those messages on the sly. Fucking fast with his hands, that one is. He is—"

"You're federal agents." Not a question. Lark barely recognized the frozen, brittle sound of her own voice.

"Agent Theo Tutweiler," the man who'd just called her brother a fool said. He put his hands on his hips, and the move pushed back his coat to show the badge clipped to his hip. And the holster under his arm. "And this is my partner, Jase Guillory."

Jase's gaze swept over her. "Did you know?"

She could only shake her head. "Know...what?"

"That your brother killed all those women. That each time he killed one, he was killing you."

Her knees buckled. She would have slammed into the ground if Oliver hadn't caught her. For a moment, she wanted to lean back against him. To soak up his strength.

But...

"No." She broke free of him. Some blind instinct had her running after the patrol car—the one that had just taken her brother away. Her twin. Her only family.

This wasn't happening. It couldn't be happening.

Wrong.

Wrong.

Wrong.

Her brother...he wouldn't...he would never...

"Lark." Oliver closed his fingers over her shoulder. He'd caught her so easily. "I'll take you to the police station, if that's what you want. But he's going to be booked. You aren't going to see Lane tonight. You...*Lark, look at me.*"

She didn't want to look at him. Her breath heaved in and out. In and out. But her gaze—her traitorous gaze—locked on his face.

"I suspected for some time, but I recently found the proof we needed. Your brother was just arrested for three murders. Do you hear what I'm saying? Do you understand?" His voice hardened. "I got you away tonight so you wouldn't witness all of this. He wasn't supposed to text you—I was going to tell you about his arrest after he'd been taken into custody."

He didn't take me to that fancy restaurant to confess his love. He took me there so I wouldn't be in the way when his men arrested my brother.

"The plan went to shit," he growled. "You got the messages from him, you were coming here, and I...fuck me, I didn't tell you before we arrived, and I should have. I should have. I should have—"

Her body wasn't cold. It was numb. The chaos around her? It no longer registered. "You think my brother is a serial killer."

"It's not what I think. It's what the evidence—"

"How long...how long did you suspect him?"

His grip tightened on her. "We shouldn't talk about this out here. You have to be questioned, but I've told my men to wait. You need some time. I'll take you to a hotel and you can rest. Tomorrow will be soon enough for the interview with you."

I've told my men... His orders. Oliver's plans. "You did...all of this."

He stepped closer. Big, strong, lying Oliver stepped closer.

"How long did you suspect him?" she asked again, but the knife that had just stabbed into her heart told her the answer even before he said—

"Before I ever walked into your flower shop."

Of course. Of course, that would be why he'd come into the shop. Tears slid down her cheeks. She wished that she could have blinked them away, but it just wasn't possible. They poured too fast from her eyes. "He's my only family."

"He's a *killer*."

She shook her head. "He wouldn't hurt a woman. Not ever."

"He did. We found evidence. Hell, *I* found evidence when I was going through those boxes in your basement—"

She was almost physically sick. Right then and there. Her hand flew to cover her mouth even as she swallowed frantically.

"Lark?"

He'd been searching her house. Not helping her. Never helping her. "I thought...tonight, I thought we went out...you said you had something to tell me..."

His jaw tightened.

"Something important to say to me...To ask me." She'd foolishly thought he might be proposing. *How* had she thought that? How?

"I needed to tell you about your brother, but I couldn't tell you *before* he was arrested. I had to wait. Thought I'd get the call long before we left the restaurant."

Another tear trickled down.

"And what I wanted to ask...It is important. Damn important." He finally let go of her shoulder. "It's...will you forgive me?"

She could not move.

"Because I know this thing between us started—it started with me working beneath the radar and investigating your brother. But I know you didn't have anything to do with his crimes. I know it, Lark. I want you to forgive me and we can move forward and...you said you loved me."

He was throwing that back in her face? Her hand lifted and she realized—

I want to slap him.

No, no, that wasn't her. Her fingers balled into a fist.

"You love me, so...I know it hurts," Oliver stated grimly.

He knew nothing about the pain tearing her apart.

"But we can get past this." A determined nod from him. "We will get past it."

She shook her head. And turned away from him. She put one foot in front of the other. Her gaze darted over the crowd. Landed on nice Ms. Hazel. A bit of a gossip, but she made incredible cinnamon rolls each Christmas. Her heart was good, and...maybe she'd give Lark a ride to the police station.

Because this was a mistake. Her brother was not a killer. He would not have strangled three women.

Never.

And especially not women...*who look like me.*

"Lark..."

Oliver's voice came from behind her. Because he was following her.

"We *can* get past—"

Her steps stumbled to a halt. "You did this." The chaos. The cops. Her brother being led away in handcuffs. "You found evidence when you were using me. You got close to me because you wanted to nail him for these crimes." She glanced over her shoulder.

"We can get—"

"Go fuck yourself, Special Agent Foxx."

Then she walked away from the man who'd just turned her life into a perfect nightmare.

***

Five months later...

"I'm not getting out of here."

She stared at her brother though the glass. Glass, plastic? What the hell was it? Lark wasn't sure and it didn't really matter, anyway. She'd just call it glass. What truly mattered was that she'd come week after week and talked with Lane through the divider. He sat on one side, clad in his bright orange jumpsuit, and she sat on the other. She gripped a phone to her ear and heard his rumbling voice drift to her.

No visitors were actually allowed in a room with her brother. No visitors but his lawyer. Not that there had been a trial, not yet. And there was certainly no bail for him.

A faint bruise slid under his jaw, and a circle of black covered his right eye.

"You were in another fight," she whispered.

"Don't worry about me."

All she did was worry.

"I have a target on me in here. I can take care of myself though."

Her gaze slid to his hand, the one that cradled the phone. His knuckles were red and scraped.

"You need to distance yourself from me," he told her. "If they are tearing me apart in the media, I know they have to be doing the same thing to you."

They were. Her shop had closed. You couldn't sell flowers when there were no customers. Her house had been egged. Bricks had been thrown through her windows. Her car had been keyed. Multiple times. Her tires slashed. "I'm fine," she told him as her left hand clenched.

His eyes closed. "You could never lie for shit."

Her lower lip wanted to tremble. She caught it with her teeth.

"I'm your older brother," he growled as his eyes slowly opened. "You have to listen to me."

Older by three minutes and thirty-two seconds.

"Take care of yourself. Don't crawl into this grave with me."

For a moment, she feared her grip might shatter the phone. "You are not dying in here."

"I am if the prosecutor has her way."

Her breath came faster. "You didn't hurt those women." Her certainty had never wavered. It would never waver.

"I didn't hurt those women," he said, voice flat. "I wouldn't. And going after someone who looks like you? *Hell, no.* Never."

"Someone framed you."

His lips twisted in disgust. "Probably the Fed who was fucking you."

She flinched. *He fucked me and fucked me over. Fucked my whole world to hell and back.* But Oliver wasn't going to win. She would not let him take her brother away forever. "I will find out who did this." Determination filled her voice. It was the same driving determination that helped her get out of bed every morning when she wanted to curl up into a ball and hide. "You are not going to be locked away for the rest of your life." *Or, worse, you will not be executed for something you didn't do.*

"Lark..."

She put her free hand on the glass. "You wouldn't leave me in here."

He shook his head. No, he wouldn't. They both knew it.

"I didn't leave you before," she whispered to him. "I'm not about to do it now."

His hand lifted and pressed over the glass. Right over hers. As close to a touch as they could get.

"I'm going to find the real killer," Lark promised him. "I don't care what it takes. I don't care what I have to do, I am going to find him. You won't go to prison for crimes you never committed. I won't let you."

"Lark—"

"Trust me?"

His hand remained pressed to the glass. "Everyone else thinks I'm a monster. Even my lawyer doesn't want to be near me."

Her chin lifted. "You aren't a monster. You're my brother."

And she would get him out.

She *would*.

She just...

Had to catch the real killer first. "I'll catch him," Lark vowed. "Or die trying."

Alarm flared in her brother's eyes. "Lark, don't you *dare*."

Oh, but she would. She was desperate, and a desperate woman would dare just about anything. "Just wait, Lane. You'll be free soon. I'm going to get the Ice Breakers to help me." She smiled for her brother. She knew he'd heard about the cold case group. Everyone had heard their success stories. "See you next week." She put the phone back into place. Stood up.

His hand remained pressed to the glass.

She turned away. Walked to the door. The guard opened it for her, as he always did. She passed down the long corridor. Headed back through the security intake area. Collected her purse. Her phone. Her keys.

There were more doors. More security checks. But then she was outside. The bright sunlight shone down on her. Her car—with its newly cracked windshield and the wonderful scratch marks that spelled out KILLER on the left side—waited in the lot.

And FBI Special Agent Oliver Foxx waited beside the car. No, actually, he glared at the car.

Then at her. Even though aviator sunglasses shielded his gaze, she could feel the fury of his stare.

"What the hell?" Oliver demanded as she drew closer to him and her ride. He waved toward the damage. "Did you report this shit? When did it happen? Who did it? How did you—"

She stepped around him. Hit the button on her keychain to undo the locks. Though, really, who was going to steal this beat up ride? Each time she got it repaired, more damage was done. So she'd stopped with the repair work. Now her vehicle just looked like shit.

Maybe it would be better if it *did* get stolen.

His hand curled around her upper arm. "We have to talk."

Lark stopped. She looked down at his hand. "Do not touch me."

His hand jerked away instantly.

"And there is nothing to say," she informed him crisply.

"Yes," he growled. "There is plenty to say. You love me, remember?"

He had not. He had fucking *not* just thrown that at her. She turned. Made herself stare at him. It was so hard. Lark had this thing...she'd always had it. When she was mad at someone—truly, deeply angry, no, enraged—she just couldn't look at the person. Her fury was too great.

Looking at Special Agent Oliver Foxx in that moment required all of her strength.

And she knew fury had to blaze from her eyes. "I love my brother."

"The courts are going to handle—"

"He's being framed. I thought you were a good FBI agent. Someone out for justice. Someone who wanted to help." She shook her head. "All you did was use me. Lie to me. Seduce me."

A muscle jerked along his jaw. "Our relationship was separate—"

She flinched. "We didn't have a relationship. We had you using me. You getting close to me so you could find evidence that you'd use against my brother. You told me all the things I wanted to hear. You probably researched me, didn't you? Before we actually met? Maybe even made a profile on *me*." Because that was what he did. He was so good at getting into the heads of people. "You figured out what I would like the most. You gave me that. Nothing with you was real."

"It *was*."

Like she could believe him. "Stay away from me. My brother's lawyer said you shouldn't be alone with me." But it was more than that. More than just following some protocol rules for the case. It was personal. "I don't want to be alone with you. I don't want you anywhere near me."

Pain flashed on his face. "I had a job to do. Listen, dammit, you and I—that's separate from everything else."

"My brother's life isn't separate." She backed up a step because she did not want to be close to him. "He has to fight in there, do you know that? The other prisoners attack him. He has a giant target on his back, and every time I come in, there are new bruises on him."

"Fuck."

Yes, indeed. "Fuck," she repeated clearly. Then, "Fuck you."

"I can pull some strings," Oliver offered. "Get him put in solitary."

Bitter laughter broke from her. "Solitary. So he can be alone twenty-four, seven? For how long? Until the trial? Because there is no bail for Lane. *Because FBI experts* said he was too dangerous. That he would kill again. That he was a flight risk because he had business in other countries. You are the one keeping him in there." Each word stirred the fire of her fury. "You took away my only family, and you dare to come to me now and talk about me *loving you?*"

Oliver squared his shoulders. "I'll make sure the guards keep an extra eye on him."

"How about you try doing your job? How about you find the real killer?" She spun away and lurched toward her car.

"He is the real killer."

She shook her head. "Screw. You." Lark opened her door. "The real killer is still out there, and when he picks another victim..." She slid into the driver's seat and—once more—forced herself to look at Oliver. Handsome, powerful, *betraying* Oliver. "When he picks another victim, her death will be on *you.*" Her breath heaved. "Stay the hell away from me. You are the last man I will ever want in my life again."

She yanked the door closed. Cranked the engine and screeched out of that lot.

As she glanced into the rearview mirror, she saw Oliver watching her.

The last man I will ever want.

And the only one she'd loved.
But how quickly love could turn to hate.

CHAPTER ONE

When it came to catching killers, Oliver Foxx liked to consider himself an expert. After all, he was a trained FBI agent. Even had his Ph.D. in psychology. He'd spent countless hours interviewing convicted killers, and he'd trained hard in the FBI's elite Behavioral Analysis Unit. Violent crimes were his bread and butter. A twisted bread and butter to have, sure, and he didn't always sleep well at night, but he got the job done.

Someone had to take the monsters off the streets.

Why not be that someone?

He knew how to defend himself. Knew how to fight hard and dirty. In his experience, most killers never went down easily. That was why he had a two-inch scar from a knife attack below his heart, and a graze from a bullet on his left hip. When you hunted monsters, you had to be ready for pain. Because pain always followed in a monster's wake.

She wasn't ready for more pain.

She...Lark Lawson. The woman he'd destroyed once upon a time.

The woman he loved.

The woman who *hated* him. With good reason, granted. Good fucking reason.

She didn't look back as she hurried down the dark Vegas street. Seemed completely oblivious to her surroundings, in fact. Something that had his already locked jaw hardening even more. She shouldn't be out alone. Not at this hour. It was freaking near midnight. And they weren't on the busy strip. No, she'd parked her car in a lot about two blocks over and was walking on the more off-beaten path. One that was mostly shuttered for the night. One with too many shadows. A light rain fell, and that rain had sent most people inside.

Lark wasn't most people.

She held an umbrella in one hand and her high heels carefully dodged the puddles. Not once did she look over her shoulder to see if...

Oh, I don't know, to see if some twisted bastard might be following her.

Because this stretch of isolated road? It was the same place where Amelia Wayne had been abducted. The last victim of the serial killer who'd hunted on the Vegas streets. A murderer who the media had dubbed the Bridal Killer because of the ceremonial way in which he'd left his victims.

Amelia had left a bar up ahead, a place appropriately titled Side Strip. Appropriate because it was on the side of the main strip and because, yep, strippers did occasionally perform for the crowds. Amelia had vanished after a friend's bachelorette party.

Only to turn up three days later, a white rope around her neck and a white bouquet clutched in her dead hands.

You shouldn't be out here, Lark. What the hell are you thinking?

But he knew. Oh, he knew exactly what her game was. After all, he'd seen her on the news that evening. As she boldly stared straight into the camera and said... *"I want the real killer to come after me. My brother is innocent. The man who did these terrible crimes? He's out there. And he's going to hunt again."* She'd swallowed. Lifted her chin. *"So if you're going to hunt, you hunt me."*

She darted around the edge of a building and the red umbrella that she carried vanished from sight.

Hell. He hurried his steps. Lunged around that building and—

Her umbrella slammed into his stomach. A hard hit.

"You think stalking a woman is fun? You asshole!" She hit him again.

He grabbed the umbrella. "Not stalking." *Dammit, I was. Best not to confess to that part right now.* "Gonna leave a mark," he groused as his fingers clenched around the wet umbrella.

"Good." She inched toward the bricks on the wall of the nearby building. "You shouldn't be *stalking* women at night. You came lunging at me out of the darkness—a whack from my umbrella is the least you deserve!"

He rubbed his injured stomach. "I wasn't lunging at you. I was trying to protect you."

She snorted. And inched back a little more. That inching took her beneath one of the few streetlamps that seemed to be working that night. The glow fell on her, revealing the long, thick, and very straight length of her hair as it tumbled over her shoulders. She wore a black coat. Black pants. Black top. Black heels. She looked like some kind of insanely sexy cat burglar, but he didn't think she'd appreciate being told that fact.

Come to think of it, he didn't think she'd appreciate anything he had to say.

"Give me back my umbrella," Lark ordered.

Yes, he should do that. He extended it toward her while he tried to think of something to stay that wouldn't piss her off even more. Tried. Failed.

She snatched the umbrella from him. "What are you doing out here? Because there is no way you're just randomly on my tail."

"Didn't realize you'd spotted me," he murmured.

"I did. You were obvious. I heard your footsteps behind me, then saw your reflection in the glass of a window I passed."

So she had been situationally aware. Points for her. What did *not* earn her points... "You think taunting a killer is a good idea?"

Her eyes widened.

"Caught the news segment. Me and most of the city, probably. You look phenomenal on camera, by the way. If possible, even sexier than you do in real life." Nah. That was a lie. She was ultra sexy in real life. The stuff of dreams and fantasies and his only weakness.

He never should have gotten involved with Lark. He'd known that he was crossing lines and risking his case.

But...

I fucked her when I shouldn't have. And she has completely fucked up my world since then. Because he missed her every damn moment.

But she hates me.

Lark stared at him. Nope. Correction, she glared at him.

He felt like he was devouring her with his eyes.

Her chin lifted. Slightly pointed. Heart-shaped face. Incredible green eyes. Green and so deep. And her lips—full. Unpainted. So soft and tempting.

He swallowed.

"How can I be taunting the killer?" Lark asked him as she tilted her head to the right. Her hair slid over her shoulder. "According to you, the killer in question is my brother. The man still locked up in a cell after all this time."

Contrary to what people saw in movies, trials didn't tend to be fast. Especially not when you were talking about a case that involved multiple murders. Months had passed since Lane Lawson's arrest, and yes, he was still sitting behind bars even though he hadn't been convicted of any crime. Yet.

Choosing his words carefully, Oliver noted, "You think someone else committed the crimes."

"Uh, yes, I do." She shook out her umbrella, flinging droplets of water in his direction. "And if your head wasn't up your ass, you'd think the same thing, too. But you just can't admit you made a mistake, can you?"

He wiped away some of the water that had landed on his cheek. "Oh, I made a mistake, all right."

She stopped shaking the umbrella.

"I should have kept my control with you," he added roughly. "You wouldn't hate me nearly as much if we hadn't—"

She flung more water at him. Deliberately this time. Though, maybe the first time had been deliberate, too. Then she lifted the umbrella up, letting it shield her head as her fingers curled around the base. "You think I wouldn't hate you as much if we hadn't had sex?" Lark asked him.

Yes, he did think that very thing.

"You think the pain wouldn't be as strong?" She twirled the umbrella. "Maybe. Maybe not. See, I have this big issue with you *using me to lock my brother away for multiple murders.*"

Right. Check. "I want to offer you a deal."

"I want you to get out of my way. Someone is waiting for me, and you're delaying my progress."

Whoa. Hold up. "You...you're out on a date?" Oliver choked out the question.

She stared back at him. "Still delaying me. But I can fix that." She took two steps to the right, clearly intending to just walk around him.

He took two steps and was in her path again. "You've got a date with some asshole who wanted you to meet him at nearly midnight? Some dick who has you out walking *alone* on these dark streets?" What a complete and total bastard. "He should have picked you up at your place. He should have taken you to the fanciest restaurant in town—"

"Where he would then distract me while the Feds and the cops stormed my house? Oh, wait. My bad. That was you. Not the man I'm meeting tonight."

She's meeting someone else. Of course, she would have moved on. A woman as gorgeous as Lark would not be by herself for long. His hands fisted. He had no one else to blame for this development but himself. *I lost her.*

"Get out of my way," Lark told him. "As I've said—numerous times to you before—if the Feds won't do the job, then I have to find the real killer myself. Only, turns out, I won't actually be working alone." She darted around him. Her heel landed in a puddle and sent a little splash up in her wake.

His head shook. "You're meeting a *partner?*" His gut twisted. During one of their angry, uh, talks, she'd said—

"The Feds consider the murders solved, but I consider them ice cold." She looked back over her shoulder at him. "I know you're familiar with the Ice Breakers."

Yes, dammit, he was. Too familiar with them.

"They solve cold cases," she told him. An unnecessary tell. Then she added, "I believe I may have even mentioned them to you before. I'm meeting with Memphis Camden at midnight." Crisply, she faced the front and began striding forward.

"Not without me, you're not," he muttered and gave chase. And even though he was *right* behind her as she marched through the darkness, Lark acted as if he was not there.

Froze him out completely.

But what had he expected? Sure, he had fantasies in which she came to him. She told him she understood. That he'd been torn between duty...and her. In those late-night fantasies, Lark offered him a second chance.

One that usually ended with them tangled in bed together.

This was not one of those fantasies. The rain picked up and pelted down on him. She kept her umbrella in perfect place.

Swearing, he flipped up the collar on his pea coat and kept his eyes on her...right up until the moment she turned and entered the door of Side Strip.

His head tilted back as he glowered up at the glowing, neon sign. No way in the world this was a coincidence. Lark was well and truly waving the red flag in an effort to draw out the "real" killer.

When would she realize there was no other killer waiting in the darkness? How long could her denial last?

The interior of Side Strip was as uninspiring as the exterior. Way too dim, with the lights focused on the lone stage in the bar. Only no one was performing that night. Probably because it was a Tuesday, and not like business was gonna be killer on a Tuesday of all nights.

A woman in black leaned over the bar and chatted with a customer. A few patrons were scattered around at the tables. Drinking. Munching on peanuts or some damn thing.

Lark paused only momentarily before her gaze swept to the far right. The back booth. Her attention locked on the man who sat back there, with his fingers lightly tapping on the scarred tabletop.

With her umbrella closed and at her side, she headed for her target.

Not exactly waiting for her to invite him along—Oliver knew no invitation would be coming—he followed on her heels. As they drew closer to the back booth, his eyes narrowed on the target. A man he knew, unfortunately, too well.

Memphis Camden. Former bounty hunter. Expert tracker. Current Ice Breaker. All around pain in Oliver's ass.

Memphis rose as Lark neared the table. He inclined his head toward her. "Great to finally meet you in person, Ms. Lawson." The faintest hint of the south brushed beneath his words because, well, Memphis *had* been born in Memphis, Tennessee. Thus, the guy's name.

Lark extended her hand to him. "Thank you so much for coming out tonight."

"No problem. Actually wanted to see the scene where Amelia Wayne spent her last night. Helps to get me in the right mindset." Memphis let her go and peered over her shoulder to smirk at Oliver. "Well, well, well. If it isn't Special Agent Oliver Foxx. With two X's because you're an extra asshole."

"That joke is really damn old."

Memphis shrugged. "Wasn't joking."

Oliver flipped him off.

And, of course, Lark would turn around right then to catch him flipping the bird to the Ice Breaker who she thought was her savior. Lark's mouth dropped open in shock. Then she grabbed Oliver's hand and pushed down his middle finger.

At her touch, warmth spiraled through him. *I have missed her far too much.*

"What are you doing?" She shook her head in obvious dismay. "I need him!"

"Bullshit." Whoops. Oh, well, he'd just called it like he'd seen it. "You have me."

She let him go. Fast. As if he'd burned her.

"Didn't know we were making a party out of tonight," Memphis drawled. "Thought the Fed was working on the opposite team. Glad to realize he's seen the light for you."

Lark whipped back around to face him. "Oliver and I are not on the same team."

She was wrong. He was always on Team Lark. That last, fateful night at the restaurant, he'd felt like his heart had been cut out. Especially when she said...*I love you*. What he would not give to hear those words from her one more time.

"He's the enemy," Lark informed Memphis bluntly. "Never mistake him for anything else."

Check. The enemy. Not the man she loved.

"Glad we cleared that up." Memphis sent Oliver a tiger's smile. "If you don't mind, we have a meeting to conduct." Memphis motioned for Lark to slide onto the bench that was opposite the one he'd been using.

She did.

Memphis sat back down. The SOB shooed Oliver away.

Funny. "Freaking hilarious," Oliver snapped as he slid into the booth right beside Lark.

She did a double take. "Why are you here?"

"Because you are."

"That makes zero sense."

"You're hunting a killer."

"Yes. I've told you that before. Multiple times."

It was too dark for him to clearly see her eyes. A fact that pissed him off. He loved her eyes. "Yeah, you have. But today was the first day you just decided to announce your intentions on the *news*. Do you have any idea how many psychos will now be at your door? People who want to harass you? Just general nutjobs who will claim they have info or who will try to hurt—"

"Do you seriously think I haven't been harassed in the last few months? I had to sell my business. My home. I've moved *three times*. People throw bricks into my windows. They carve crap on my car. I have break-ins. I have—" She stopped. Her delicate nostrils flared. "Don't you dare look at me that way."

What way?

"Don't you feel sorry for me. I'm going to get my brother exonerated. The truth will come out."

He could feel her pain. Living, breathing right between them. He wanted to take away all her pain. If only he could.

I caused her pain.

No, no, her demented brother had done that when he'd killed three women—women who all looked far too much like Lark.

"Ahem." Memphis.

Oliver and Lark turned their heads toward him.

He waved. "Hi. This is certainly, well, not fun for me to watch. So, how about we move along, shall we? I do have a wife at home. Or, technically, at a hotel in Vegas. Sleeping like the perfect angel that she is. I want to get back to her sooner rather than later."

Oliver knew all about Memphis's "perfect angel" of a wife. A society princess who'd been kidnapped but she managed to escape her abductor and find her way back home. Only once she got home, no one had believed Eliza's story. No one, until Memphis and his team came along. Because the Ice Breakers had realized a killer was hunting. They'd connected other missing women to Eliza's abductor. And, eventually, Eliza and Memphis brought the bastard down.

It wasn't the first time that the Ice Breakers had closed a case. In fact, Oliver had even thought about joining their group. Especially right after the nightmare went down with Lane Lawson. Sometimes, being able to play by your own rules was truly the best way to go.

The Ice Breakers had originally started online. The members of the team all came from different backgrounds. Memphis was the bounty hunter. But there was also a reporter—and her freaking billionaire husband who now happily backed the group. Happily, because his wife had cleared him of an old murder suspicion. One of the most interesting players on the Ice Breaker team? That had to be the doctor of the dead. Dr. Antonia Rossi could make the dead speak. She was one of the best—no, she *was* the best forensic anthropologist in the country. She'd cracked dozens of cases. She'd worked over and over again with the Feds. Oliver respected the hell out of her.

Honestly, he respected the hell out of all the Ice Breakers. Even when Memphis got on his nerves, Oliver still admired the jerk. Hell, Memphis had been the main Ice Breaker trying to recruit Oliver.

The Ice Breakers didn't take just any case. They were highly selective. And in order for them to be working with Lark...

What the hell does Memphis think I missed? What *could* have been unease slithered down Oliver's spine.

"Shall we get down to business?" Memphis asked smoothly. "Or do you two want to waste more of my valuable time by bitching and moaning at each other?"

They hadn't been bitching and moaning. Oliver narrowed his eyes on Memphis. "Watch it."

"Oooh. So scared." He shuddered. "Wait, I'm not. Just getting bored." He pointed at Lark. "You realize that you just put one giant-sized target on your back today with that news story?"

Yes. Finally. The voice of reason. Even if the voice came from Memphis.

"You already fit the killer's profile to a perfect T," Memphis added because the man had never learned how to pull a punch. "Now you're on the news, taunting him. Practically begging the guy to come for you." He whistled. "If you'd run that plan by me first, I would have advised against it."

"The real killer *is* out there. Only none of the cops or the Feds are looking for him." Her hands flattened on the table. Unpolished nails. Delicate fingers. "I had to do something. I wasn't just going to keep wringing my hands while my brother is trapped in hell."

Memphis dipped his head in a slow nod. "Got to say, I admire the loyalty you've got for your brother. It's actually the reason I agreed to take your case."

Damn. Now the puzzle pieces made sense. Oliver knew all about Memphis and—

"Got a brother myself. Once upon a time, he was wanted on a murder charge." No emotion entered Memphis's drawling voice. He was always good at keeping his real emotions hidden. "I was the one who tracked him down and threw him in a cell."

Lark sucked in a sharp breath.

"But I got him out, too." Another dip of Memphis's head. "Because I believed he was innocent. Didn't give up until I cleared him." His expression softened, just a bit, as he studied Lark. "Like I said, I admire your loyalty."

Great. Now Memphis and Lark were bonding. Oliver couldn't remain silent. "Memphis, there's a big difference between your brother Saint and Lane Lawson..."

Memphis raised his brows.

"Saint was innocent." Oliver turned his head to stare at Lark. To drink her in even as he said words that he knew would hurt. "Nothing suggests that Lane is innocent."

She didn't flinch. Didn't rage at him. She sucked in another deep breath and her shoulders squared. "I know he is."

"Knowing isn't evidence." *What you've got is jack and shit.* But he could be tactful enough not to say that. "You think you're the first family member who doesn't want to see a loved one's guilt? You're not. Not even close." He'd witnessed this time and time again. "They count on that," he added gruffly. "Count on your love to blind family and friends to the crimes they've committed. Lane is counting on *you* to be blind to what he's done." And that pissed off Oliver. "Don't let him drag you down with him. See him for what he is."

Her jaw hardened "I do. I see him perfectly. You're the one who doesn't."

"I'm the one who made the profile on him."

Now she did flinch.

But she must have known that truth already.

"Ahem." From Memphis once again.

And, again, both Lark and Oliver turned to look his way.

"Hate to say it, but the Fed makes a good point. I need more than just your belief in your brother. I need stone-cold evidence if I'm going to find the perp you think set him up." He folded his arms over his chest and leaned back in the booth. "So what do you have?"

"M-mementos were found at my house. Jewelry from the v-victims..."

Her stutter made Oliver's stomach clench, but he had to tell her, "We call those trophies, sweetheart."

"Not your fucking sweetheart." No stutter there, just fury.

Right. She wasn't. Not in reality, anyway. But in his head? *You are still mine.* He cleared his throat. "Serial killers often take trophies so they can relive their crimes. When I was helping you organize those boxes in your basement, I came across the—"

"You weren't *helping.* You were searching for evidence to convict my brother. I think that counts as an illegal damn search, and I know Lane's lawyer is working to get that evidence tossed out."

"You *asked* me to help you move those boxes. You asked for help organizing. It was your house. Not your brother's. He had only moved in a few days before because he'd sold his old home and was in the process of buying a new place. I thought I was helping *you.*" On this, he wanted to be clear. "I never lied to you about who I was. You knew I was a Fed the minute we met. You knew I was working on the Vegas abductions and murders."

She leaned toward him. "And *you* had my brother pegged as a suspect even before you walked into my florist shop, didn't you? You lied about looking for flowers for your mom. Your mother is dead."

"I wanted something for her grave."

"That is such BS! You lied to meet me. And you were nosing around in my house looking for evidence to use against my brother under the pretense of helping me because no judge would give you a warrant. You were just busy digging on your own without—"

"*Ahem.*"

Their heads whipped to Memphis.

"That is my third 'ahem' of the night. Third and final." He grimaced. "You two really need to separate. Or fuck. Don't know if you've realized it, but there is a whole lot of tension in the air between you."

Lark scooted away from him. As far as she could scoot in the booth. "Special Agent Foxx assumed the box with the jewelry belonged to my brother."

"I assumed it belonged to the vics." With good reason. He'd recognized one of the missing jewelry pieces. A cross that had belonged to Susan Peters. Victim number two.

"It was *mine.*"

Now he shook his head. "Lying for your brother will do no good. Susan's DNA was found on the cross. It belonged to her. Obviously. Your brother brought the box with him when he moved into the house with you because he couldn't stand to be separated from his trophies. He probably relived the rush he got from the kills every time he looked at the jewelry." Lark's prints hadn't been found on the jewelry. Neither had her brother's. But—

"You're not listening to me. Just like you and your team didn't listen to me before." Her voice rose. "The box was *mine.*"

His stomach knotted. "Are you trying to incriminate yourself? Are you saying you were—"

Her head angled toward him. "I'm saying I forgot about that box. It was in a pile of materials I brought home from my store when I was cleaning up. I thought it had old Halloween decorations inside of it. Decorations like that were in the other boxes, *if you will recall*. I brought that box—and three others—home with me. But then Lane moved in. I met you. Things got...intense." She wet her lips. "I forgot about that box because it wasn't important. Only then, we started organizing. You actually opened it. I remember when you opened it because I *told* you the jewelry wasn't mine. I thought it was so strange, and I was trying to figure things out and then you said..." Her words trailed away.

"Must be your brother's," he muttered.

"Only it wasn't. *I* brought the box home. It was in my store. *Mine.*"

"That doesn't mean that Lane hadn't put it in your store." An obvious explanation.

But she shook her head. "You think I haven't been digging? Every single moment and every single way that I can? Racking my brain over and over again? After Lane's arrest, my assistant and I scanned through hours and hours of security footage. Not like I had customers coming in, so we had plenty of time to watch the recordings. So we watched and we discovered proof that box was originally delivered to us."

He straightened.

"Katya found the box outside the shop and assumed it was a delivery. We recovered video footage of her putting it down next to the cash register. All of this happened when we were taking down the Halloween decorations at my shop. In the video we recovered, a customer came up after Kayta had put the box on top of a few others at the register...then I appeared in the footage and moved everything to the storage room. *I never even looked inside the box she'd found.* Neither did she."

"Don't lie for him." But his heart was pounding, way too fast.

"I'm *not,*" she gritted. "That box wasn't his. It was sent to *me.* My shop. Only I never even opened it. If I had, hell, I don't even know if I would have understood its significance. A cross. Two pearl earrings. A gold bracelet. I would have thought it was a mistaken delivery but..."

But if what she was saying was true... "No mistake." *All the vics had looked like Lark.*

"I think the killer sent that stuff to me deliberately. Me, not my brother. I don't *think* I caught his attention by going on the news. I think I've had his attention for quite some time."

Sonofabitch. *If this is true*...Ice spread through his veins.

"Ahem." Memphis.

Only this time, Oliver didn't look his way. Neither did Lark. Oliver and Lark kept right on staring at each other.

"And here I said I wouldn't go for a fourth time," Memphis muttered.

Oliver ignored him.

"As soon as I figured this out, I called the Ice Breakers," Lark informed him. "I started working to get a meeting with them."

"You didn't tell me," Oliver snapped.

"I'm telling you right now."

Fuck. Fuck. "If this is true—"

"It's true."

His fist slammed into the table. "Then the sonofabitch has had you in his sights all along." *And I left you on your own. You've been unprotected, and he could have taken you at any time.*

If it was true. If she wasn't just a desperate sister trying to save her brother. If this wasn't part of some strategy to provide reasonable doubt. If, if, if...

But looking into her eyes, he stopped thinking about all of the "if" situations. He just thought about...

Lark.

In danger.

Unprotected.

Screw this.

"Judging by your expression," Memphis said, voice quiet and a bit sly, "I think I should now consider you an honorary Ice Breaker?"

Oliver kept his attention on Lark. "I'm an FBI agent. I follow evidence wherever it may lead me."

"Uh, huh. Great for you. But you *will* be looking into this case more, yes?" Memphis pushed.

"Yes," he hissed.

"Fantastic." Memphis slapped his hands together in a clap. "Glad to have the team together." He raised his voice and said, "Uh, waitress, can you bring us something to drink? Because I think this night could go long."

Oliver slowly slid his gaze over Lark's face. There had been no tells to indicate she was lying. No stutters in her voice. No hesitations. Her gaze had held his. No nervous motions. No twitches.

His stare darted down. And he noticed that her left hand had curled in her lap.

As he watched, her fingers slowly unfurled.

And he saw the deep, red indentions that her nails had left on the inside of her palm. So deep that there was even a little blood.

His eyes narrowed.

"If the guy sent you the trophies," Memphis said, "and if he's abducting and killing women who look just like you, then we need to start by taking a hard look at your personal life, Lark."

Lark glanced over at Memphis.

"Got anyone in your life who might be obsessed?" Memphis asked. "An ex who maybe just can't let the fuck go?"

Great. Fabulous. Oliver exhaled. "That would be me." Better to just be clear on this point now. He knew how the Ice Breakers operated. They would leave no stone unturned. And they would know about his obsession. *If they don't already. Memphis could be testing me right now.* So better to just put the truth out there.

And in response to his confession?

Silence. Absolute silence.

"Only I'm not the killer you're after." His attention swung to Memphis. "But I will help you to find the bastard. Provided he exists." Lark's brother could have sent the package to her shop. All the evidence still pointed to him as being guilty as sin.

Or...

The lovely Lark could be lying.

Oliver would get to the truth, one way or the other. That was his thing. He didn't stop until the guilty person was locked away. Until the final verdict was delivered.

But I will not risk leaving her unprotected. Just in case...in case he was wrong. In case the wrong man was in a cell.

In case a killer is hunting the only woman I've ever loved.

CHAPTER TWO

"Yep, okay, this is probably enough for tonight. It's a good start." Memphis had been keeping notes on his phone, but he shoved the device into his pocket. "I'll want a copy of that video footage you have from the shop."

Lark tensed. "There isn't anything useful in the video. Just the package itself. The Feds already have the box. No return label or anything like that are on it."

"I'd still like to see the footage."

She swallowed. "Of course, I'll get it to you right away."

"And you make sure that you're staying vigilant at all times, got me?" Memphis pointed at her. "Now that you're just full-on taunting the creep out there, who knows what the hell he will do?"

Goose bumps rose on her arms, but Lark insisted, "I'd rather he come after me than someone else." Because she was on her guard. A gun nestled in her small bag, a cross-body bag that had been over her body during their entire chat. She'd been taking the gun to the shooting range every other week, ever since the first brick had come flying in her bedroom window.

"She's not going to be alone," Oliver said in that deep, rumbling voice of his. A voice that she'd once thought was like pure sex appeal. "I'll be with her."

"The hell you will," she returned without glancing his way.

"Oh, yes, the hell I *will*," he said flatly. "You think I'm gonna let you walk alone through the city at this hour? And, really, Memphis, what the fuck? You *had* to pick this place for the meeting?"

"He didn't pick it." She liked that her voice didn't tremble and that she didn't stutter. "I did."

"Why would you...?" Oliver started roughly but his words trailed off when the waitress reappeared.

"All virgin drinks? Don't usually get that from crews in here." She flashed a sunny smile. Her long, red hair hung in a braid that slid over her right shoulder. "You guys ready for the check?"

"It's on me." Memphis smoothly handed over his card. Before she could take it and disappear, he asked... "Sia, wasn't it?"

That was what the nametag on her left breast said. But Lark had already known the other woman's name. She'd made a point of learning it while trying to help her brother's case. Yes, she knew the woman's name.

So did Oliver. After all, he'd interviewed Sia after Amelia Wayne had gone missing.

Lark also knew that Memphis realized exactly who she was, too.

Sia was the waitress who'd told the FBI that Lane had been in Side Strip the same night that Amelia had vanished. Another nail in Lane's coffin.

"Yep, I'm Sia. What can I do for you?"

Oliver growled.

But Memphis just smiled a truly killer smile. "You remember the guy across from me?"

Her gaze slid to Oliver. She peered toward him with zero recognition on her face. Then shrugged. "Sorry, but I am terrible with faces." She laughed. "Did we meet before? And it's super dark in this place, you know. Hard to tell a lot about a person."

"Fuck," Oliver rumbled.

"Indeed," Memphis returned. His hand scraped over his jaw. "You did meet before, actually. You met FBI Special Agent Oliver Foxx—"

"When I questioned you about the disappearance of Amelia Wayne," Oliver snapped. "When you *told* me that you'd seen a dark-haired, Caucasian male, probably in his late twenties, who kept buying drinks for the women in the bachelorette party."

Sia jerked back. She also dropped the credit card. Bending swiftly, she scooped it up. "Right." Too bright. "Now I remember. Sorry. Yes…that was so terrible. Just terrible." Her gaze darted to the card. "I'll just run this transaction for you."

Oliver's hand flew out and curled around her wrist before she could rush away. "You later picked the man's photo out of a lineup."

"He's guilty," Sia whispered. "I read online that he had jewelry from those poor ladies in his house. He stole it from them after he killed them." A shudder slid over her body. "What a twisted freak. He was killing women who looked like his sister. Glad I could stop him. Glad I could send the Feds after his sorry ass even if I...I wasn't real sure when I first saw the photos."

The pain came, as it always did when people said those words about Lane. Everyone thought he was guilty. *Everyone but me.*

And now, maybe...the Ice Breakers.

"You weren't *real* sure?" Oliver seemed to be choking.

"You guessed when you saw the photo lineup, didn't you?" Memphis asked. "Then told yourself to stop feeling guilty once you read the news stories. Had to be the right guy, didn't it?"

Sia swallowed. Twice. "Damn straight, it was the right guy. Like I said, people were talking online about how he had the jewelry that belonged to those poor women. It was *him*."

No, it's not my brother.

"Now if there is nothing else, I'm running the card." Sia yanked away from Oliver and practically ran toward the bar.

Lark noticed that Memphis was suddenly studying Oliver with a whole lot of focus.

"What?" Lark demanded when the silence stretched a little too long.

"She won't ever admit it was a guess." Memphis pursed his lips. "But we all know it sure as shit was. In one breath, she told us that she can't ever remember faces. That statement alone will be a defense attorney's wet dream, and she just made the confession right in front of our friendly FBI agent."

A defense attorney's wet dream? Lark would be telling Lane's lawyer, Holly Ashford, about this development right away.

Memphis pointed at Oliver. "You don't make mistakes like that one. If a witness is uncertain, you'd see it. And since you *didn't* see it, I suspect you had one of your junior FBI squad actually get her to do the photo ID'ing. You weren't there at all." He shook his head. "Bad. So bad. Sloppy. Because the junior agents are too eager to gain your approval. The case was too big. They'd want it shut down as fast as possible. So fast that they might have even given the witness a little nudge."

Oliver leaned over the table. "A security camera at the bank half a block away caught footage of Amelia Wayne walking down the road after she left the bachelorette party. Approximately two minutes later, the same camera caught an image of Lane Lawson. That's no mistake. That's a fact."

"True." Memphis tapped his fingers on the table. "But it also doesn't prove that Lane was the one *in* this place, buying those drinks. They were paid for in cash, right?"

She knew they had been. Another point in the reports she'd read. The drinks had been purchased in cash—cash that had been long gone by the time the Feds came to investigate. So there had been no chance to investigate by finger printing. Of course, finger printing cash would have probably turned up hundreds of results.

"Lane was following her," Oliver insisted.

"Or he was just taking a stroll." Memphis shrugged. "Proximity doesn't equal guilt. Don't worry. I plan on talking to the man myself. See what he has to say. I'm pretty good at getting folks to open up to me." Another shrug. "I think it's my winning personality."

The waitress came back and practically hurled the credit card and receipt back on the table before storming away.

"Sure," Oliver said easily. "Got to be that."

***

Excitement had Lark's knees shaking as she exited Side Strip. The rain had stopped, so she kept her umbrella down and gripped in her right hand. Her small cross-body purse bumped lightly against her left hip.

"I'll check in with you when I have more info," Memphis told Lark.

He's working on the case. The Ice Breakers are going to help me. Impulsively, she threw her arms around him and held tight. "Thank you." Tears wanted to fill her eyes, so she blinked them away quickly. "I can't tell you how much this means to me."

"I can tell you..." Memphis whispered into her ear. "That a certain FBI agent looks like he'd enjoy ripping my head off right about now."

She whipped away from Memphis and whirled to catch Oliver glaring. He did, in fact, appear to be in the mood to rip off Memphis's head.

Memphis laughed. "I trust you'll see her to her car safely, Agent Foxx? You certainly seemed focused on guarding her earlier."

"You sure don't seem concerned with her safety," Oliver snapped back. "If you had been, she wouldn't have been walking alone tonight. You could have picked her up."

"I can take care of myself," she assured him. With that, she started making her way back to her car.

"The lady made the plan. I followed it." Memphis's voice drifted to her. "I'll be in touch, Foxx." His footsteps padded away.

Lark kept striding forward and avoiding the puddles as best she could. Only she wasn't striding forward alone. Oliver trailed behind her. Without glancing back, she asked him, "Are you really going to follow me all the way back to my car?"

"Have to."

Treacherous warmth started to spread inside of her. Maybe he was really concerned—

"I parked in the same lot."

The warmth stopped spreading.

She started walking faster.

Only it wasn't fast enough because he moved to keep pace at her side.

Silence reigned at first from him, then, as if the words were pulled from him, Oliver said, "You think I'm a total asshole."

She didn't argue.

"That's fair. Is there any chance we could start over?"

Stunned, she froze. Then swung toward him.

Shadows and darkness covered Oliver as he told her, "I've wished a million times that we could start over. No, correction, I've wished a million times that things had been different."

"We're not starting over *anything* until I get my brother cleared." With that, she went back to her marching. What time was it? Nearing two? The streets were absolutely deserted. Every now and then, a vehicle would slowly drive down the road, kicking up some of the leftover rainwater that still glistened on the street.

His pace perfectly matched hers and soon they were nearing the parking lot. Just one more crosswalk and she'd be home free. Lark reached the corner and prepared to walk across.

"You want your brother cleared so badly." A pause. "Is that why you lied to Memphis?"

Don't look at him. Don't.

But Oliver caught her hand. Her left hand. He uncurled her fingers. "Didn't think there was a tell, at first. Then I saw you were digging your nails into your palm."

"I was *stressed*." A white sedan approached. Dammit. She had to wait for the vehicle to pass. Great.

"You were *lying*. I interviewed your assistant Katya. She never said anything—"

"She'd forgotten about the delivery. I'd forgotten. We both had. You know what? Screw this grilling routine." The white sedan passed. "You never believed me or Lane, anyway." Lark ran over the crosswalk.

And he kept his perfect pace.

When they got to the lot, he started heading for her car.

She stopped. "No, no, this is it."

He stilled.

"You walked me to my car. It's right there." She used her umbrella to point toward her small SUV. "You've done your due diligence. Even as you called me a liar."

"Sweetheart, we both know you were—"

"Get away from me," she snapped because it actually *hurt* when he called her sweetheart. *How dare you? And why does it keep hurting?* "Go to your car. I'll go to mine. Just *go.*"

But he didn't. "I said I was going to help you. I meant it. I will either prove that he's innocent or I will prove your brother is guilty beyond every possible doubt. One way or another, this is ending."

His words held such an ominous ring. She turned and double-timed it to her vehicle. Then she heard the thud of his steps behind her. "Don't even think it!" She had hauled her keys out of her purse. Clenching them in her hand, she lifted her fist so he could see that she had her keys and was ready to go. "Leave me alone right now, Oliver. Do not come even a step closer." *Because he thinks I'm lying.*

Of course, he did. He thought her brother was a killer, and he thought she was a liar.

How perfect.

Perfectly heartbreaking.

When will I learn?

She hit the button to unlock her car. Barely pausing, she wrenched open the door and climbed inside. Lark tossed her umbrella into the passenger seat and yanked the cross-body bag over her head. It landed on top of the umbrella. Her breath heaved in and out as she stared blankly at the steering wheel for just a moment.

He hadn't followed her.

Good. He'd gone to his own vehicle. He had...

I hit the button to unlock my car. Only when she'd done that, the lights hadn't flashed. She hadn't heard the little *swish* of her locks disengaging the way she normally did. She'd just opened the door, though, without any problem.

Because the locks had already been disengaged?

Her gaze darted to the rearview mirror. She could see Oliver approaching his waiting vehicle, an Audi. She could see him because his headlights just flashed and illuminated the scene.

Mine should have flashed, too.

Even as she had the thought and stared in her rearview mirror—

"Took you forever to get back," a man's voice groused. Then a head appeared in her rearview mirror. Dark and shadowy. Covered in a ski mask.

She opened her mouth to scream, but a gloved hand slapped over her lips to muffle the cry. For an instant, her fingers flew up to try and pry those fingers away.

"You're going to sleep, and when you wake up, you'll be mine." A whisper in her ear.

And...

His other hand came up, fast, rushing toward her neck.

She stopped clawing at the glove over her mouth, and, instead, her fingers slammed into her steering wheel. The horn sounded like a desperate cry. She hit it once, twice. Then she twisted in her seat, frantic because she'd just realized that her attacker's other hand—it held a syringe.

Desperate, terrified, her fingers stretched for her purse.

For the gun inside.

***

When the horn sounded, Oliver whirled around. His gaze immediately flew to Lark's car. Fear flooded through him even as he bounded toward her vehicle. *"Lark!"* He hauled out his weapon.

Boom.

A gunshot blasted, and he hit the ground. Fuck. That bullet had seemed to come tearing right toward him. He swore that he'd even felt the heat of it lance over him. He looked up and saw the hole in the back of Lark's rear windshield. *"Lark!"* He leapt to his feet and ran to her.

Her driver's side door opened. Lark fell out. Spilled onto the ground.

He grabbed her and dragged her into his arms.

And some sonofabitch jumped from the rear of her vehicle. The right passenger door—the rear right passenger door. He erupted from the vehicle and raced away.

Every muscle in Oliver's body tensed. *Give chase. Catch the bastard*. But he couldn't leave Lark. His hands flew over her.

Something crunched beneath Oliver's foot.

"H-he had a syringe!" Lark's voice shook. "Tried to jab me. He was waiting in my car!" Fear trembled beneath every single word.

Tried to jab me. She'd said *tried*. "He didn't inject you?"

"No. He—we have to catch him!" She twisted and fought to break out of his arms.

Nope. He just held her tighter. "Are you injured?"

She frantically shook her head. Her hair whipped around her shoulders. "No! He's getting away! We have to stop him!" Once more, she heaved against his hold.

"Stay behind me," he barked. "Every second." And, with his gun in hand, with Lark behind him, he took off after the SOB. The guy had gone north, cutting across the parking lot and zipping back toward the left. Oliver had seen him flee that way, and he barreled after his target even as rage beat in his blood with every step.

You tried to hurt her? You tried to take her?

While Oliver had just been steps away.

Steps fucking away.

He jumped over the small chain that sectioned off the rear of the parking lot. Lark hopped over right after him. A quick glance back showed him that she gripped a gun in her hand, and her shoes were gone. She'd kicked off her heels as she gave chase with him.

His head whipped back to the front. He searched for his prey. The bastard had been wearing black. A ski cap had been on his head. *Ski mask?* And it was so damn dark that the jerk would blend easily with the shadows.

I need to call for backup.

He ran onto the street. Lark rushed right behind him.

Bright lights hit him and momentarily blinded Oliver. He squinted against them but didn't lower his gun. The growling of an engine reached him right before he heard the piercing shriek of spinning tires and smelled burning rubber.

The bastard is coming right at us.

And Lark was in the road because she'd run out after Oliver.

Oliver grabbed her. His left arm locked around her waist as he hauled her against his body and hurtled them both toward the sidewalk.

The vehicle whipped past. The scent of burning rubber hung heavily in the air.

Oliver twisted his body and glanced up. He'd hit the sidewalk hard with Lark, but he'd turned to take the brunt of the impact. Now he moved so that she was half beneath him—instead of on top of him—and his eyes went immediately to the back of the fleeing vehicle.

No license plate.

The vehicle barely slowed at the corner. Instead, it hurtled around the turn so fast that Oliver expected it to go onto two wheels. Only, it didn't. Somehow, the driver kept the car steady.

Tires still squealing, the vehicle disappeared from sight.

Oliver's jaw locked. He'd noted the make and model of the ride. He'd get an APB out immediately. There had to be security cameras in the area. Street cams. They'd find—

"You let him get away!" Lark charged.

His head jerked back toward her. "You mean...I saved your life?" Because he had a quick flash of her standing in the middle of the road and lifting her gun toward the car. Didn't she realize that even if she'd fired, the car would have kept coming? It would have barreled into her. The distance between them had been too short.

"That was the killer! If we'd caught him, my brother would be clear." With one hand, she shoved against his shoulder. "Get off me!"

Slowly, he did. Oliver rose and then he reached down to offer Lark his hand.

She swatted it away.

"Lark..." He shook his head. "Protecting you is the priority. I don't sacrifice civilians to catch bad guys." He wouldn't sacrifice her for anything. Though this was clearly not the time to tell her that fact.

She stared down the dark road. "He got away."

But you're alive. You're safe. And I'm not letting you out of my sight again.

Light raindrops began to fall.

***

"I want the car impounded. I want it checked for prints inside and out." Oliver pointed to Lark's small SUV. "He was inside, so maybe we'll get lucky and find something we can use. Though Lark said the bastard was wearing gloves and a ski mask."

FBI Special Agent Jase Guillory scratched his chin. "Uh, not to speak out of turn..."

Oliver narrowed his gaze on the other man.

"But are we sure this wasn't just some carjacking gone wrong? I mean, this area is known for that—"

"The area is also where another woman was abducted. I know you have *not* forgotten about Amelia Wayne," Oliver snapped back.

"And carjackers don't usually bring hypodermic needles to use on their targets," Theo Tutweiler announced as he joined Oliver and Jase. He pointed to the left. "Crime scene unit bagged and tagged the syringe they found near her car. But don't get your hopes up. It was crushed to hell and back."

Yeah, courtesy of Oliver's shoe. He remembered stepping on something near the car and hearing the crunch.

"The rain is not helping." Theo glanced up. The rain kept falling in a steady pattern. Light, but steady. Washing away evidence they needed. "The techs are gonna do their best." His head lowered as he looked over to where Lark huddled beneath her umbrella as she talked to two uniformed cops. "She can't give us much to go on."

"The woman was fighting for her life. The bastard attacked her from behind." *Waiting in her car.* Shit. "We always thought the women were abducted on their way back to their vehicles. The cars were found undisturbed, but, dammit, he could have been waiting *inside* the whole time. He pops up from the backseat while they are distracted. Shoves a needle in their throats—"

"Dexter style," Jase murmured.

Oliver's brows shot up. "Excuse me?"

"Oh, come on." Jase chided. "You're the horror buff. I *know* you're familiar with Dexter Morgan. You know, boss, the serial killer on TV? He was super big a few years ago, and I remember that he'd lurk in cars sometimes. Jab his victims with—"

"Etorphine hydrochloride," Oliver finished.

Jase rocked back on his heels. "See, you do know the show."

Yes, he knew it. And he also knew his tranquilizers. In the TV show, the main character had used Etorphine hydrochloride, or M99, to dose his victims. An animal tranquilizer, the M99 acted swiftly and could have a person slipping into unconsciousness within a matter of seconds. No wonder the writers had used it in their scripts.

"If he drugged them fast enough," Jase mused, "they wouldn't fight in the cars. They'd just slump forward. He could carry them out. There'd be no sign of a struggle."

Oliver's gaze returned to Lark's car. The bullet hole in the back was clear to see. "There's a definite sign of a struggle with her." Because Lark had known that the killer might come after her. She'd been ready with her weapon.

Only not ready enough because the sonofabitch still got killing close. I walked away, and he attacked her.

I will not be walking away again.

In his head, he could still hear that sudden honking of her horn.

Jase sidled closer and asked, "You really think this is our guy?"

Theo angled closer, too. Rain had soaked his slicker. Theo and Oliver both wore the FBI issued slickers.

"Is this him?" Jase asked. He hadn't bothered with a slicker or umbrella. His clothes had been soaked. "Is her brother innocent?"

Oliver didn't know what the fuck they were dealing with, not yet. Could be just some freak who'd been drawn to Lark because of her story on the news. He wasn't prepared to make any judgments yet. "We're going to find the bastard." Yeah, he got that didn't sound professional. Too bad. He wasn't feeling professional. This was personal. She was personal. "Then we're going to nail his ass to the wall."

The vehicle that had nearly mowed him down had been exceedingly distinct, even with the license plate removed. A hulking Cadillac Escalade. The grill had gleamed between the bright lights. Oliver wasn't sure about the color of the ride. Could have been black. Could have been blue. Just—dark. "Get access to all the street cams. If you can't find the vehicle on them, then we'll hit the stores in the area. I want to know where this vehicle is ASAP, got me?"

"On it," Jase assured him.

Theo nodded. "You can count on us."

Jase and Theo had been assigned to his task force shortly after he'd taken over the investigation into the Vegas murders and abductions. Currently, there were two more members on his primary team, Shannon Steele and Everett Callen. Agents tended to rotate in and out with him as they finished their training and got firsthand experience with serials. That was one of the things he was supposed to do, after all. *Train more agents to hunt monsters. Then send them out on their own to track killers.* No agents ever stayed on a permanent rotation with Oliver.

There was a saying at the Bureau...*When you pull duty with Oliver, you're in for a dark ride to hell and back.* But that ride would sure as shit teach you about the twisted nature of killers.

His crew had worked hard on the Bridal Killer investigation. When Lane Lawson had been arrested, they'd all thought the nightmare was over. *A trip back from hell.* Because the case had seemed over.

And now this had fucking happened.

"Ah, boss, not to speak out of turn..." Jase cleared his throat. "Not trying to piss you off or anything..."

Clearly you are about to piss me off. No one said words like that unless they were, indeed, about to piss off someone. And Oliver had told the man not to call him "boss" multiple times. Jase was new to the Bureau. Not quite steady on the lingo yet. He'd been a lawyer before joining. Had practiced at a high-priced law office. Only he'd gotten tired of defending the criminals, and, at twenty-nine, he'd made a huge life change.

Welcome to the Bureau.

"But, ah...were you on a date with Lark Lawson?"

No. "We happened to be at the same place."

Because I was tailing her sweet ass.

"I get that you were working a cover before..." Jase added quickly.

Of course—of fucking *course*—Lark would have chosen that moment to walk closer. And Jase had a loud-ass voice.

Oliver growled.

But Lark was behind Jase, and he just kept running his mouth. "You did what you had to do," Jase told him. "I admired that. But...with her brother getting ready for his trial, should you be—"

"Keeping a victim safe?" Oliver threw back. "Yes, yes, I absolutely should. And that's what I'm doing. I will be escorting Lark Lawson back to her home. I will be making sure that she is protected, you can rest assured of that." He took a step to the side so that Lark would see him clearly. "*Everyone* can be assured of that." And by everyone, he meant her.

You are not getting away from me, sweetheart.

"Ready to go, Lark?" he asked.

She twirled her umbrella. A deliberate twirl that sent an extra cascade of water toward Jase. "Shockingly, yes, I am eager to get out of the parking lot where I was nearly abducted." A pause. Then, voice louder, she added, "By the man who *actually* abducted and murdered those other three women. The real killer. I told you he was out there." Her gaze slid to each FBI agent's face. Then lingered on Oliver. "Now, I guess you have to believe me."

CHAPTER THREE

"Why do you live...here?" Oliver glowered at the small apartment complex. He leaned over the steering wheel to peer out of the windshield. "No security. Easy access to every room. Hell, I'm betting one kick, and the front door of any apartment in the place will go flying inward."

She unhooked her seatbelt. "Thanks for the reassuring pep talk. I'm so glad that you enjoy my new home. I can only assure you that I love it just as much as you do."

His head whipped toward her. "Are you making a joke right now?"

Wearily, she rubbed her left temple. "I don't know what I'm doing. Pretty sure it's close to four a.m." Because they'd talked to the Feds and the local authorities forever. "I'm dead on my feet, plus I've got a ton of scratches and bruises both from my fight with the jerk in the car..." A nightmare she was sure would play in her head over and over again. "And from our lovely tumble onto the pavement when the Escalade was charging at us. I want to get inside. Take an exceedingly hot shower. And pass out." Though she feared her sleep wasn't exactly going to be peaceful.

It never was.

"Why the hell did you move *here*?"

The man had obviously gotten obsessed on that point. So she'd help him out. "I'm trying to conserve money. After my brother's arrest, my customers stopped coming to the store. I had to close it." What did he think? That she was drowning in cash? "My brother's money has all been frozen." And as for the business Lane ran...another nightmare. "I sold my house because I was getting harassed." Her lips twisted in a humorless smile. "The listing agent told me that I got lucky. Someone actually *wanted* to buy it because it was a serial killer's home." Just saying those words *hurt*. "He's not a killer," she whispered.

"But we both know that he is." Quiet.

She flinched.

"And I'm not talking about those three women. I'm talking about what happened long ago. The very thing that made him fit my profile."

She closed her eyes to hold back tears. "I'm exhausted. And really, really not up to another one of our battles right now." She was also not up to facing the past. After a few bracing moments—when she was steady—Lark opened her eyes. She turned and reached for the door handle. "Thanks for the ride home." Her mother had been a stickler for manners. Even though she really wanted to tell Oliver to go fuck himself, the thanks just rolled out.

Some things, you never forgot.

His hand flew over and curled around her wrist before she could open the door. "Do you seriously think I'm just dropping you off? After what happened tonight, consider me on high alert."

"What, exactly, does that mean?"

"It means I'm not leaving you in a shithole with zero security and a flimsy lock right after some creep was just waiting to attack you in your car," he bit out. "We're going inside—together— and you're packing a suitcase. Then you are coming home with me."

We made love at his home. "No." She jerked her wrist free. "I'm good." This time, she succeeded in shoving open the passenger side door and darting out with her umbrella and bag.

Only he'd jumped out from his side, and he rushed to meet her. "You are *not* good."

Her stomach dropped. He had no idea how very, very true those words were.

"You were just attacked. The perp got away. That means he could come for you again." He glared at the parking lot and the assortment of vehicles that filled the area. "For all I know, he could be waiting inside your place right now."

Her gaze darted to the right. Her apartment was number thirteen. Unlucky, right? Story of her life. And it was on the ground floor. The locks *were* flimsy. The windows in her bedroom could easily be broken. And...

And I'm scared. "Fine. You can walk me to the door." She rolled one shoulder in a shrug as if she was not absolutely terrified. *But I am.*

He grunted. Caught her hand with his. Threaded their fingers together and started walking straight to number thirteen.

At first, she took a few sluggish steps with him, then she dug in her heels. "How do you know I'm in thirteen?" A low whisper because, as she'd discovered days after moving in, the walls were paper thin.

He tightened his hold on her. "Because I've been stalking you."

Automatically, she tried to jerk away.

"Fuck, wrong thing to say."

"You think?" Lark demanded as her heart lurched in her chest.

The door to apartment fourteen flew open. "Shut the hell up!" A drunken voice raged. All of the words flowed together. *Shutthehellup*.

Oliver yanked out his FBI ID. "Federal agent. Go back inside!"

Her neighbor swayed in the doorway. "Federal agent can...*shutthehellup*." She slammed her door.

Oliver stared at her neighbor's closed door, then swung his attention back to Lark. "*Why* are you here?"

"Because it's cheap. Because I'm trying to make my money last. Because I have to help with my brother's defense. Because, shocker, a lot of people were not thrilled when the sister of a suspected serial killer wanted to move in next door to them." She huffed out a breath and tugged away from his grip. She ignored the warmth that had come from his touch. The way she had to keep ignoring the heated awareness that would not stay buried.

She hated him, yes, no doubt.

But she'd also never stopped wanting him. And maybe that just made her hate him all the more. Lark dug her key out of her bag. She shoved it in the lock.

"That damn thing won't stop anyone who wants inside."

Like she didn't know that. Lark twisted the knob and darted over the threshold. Automatically, her fingers flipped the light switch. She'd only been there a few days, and an alarm system *would* be installed soon. She'd already scheduled the installation. Along with the installation of new locks. But she didn't tell him that. At this point, she was done explaining. Too dead tired. "Thanks for seeing me to the door. I'm safe. Good night."

She started to slam the door shut.

His hand flew up and caught the door. "What. The. Hell?" Fury hardened every word.

"What are you doing?" Lark pushed harder on the door in an attempt to try and shut it. But he just pushed back. "Oliver!"

"Behind you," he gritted out.

She let go of the door. Whirled around. And saw the garish spray paint above her couch. *You will die, too.*

Her shoulders sagged. "Wonderful."

"That's not fucking wonderful. That's a death threat."

Her lower lip trembled. "It just means people know where I am. I've gotten lots of spray-painted messages since Lane's arrest. Some are quite...creative." *If you think threats of violence are creative.*

His hands locked on her shoulders, and he whirled her to face him. "Why didn't you come to me?"

"Do you really have to ask that question?" A sad shake of her head. "I reported the incidents to the cops. Their response was basically for me to move. I did. But people hate me. They hate my brother, they think I was probably involved somehow, and this shit just keeps happening no matter where I go." She swallowed. "No worries, I can get the paint off. Gotten pretty good at doing that very thing." But not tonight. She'd scrub tomorrow.

"You're not touching it. I'm getting a crime scene team here. This is breaking and entering. That's a *death threat*. For all we know, the same fucker who was in your car left the note."

Doubtful. "A woman in her early fifties left one of the first messages. She spray-painted '*Bitch killer*' on the outside of my house. And the first time eggs slammed into my front door, they came from a neighbor. Tim Holloway. Thought he was a nice guy. Turns out, he didn't want me staying in the neighborhood."

"*Come with me. But don't touch anything.*"

That was a flat order, and she just followed along because...why not? If he wanted to investigate, then, by all means, the Fed could investigate. He darted down the small hallway. She trudged along with him. Then he turned into her bedroom.

The window was still open.

"Fuck," he breathed.

Yep.

"You're coming home with me."

She shook her—

"That wasn't a question. This is a crime scene. I don't care who threw shit before—actually, I do care. All of that pisses me the hell off. But *my* team is investigating this. Two attacks in one night? They could be linked. It's not *safe* here. And you are coming home with me."

She opened her mouth.

"Argue and I'll just cuff you to me. *This shit isn't up for debate.* You are getting protection, whether you want it or not."

***

He'd searched to make sure the perp wasn't still in that piss-poor excuse for an apartment. But the place had been empty. A cop had arrived to secure the scene, and the crime scene crew Oliver ordered had promised to report to him with their findings.

You will die, too.

The words had burned into his mind, and by the time Oliver arrived at his rental house, rage pulsed in every cell of his body. It wouldn't be too long until the freaking sun was up. Lark had to be completely exhausted. Soul weary. As for him, all he wanted to do was find the person after Lark...

And rip him apart.

He drove the car into his garage. Killed the engine and then heard the grind of the garage door as it lowered once more. The last time he'd had Lark in his home, he'd lost control. He'd *known* he shouldn't cross that final line. Known that he shouldn't have sex with her.

But...

But when it came to Lark, he wasn't reasonable. Hell, some days, he wasn't even sure he was sane. And he missed her so much. Longing for her ate at him.

She unhooked her belt and exited the vehicle without saying a word to him. A long sigh slipped from Oliver. He definitely could have handled the situation at her apartment with more tact. But when he'd seen those words, so soon after the attack on her...

You will die, too.

He'd lost it.

Oliver climbed from his vehicle. Gripping his keys tightly in his hand, he made his way to the door that led into the house. Lark remained silent as he unlocked the door and crossed the threshold. He typed in the alarm code, all too conscious of her stare on him.

Did she have any idea that he saw her every place he looked in his house? And when he went to bed at night...

I swear, I still smell her jasmine scent on the sheets.

"We both know you were lying about the cuffs."

His shoulders stiffened, and he glanced over at her.

"You weren't going to cuff me. And that idle threat certainly isn't what made me come along with you."

Her husky voice raked right over him. But she was misinformed. He turned to fully face her. "Lark..." *Sweetheart*. "If it meant keeping you safe, I'd cuff you any day of the week."

Her amazing green eyes—now lined with dark smudges that he hated to see—narrowed. "Excuse me?"

He took a step toward her. Then another.

Her chin notched up, but, points for Lark, she didn't retreat. Not an inch. God, she was so incredibly beautiful to him. The person he wanted most in the world. *And I've finally got her back in my house*. Now, if he could just get her back in his bed. But first...His hand lifted.

She flinched.

Fuck. First, he had to get her to trust him completely again. A seemingly impossible task.

He gently tucked a lock of hair behind her ear. His fingers brushed over her silken cheek. Oliver found himself leaning closer to her, drawn helplessly by her tempting jasmine scent. Hell, just drawn by her. "Also..." His voice was too gruff. Too rough. "Just so we are clear..."

Her head tilted to the side. Tilted *into* his touch.

He wanted to kiss her so badly. Instead, he told her, "There is never anything idle about the threats I make."

Her dark lashes flickered. "I will remember that."

"Good." His eyes dropped to her mouth. Lingered.

"Don't you want to know why I agreed to come here with you?"

"Because you still want me, and you don't want to fight the temptation anymore?"

She sucked in a sharp breath. "What?"

"No? My bad. Guess that's just the way I feel." His hand pulled away from her. He eased away, giving her space. Giving himself space, too. Because being close to Lark was heaven and hell all tied in a big, beautiful bow. "You kicking me out of your life didn't stop me from wanting you. Pretty sure nothing could ever do that."

She stumbled back a step.

He shook his head. "You don't need to retreat from me. I know how to keep my control." Oh, wait. Total lie. If he'd known how to keep his control, he would never have crossed the line and fucked her in the first place. He spun on his heel and marched for the den. After flipping on the light switch, his gaze went straight to the fireplace. Right there. He'd taken her right there, right in front of the flames.

And she'd burned him alive.

He heard the soft tap of her footsteps behind him. Without looking back at her, he asked, "Why did you agree to come here with me?"

"Because you know killers."

His shoulders stiffened.

"You profile them all the time. That's your *thing*, right? Getting into the minds of modern-day monsters?"

"Yes." Soft. "My thing."

"You were wrong about my brother."

He didn't argue with her. *Baby, don't you wish I had proof that I was wrong?* Instead of arguing, he asked, "Do you think I *wanted* to lock away the person you love most in the world?"

Silence.

So he had to turn toward her.

And when he did, Oliver discovered that she wasn't watching him. Her gaze was on the fireplace. Or, rather, on the floor in front of the fireplace. They had wound up on the floor. Eventually. First, though, he'd fucked her standing up.

Red stained her cheeks.

"Forgetting is impossible." A grim truth. Not that Oliver wanted to forget. Sex with Lark had been incredible. It had been the part *after*—the part where he broke her heart—that was the part he wished he could forget.

Her stare jumped to him.

"I see you wherever I look." Flat. "And I never wanted to lock up Lane. I had no choice. Every bit of evidence I found pointed to his guilt. If I had tipped you off about his arrest..." Impossible. He'd had a job to do. Rules to follow. As for Lark...

"You think I would have warned him. Told him to run." She wrapped her arms around her stomach.

Yes, that was exactly what he thought.

"You are right," she whispered.

His brows flew up. "Excuse me?" He took a step toward her.

"I would have told him to run..."

Well, damn.

"But I should have told him to fight, not run. And that's what I'm telling him now. *Fight*. Because Lane is not guilty. I know it. And the reason I came with you? It's already almost dawn. I didn't need shelter."

"You need rest." She had to be dead on her feet. "You need—"

"You," she finished. "You're what I need."

And the world stopped spinning. *Was this a dream?* If it was, then no one had better wake his ass up. He lunged for Lark. Oliver's hands wrapped around her shoulders as he hauled her close.

CHAPTER FOUR

His eyes were hungry. His expression savage. And his hold? Tight. Hot. He pulled her toward him. Their bodies brushed and traitorous longing pulsed through Lark, but she still managed to say, "You. I need you to prove Lane is innocent."

Oliver blinked. He didn't let her go.

"You know killers. I've read as much about you and your past cases as I could." He was actually damn good at his job. Scarily good. But in this instance, he was wrong. "The Ice Breakers are wonderful, and I am grateful to Memphis, but I came back here with you because I think you're starting to see—you *have* to see—that someone else is out there, hunting. The real person responsible for those terrible attacks." She swallowed because her throat felt so dry. "He was in the car with me. I know it was him." *It must have been.* "And if I have his attention, if he's going to come after me again, then I think having an FBI agent at my side is pretty important. Because I can defend myself, yes." She'd taken classes in college and after. But basic self-defense didn't compare to the kind of training that she knew a federal agent had experienced. "But you can do a lot more than just defend me. You can help me catch the bastard."

Silence.

His head was so close to hers. *Because he'd been about to kiss me.* Right here, in this same room where they'd crossed the line before. She'd wanted him so badly that night. More than she'd wanted anyone in her life. And things had just—just exploded. One minute, they'd been drinking wine. The next...

He had me up against the wall. His hands gripped my ass. My legs wrapped around his hips. His dick pushed against me. That hard, heavy length. And I begged him to take me.

Begged.

Her eyes closed, but closing her eyes didn't shut out the memory. If anything, it just burned hotter in her mind.

"Oh, there is no doubt that the bastard waiting in your car *will* be caught." The grim promise in his words had a shiver chasing over her. "But I'm not saying he *is* the man who committed the other crimes..."

Her lashes lifted. "Because of your profile, right? The profile that says my brother has to be the guilty one. He ticks off every box you have."

Oliver put distance between them. "You're exhausted."

Beyond exhausted. But that was the way she'd been living ever since her world had become a nightmare.

"Get some rest," he said, voice still gruff. That rumbling, deep voice of his was sexy as hell. She hated to still find things about him to be sexy, but...*it is what it is*. Oliver was gorgeous, strong, and he had a voice that made her panties melt. Damn him.

Oliver raked a hand over his face. "After a few hours of rest, we'll talk. The crime scene teams will hopefully have more info for us by then. We'll go forward and come up with a game plan."

A game plan. That seemed promising. But... "I'm *not* sleeping in your bed."

"In my dreams, you are."

They stared at each other.

"But for now," his head inclined, "the guest room is down the hallway. It's the door just past my bedroom. You can crash in there."

What did he think? That she'd just close her eyes and drift off to sleep? Even as tired as she was, sleep tended to elude her. She feared too much. *Like bricks flying through my window.* That had happened one night when she'd been in bed. The brick had hurtled through the glass. The shards had flown onto the bed. One had sliced her cheek. And the brick? It had missed her head by about five inches.

Now, she'd have a new, terrifying memory to stop her from sleeping—or, if she did sleep, to haunt her nightmares. The memory of the man in the mask. *You're going to sleep, and when you wake up, you'll be mine.* She'd told the Feds those words. Oliver had sworn—long and viciously— when she'd spoken.

I want to swear, too. Want to swear and scream and make this nightmare end. Only it wasn't ending. It was just getting so much worse.

She turned and headed for the hallway, but Oliver's voice stopped her just as she reached the doorway.

"The profile does match. Perfectly. But it wasn't just about the profile. It was about the evidence."

She'd explained that the box hadn't been her brother's—

"And the lack of an alibi. Your brother was seen on a street cam very close to where Amelia Wayne was taken. That put him near the scene of the crime."

"Proximity doesn't make you guilty," she whispered.

"He didn't have an alibi for the night the other two women were taken. Said he went out for a late-night jog both times, alone."

Her hand rose to grip the doorframe. "Nothing wrong with running."

"After midnight. All alone."

She looked back at him. "Sometimes, we run to escape our demons."

"Sometimes, you can't escape them, and those demons turn you into a monster."

She didn't flinch. "Good night, Oliver." Though it wasn't really night. Too close to dawn. She faced forward and took a step—

"I know you see him as a hero because of what he did when you were kids. I know you can't get past that. But...but the very thing that makes him a hero also made him a killer."

She did flinch. "You are wrong." Her words were so soft that she didn't think he heard them.

"I'm sorry about what happened to your parents."

No, not now. I can't deal with this now. It was too late. Too much terror from the night had left her shaken. Too much adrenaline spiked her blood.

"Your father attacked your mother." Sympathy slid beneath Oliver's words.

Her stomach dropped. Seemed to just hit the floor.

"You were there. You and your brother. You tried to get him to stop, but your father was enraged."

He'd been jealous because her mother had smiled at a stranger when they'd gone to the store. Jealous, then violently angry as soon as they'd all gotten home. "He was so mad all the time." A change that had terrified her. Her once smiling, easy-going father had turned into a stranger. One who hurt her mother. *And who wanted to hurt me.* But they hadn't known...couldn't have known...

"The brain tumor wasn't found until the autopsy." Oliver's voice was louder. Because he was closer.

She wanted to break and run to the guest room. To slam the door shut and hide.

But there was no hiding from her own past.

"The location and size of the tumor in your father's brain—it led to his behavioral changes. The violent outbursts. The paranoia. He couldn't control himself. And he would *not* have stopped that last attack."

The last attack. When he'd been hitting and hitting her mother. Lark could still hear her own voice, begging her father to stop.

Only he hadn't. Not until—

"Your brother ran upstairs. He took the gun out of your father's nightstand drawer." Oliver's voice came from right behind her now. "When he came back down the stairs, he shouted for your father to stop."

Stop! Please, God, just stop!

"But your father was far past listening. Far past his normal sanity. And he'd stopped using his fist and was armed with a knife."

Blood. Everywhere.

"Your mother was still alive. Barely. Your father whirled at your brother's voice—"

You won't shoot me!

"But you were standing there. Standing too close to your father because you'd been trying to reach your mother and help her."

I can see the madness in his eyes.

"Your father lunged at you. He locked one hand around your throat even as the other raised the knife and—"

My father had my eyes. Same green color. But that madness...that rage...

"You broke from his grip. He swung the knife—"

Boom.

"Your brother shot him. Killed him with a bullet that went straight in your father's heart."

Her body trembled. She let go of the doorframe. "I'm really too tired to relive one of the worst moments of my life right now." Her voice was hoarse. Rasping.

"Your brother saved your life. He became a hero to you. To everyone, at first. But then the truth of your father's brain tumor reached the media. It reached your brother. And the guilt...The guilt must have been unbearable. He'd saved you. And killed the father he loved so much. If only the bullet had gone somewhere else. If only he'd missed your father's heart. If only..."

She whirled. "You know *nothing* about my brother or about me."

A furrow appeared between his eyes.

"This is what you based your big profile on? That my brother felt *guilty* for saving me?" A bitter, disbelieving laugh slid from her. "So, what is he supposedly doing now? Murdering me over and over again because he wishes I had died instead of my father?"

"He—"

She lunged at him and jabbed her finger into Oliver's chest. "You are wrong."

"Lark—"

"My brother has never killed anyone," she whispered. "But you have him locked up with murderers and rapists and drug dealers."

"Lark—"

"Not anyone," she said again, voice barely above a breath.

The furrow between his brows grew deeper.

"But I have," she confessed. "Yet I'm the one walking free." Her finger still pushed into his chest, so she pulled her hand back and let it fall. "The profile you made? The one based on the murder of our father? It was wrong. Or maybe it was right. Maybe you just had the wrong twin. I'm the one who's guilty. Not Lane. Never him."

Oliver's gaze swirled with so many emotions.

"Gonna arrest me now?" she asked. She looked down at her hands. Slowly, they lifted, with her wrists up. "Want to slap those promised cuffs on me?"

He didn't speak.

"Because that's what you do, isn't it? You lock up killers." She licked her lips and forced herself to peer into his eyes once more. "Are you going to lock me up? Because I just confessed to murder."

A muscle jerked in his jaw.

She nodded. "Think about it. Promise you, I won't be running. In fact, when you're ready to put those cuffs on me, I'll be just down the hallway." She turned away. Kept her spine completely straight and her shoulders squared. And she left him. When Lark reached the guest room, she pushed open the door. He hadn't followed her. Probably was too stunned.

I just told him the biggest secret of my life.

She closed the door.

Only then did she cry.

It had really been one hell of a night.

***

Fuck me.

Oliver waited until he heard the soft click of the guest room door closing, then he rushed toward his study. *Away* from the guest room. In the front of the house. He threw open the French double doors that led to his study and hurried around the desk. His fingers flew over the keyboard as he pulled up his case files.

Or, rather, one very specific file.

The death of Roger Lawson, Lark and Lane's father.

He read through the details. Details he'd already reviewed over and over again. But this time...

Investigating officer Derek Lashay noted that Lark Lawson and Lane Lawson both claimed responsibility for the shooting.

Fuck, fuck, fuck.

Lashay noted that there were bruises on Lark's arms. Thick fingerprints as if she'd been grabbed. Bruising on her face and neck.

Fuck.

Lashay and his partner, Jo Wells, both agreed that Lark was traumatized at the scene. They had her transferred to a local hospital for evaluation. And for treatment of a possibly broken jaw.

Lane stayed at the home while the body of his mother was bagged. He confessed over and over. Said everything was his fault.

The responding officers surmised that a traumatized Lark tried to cover for her brother.

Oliver's fist slammed into the desk.

The shooting had been deemed self-defense. Neither Lane nor Lark had ever been charged. And what she'd just told him? *Still fucking self-defense.*

Only...

My profile has to change. Because what he'd thought before was wrong. What he knew about Lane Lawson was wrong.

And the way he felt for Lark? *That sure as shit has changed, too*. Because now, hell, now he felt even more protective. Her pain had been a living, breathing beast between them. All he'd wanted to do was pull her into his arms. Hold her tight. Never, ever let anything or anyone else hurt her again.

And I will. I will stand between her and hell itself. Nothing will hurt her.

Not on his watch.

She'd already been hurt enough.

***

Lark swirled the wine in her glass. "It's late. I should probably be getting home."

Oliver watched her from his position on the couch. She was so fucking beautiful. And he was lying to her. *One day, I won't be lying. One day, it will all be real.* He cleared his throat. "I'll drive you back."

She put the wine glass down on the nearby coffee table and rose to her feet. The black dress she wore hugged her curves perfectly. Like those curves didn't fill his fantasies every single day and night. Her head tilted as she studied him, and her thick, dark hair slid over her shoulder. "You're always the gentleman." She put one hand on the arm of the couch and leaned toward him. Her other hand rose to press lightly against the stubble on his jaw. "How long are you going to keep pretending?"

His heart slammed into his chest, and, for a moment, fear clawed at his insides. *She knows*.

But Lark sent him her slow, tempting smile even as her jasmine scent wrapped around him. "Always being so careful with the way you touch me."

He was careful. She deserved care. Compared to him, she was delicate. So much smaller. Fragile.

"Always so careful with the way you kiss me."

He had to be. If he let go of his control, he'd kiss her like a man possessed. Deep and hard and consuming. The same way he wanted to fuck her.

But he couldn't.

Not with so many secrets between them. He had to walk a fine line.

So very fine.

Lark leaned forward a little more. Her lips pressed lightly to his. Such a sweet, sweet kiss.

When he wanted to consume her with fierce passion.

"How much longer," Lark murmured against his mouth, "are you going to be careful?"

Then her hand slid from his cheek. Moved down, down...and curled around his fingers. He'd been making an effort *not* to touch her. Because when he touched her, his control always started to crack.

"Can I tell you a secret?" Lark asked softly as she lifted his hand—and brought it to rest on her thigh.

Her legs were parted. The dress she wore ended about four inches above her knees.

His head moved in a jerky nod.

"I think about you all the time." She began to drag up his hand. Slowly. And his fingers caught the hem of her dress and pulled it up. "I don't want you to be the gentleman tonight. I don't want to end the evening with a sweet kiss on the lips."

Higher, higher, her dress and his hand went.

"Guess what?" Lark whispered. Her right hand was still on top of his. Pushing *his* hand and her skirt ever higher. "I'm not wearing panties. Didn't want to wear them because I want to make it easy for you to touch me." She kissed him again. A tease as her tongue slid past his lips.

And his fingers went higher. Touched *her*. No panties.

Slick.

Hot.

Mine.

He shouldn't. He knew he shouldn't. He should pull back. He should...

"I want you," she breathed against his mouth. "In me."

Lost. He was lost in that instant. All his fucking good intentions. All of his plans to not cross that final line between them...gone.

Because his fingers had just dipped inside of her. Nothing in the world could have held him back when she moaned and kissed him again. Ever harder. Ever deeper.

He lunged off the couch. Grabbed her and twisted. Then she was the one on the cushions. Spread out for him with the dress showing him that, yes, she was *not* wearing panties. He shoved her legs wider apart, hit his knees, and put his mouth where his fingers had just been.

And he went wild. Licking. Sucking. Taking. Driving her toward her orgasm with every hungry stroke of his tongue. She arched into his mouth and choked out his name. Her orgasm was close. He could feel it building. Wanted to taste it on his tongue.

"No!" Lark called out. "Want...first time...*Want you in me.*"

His tongue had dipped into her. So had his fingers.

And his dick? Oh, hell, yes, he wanted *in*.

But he also wanted her ready because the way he felt...

Too rough. I'll lose control.

He strummed her clit with his fingers. Plunged his tongue into her again. And she...

Her body trembled. Her hips arched. But her hands locked around his shoulders. "Want us...*together*...*want*..."

He pulled away. *I'll give you anything you want.* Did she get that? Did she have any clue how far gone he was when it came to her?

Oliver stumbled to his feet. For a moment, he just stared at her. So fucking perfect with the dress hiked to her waist.

She licked her lips. Rose beside him. "You have on too many clothes."

Yeah, he could fix that problem. In seconds, he stripped. His clothes went flying, and he didn't care where they landed. He *did* pause long enough to take a condom from his wallet. To roll the thing on as quickly as he could.

She unzipped her dress. Let it fall to the floor.

No panties. No bra. She was like that all night long.

If he'd known, he would have gone insane. He would have fucked her in the car. At the restaurant. *Hell, we might have never even made it out of her driveway.*

His arms locked around her. He lifted her up. He kissed her. Held her tight. Her breasts pressed to his chest even as Lark's legs wrapped around him. Her sex rode his dick. Slick, so freaking hot. She arched against him, and the head of his cock dipped into her.

"Please, Oliver. *Please*. I want this. I want you. I *need* you."

There was no more control. She felt too good. Better than good. Better than anything he'd ever experienced in his life. And he *should* have carried her down the hallway to his bedroom.

The flames crackled in the fireplace.

I'm taking her. Here. Now. And never letting go.

Oliver knew he shouldn't. He knew it but...

She kissed his neck. Licked him. "*Please. Give me everything.*"

He sank fully into her. There was no turning back. No stopping. No sanity. There was only need and desire and desperation. The frantic drive of his hips against her. The drive of his cock *into* her. His hand slid between them so he could stroke her clit. The moans that slipped from her just inflamed him more. He thrust into her again and again.

Her heels dug into his ass. Her cries urged him on. Faster. Harder.

She came for him. The clench of her inner muscles around him and the sharp cry that burst from her lips were hotter than anything he'd ever experienced. He watched the pleasure rush over her face and then kissed her.

Even as he came in her. An orgasm that shook his whole body and consumed him—

***

Oliver's eyes opened. "Fuck." He glared at the bedroom ceiling above him. Then his gaze dropped down to his own body. And to the freaking tent he'd just made with the bed sheet and his dick. "Fuck," he said again.

Not a dream. A memory that just kept haunting him. One that was going to ruin him for life. Because how the hell was he ever supposed to want another woman when he knew what it was like to let go and explode in Lark?

His Lark.

The woman who'd kicked him out of her life.

The woman he'd betrayed.

The woman who was back in his house. Sleeping in the room next door.

He climbed from the bed and marched for the bathroom. And he turned on the iciest water that he could.

With every cell of his body, he wanted her. But he was also not about to screw things up again. Not with her.

The icy water hit him when he climbed into the shower. Oliver closed his eyes.

And saw her.

He could play the gentleman, dammit. He'd done it before. He would do it again.

Only...before...

I didn't know what it felt like to come inside of Lark.

Now, he did.

But he also knew how much it sucked to lose her. How it felt to have his heart cut out of his chest when she walked away.

No way would he go through that hell again. This time, he would do whatever it took to keep her.

Because I will not lose Lark again.

CHAPTER FIVE

Lark didn't know what to expect when she walked into the kitchen a little after nine a.m. She'd showered, dried her hair, and when she'd come out of the bathroom, clothes had been waiting for her.

A pair of jeans. A black blouse. Black boots. Underwear. All *her* clothes. She figured Oliver must have made a run to her apartment, but he hadn't said anything to her about the trip.

The clothes had just been on the bed when she opened the bathroom door. The boots had been on the floor.

The house seemed eerily silent as she pushed on the door that led into the kitchen. And when it swung open...

Oliver sat at the kitchen table, sipping coffee. His long, tan fingers gripped the white mug. His gaze slid to her. Was it her imagination or was there heat in his gaze?

She tucked a lock of hair behind her ear. "I...thank you for bringing my clothes over."

"Theo did it. He was coming by to check in, and I asked him to pick up a few items from your apartment."

Fabulous. So someone else had gone through her underwear drawer. Like that made her feel super comfortable.

"We'll be going back to your apartment today and clearing everything else out. You can't stay there." He put down the coffee. "I don't have anything here you're gonna want to eat. I was waiting for you to get up so we could go out for breakfast."

Her gaze slid around the kitchen. Landed on a box of cereal. She wasn't hard to please, and he didn't need to take her out for a meal. "My favorite," she murmured. "Mind if I help myself?"

"Take anything you want."

She could feel his eyes on her as she got down a bowl. Took out a spoon. Poured the milk. She still remembered where everything was. Like they'd never been apart.

Her fingers trembled a little as she carried the bowl of cereal back to the table and sat down. Only to meet his disapproving stare. "There a problem?" she inquired.

"You need more than cereal. You look...hell, beautiful, always beautiful."

She almost dropped her spoon.

"But I know you've lost weight. You seem too fragile. Let me take you out—"

"I'd rather you take me to hunt a killer." That was on her agenda. Not breakfast.

His lips thinned.

She devoured her cereal because, honestly, she was starving. And eating meant she didn't have to talk about the big bombshell she'd dropped last night. The one where she'd just casually confessed to killing her father.

My fault. All of it. I tried to tell the cops, but they wouldn't listen. Then I was sent to the hospital. Her father had fractured her jaw with one of his hits.

And I pulled the trigger. I saw his eyes widen. I swear, for a moment, I saw the madness fade from his eyes, and he just looked...confused.

The spoon clattered into the bowl.

"Lark?"

She stared at her already soggy cereal. "Are you going to arrest me?" Her eyes raised. "Where are those cuffs you love?"

"No one is fucking arresting you," he growled. "That case was ruled self-defense. And I read through the case file again after you went to bed."

Of course, he had. She was sure he had a copy of the file on his computer. *He used it in his profile.*

"You told the responding officers that you'd shot your dad. Your brother also said *he'd* shot him. You didn't lie, he did."

"But when I got out of the hospital, I didn't correct anything."

"What was the point? You or your brother— same ending. Self-defense."

She placed the spoon beside the bowl. "I expected a different response from an FBI agent. Aren't you always supposed to be looking for the truth?"

His eyes glittered. "An FBI agent isn't talking to you right now."

Her heartbeat quickened.

"A man who is damn near obsessed with you—he's the one talking to you. You're not getting arrested. But I need to know if there are more secrets. I can't help you if I don't know the truth."

"The truth...is that Lane thought he was protecting me. He was afraid I would go to juvie for what I'd done. He tried to take the rap for me, but by doing that, he ruined *his* chances." Her lips pressed together.

"What do you mean?"

"Everywhere we went, the foster families always watched him extra intently. They whispered. Talked about him when they thought no one could hear." But she'd heard. "The boy who killed his father. They said that had to leave a mark on him. That he'd always be troubled. That was when the labels started. Social workers put in his file that he exhibited signs of attachment disorder, oppositional defiance—"

"He only attached to you. Your brother only loved you."

"Love isn't easy." Her heart broke thinking about him. "Everything they wrote about Lane? It was all true of *me*. But they looked at me and saw a victim. They looked at him...and instead of seeing a hero, they saw...they saw the boy who'd killed his sick dad."

He gripped the edges of the table. "I'm sorry."

"He fired the gun after I killed our father. I didn't realize why he'd done that but later...one of the cops said Lane had gunshot residue on him. I did, too, but no one ever tested me. Lane set the whole scene. He did *everything* to protect me. I tried to get the cops to listen to me, but they wouldn't." *Lane had been too good at convincing them. And then...*She swallowed the lump in her throat. "Three different families wanted to adopt me." Now that she'd started talking about her past, the words just wouldn't seem to stop. "But they didn't want *him.*"

Oliver nodded. "And you were a package deal."

"Yes." Low. "We still are." Did he get what she was saying? "I won't abandon him. I can't. By taking the fall for my father's death, Lane was the one shunned by everyone. In school, in the foster homes, he was the one everyone always talked about. He has walked in shadows for years because he was trying to make things better for *me.*"

Oliver's gaze cut away from her.

And the cereal she'd eaten suddenly felt very, very heavy in her stomach. "What is it?"

"We should go to that piss-poor excuse for an apartment. Clear everything out. Then I want to check in with Memphis. And with Theo and Jase. I need to see if the crime scene techs have unearthed anything we can use—"

"I thought you didn't want secrets."

Slowly, his stare returned to her.

"I don't want them either." Secrets just dragged you down and weighed on your heart. "*Tell* me what you are thinking."

A long exhale. "You think you cleared Lane by telling me about your father's death, don't you?"

"I..." Hadn't she? She was the killer, not her brother.

Oliver shook his head. "If he lied to protect you, and that lie...it made him become ostracized, it made him the villain, if it made him the one that the families wouldn't choose to adopt, the teachers didn't trust...baby, don't you see? It still all points to him resenting you. To him developing a deep-seated anger toward you. To him hating—"

She shot to her feet. "My brother loves me."

"Yeah, he does." Oliver didn't rise. His head tilted back as he studied her. "But don't you understand, some people can hate the very things that they love?"

No. "Not Lane."

"Right. Not precious Lane."

Her eyes narrowed. "What is that supposed to mean? My brother is in *jail*. You don't get to say things like that about him! You don't get to mock him."

Now he did rise. "Oh, I'm not mocking him." The legs of the chair scraped as he shoved it back. "I'm jealous as hell of him."

"What?" In what universe did that make sense?

"What would it take for you to ever defend me the way you defend him?"

Her lips parted.

But no answer came.

Grimly, he nodded. "That's what I thought. With you, your brother will always come first. You choose him over everyone else. I don't think you did have attachment issues. I think you could probably attach just fine."

He didn't know her. He didn't—

"But you didn't want Lane to be alone. You never wanted him to feel like you weren't there for him. So you kept everyone else away, didn't you?" And he began to close in on her. One slow step at a time.

Those slow steps made her feel hunted, but Lark refused to retreat.

Then he was right in front of her. Looming over her. Seeming to suck all of the air out of the room. "But you couldn't keep me away, could you? I got close." He leaned toward her. "I'm still close."

He *was* close. So close that it almost seemed as if he was going to eliminate the last bit of space and kiss her. And he wasn't. No way was he going to do that.

She didn't want him to do that.

Liar, liar.

"Here's a newsflash for you, Lark. I intend to *stay* close."

For one wild moment, she wanted to grab him. Yank him to her. Kiss him. Pretend that they were lovers once again and that everything was okay. But...

Nothing is okay.

A phone rang. His phone. The faint lines near Oliver's dark eyes tightened as he shoved his hand into his pocket and hauled out the device. He looked at the screen and swore. "Dammit, I have to take this. It's Executive Assistant Director Ballard."

"By all means, answer. I know he's important." She began to turn away.

"You're important."

Those words wrapped around her. She looked back.

He'd put the phone to his ear. "Executive Assistant Director," Oliver began. But then he stopped. Winced. "Sir, I can hear you just fine."

She could hear the guy, too. Hard to miss those angry snarls.

Oliver's jaw clenched. "Yes, she is with me." His eyes were on her. "She's under my protection." A pause. "No, I don't think another agent needs to take over. There is no conflict for me."

No conflict. Of course. There was nothing personal at all between her and Oliver any longer.

"No," Oliver snapped back. "I don't think you understand. This isn't something that is up for debate."

Uh, he was talking to his *boss* in that biting tone?

"Lark stays with me. She was attacked last night. I'm not leaving her safety in anyone else's hands."

Lark took a step back.

"I am well aware of my position," Oliver returned in response to something the Executive Assistant Director told him. "And, yes, we will *both* come down to the office in order to see you." With that, he hung up.

She rocked back on her heels. "Let me guess." As if she had to guess. "Your boss isn't pleased because you let a suspected serial killer's sister spend the night with you last night? That gonna be some bad PR for the Bureau?"

"The press has already talked about our relationship."

They had. The FBI agent—the superstar profiler—and the killer's sister had made for a tantalizing tale in the media.

"Executive Assistant Director Ballard thinks that, with the court case looming, it is in the best interest of the Bureau if I distance myself from you."

Oh. So... "I should go." A brisk nod.

"You're a victim of a crime. You were attacked last night. I don't abandon victims." A hard, negative shake of his head. "You're getting my protection. No one is going to separate me from you. *No one.*"

***

"What in the name of heaven do you think you're doing?" Executive Assistant Director Colby Ballard slapped his hands onto his desk as he glared at Oliver. His wedding ring clinked when it made contact with the hard surface. "Are you trying to screw this case to hell and back? Do you *know* what the jury will do when they find out you're still sleeping with the suspect's sister?"

"I'm not sleeping with her." Oliver kept his relaxed pose in the chair across from Colby. Even on good days, he didn't particularly like the Executive Assistant Director. The guy was a pencil-pushing prick who'd had zero time in the field. Colby loved bossing agents around and claiming responsibility for the successes that others made. Something that extra infuriated

Oliver? The man couldn't profile his way out a paper bag, but he liked to act like he was some genius full of insights when it came to criminals.

"You're not sleeping with her." Colby leaned forward. "She was at your house all night—"

"Actually, she arrived close to dawn." Details mattered. Colby had never seemed to understand how very important small pieces could be to the big picture. "That would have been *after* a masked man attacked her in her vehicle. Her vehicle was taken so the crime scene techs could check it for evidence." With her vehicle out of commission, she'd needed a ride home. What should he have done? Left her stranded? Unprotected? Left her waiting for another attack? *Oh, the fuck, no.* "Lark fully believes that the man who attacked her is the same man who killed Amelia Wayne, Susan Peters, and Casey Gallows."

Colby opened his mouth. Closed it.

"I drove Lark home after the attack, but when we arrived at her apartment..." Now anger slipped into his voice. "Someone had broken in. Apparently, she's had a series of attacks. People throwing bricks into her home. Damaging her vehicle." *She'd been scared. Alone.* Yet Lark had said that she'd reported her attacks to the local cops... "*Why* was I not informed of these situations?" He'd realized that someone in power must have been deliberately keeping him out of the loop.

Oliver strongly suspected he was staring straight at that someone.

"The incidents are being investigated by the local police department. They did not fall in your purview," Colby responded in his arrogant, slightly nasal, I'm-a-prick voice. "I assure you, the local cops are quite capable of dealing with vandals. Your job is serial killers, remember? That is your famous specialty."

Oliver narrowed his eyes.

Colby beetled his brows. "After all, you had the chance to advance higher up in the Bureau, but instead, you basically had a position hand carved for you. You go to where the monsters are, am I right? That's what the people in power at the FBI want for you. They want their monster hunter to hunt at their command. Well, the Bridal Killer has been captured. You should have moved the hell on by now."

Oliver cocked his head to the right. "You're still mad because they offered me the Executive Assistant Director job first, aren't you?" The job that would have put him over the Criminal, Cyber, Response and Services Branch at the Bureau. Only Oliver had never wanted that job. And Colby was right—the people in power at the FBI really wanted Oliver out hunting. Not pushing the papers that Colby loved so much.

A muscle jerked along Colby's jaw. "I'm *pissed* because your personal relationship with Lark Lawson could very well jeopardize the case the Bureau has built against her brother. If he walks, are you going to talk to the families of his victims? Are you going to tell them that a killer went free because you wanted to fuck the guy's sister?"

Well, the gloves were clearly off. "I want to be sure he's guilty."

Colby's chin almost hit the floor as his jaw dropped. Then he rallied even as his face flushed to nearly match the color of his red hair. "You're the one who built the profile! You're the golden boy! You're—"

"After the attack on Lark last night, we need to make certain we are not about to send the wrong man to death row. Details like that matter to me. When I leave here today, I'll be going to visit him. Having a one-on-one chat with Lane."

Colby snorted. "Like the guy's lawyer is gonna ever allow that."

"It will be allowed. Lane will want to talk to me."

"The man probably wants to beat the hell out of you. But, hey, you know what? Go for it." A taunting smile tipped Colby's lips. "You go in there, tell the guy you used his sister to build your case against him, tell him how much you fucked them both over, and when he starts swinging, we can have him for assaulting an officer. Win, win."

"You're a dick, you know that?"

"You shouldn't talk to your supervisor that way. That kind of thing will get you reprimanded." Colby walked around the desk. Moved to tower over Oliver as he continued to sit casually in the chair. "Even your golden boy status won't save you."

It was Oliver's turn to smile.

Colby's brow furrowed in the face of Oliver's smile. Uncertainty flashed in his eyes. "What is your problem?" he groused. "Does anything intimidate you?"

"You don't," Oliver assured him. "I've been toe-to-toe with the worst monsters in the world. Twisted killers who slice up their prey, who torture for hours, and who get off on pain."

Colby flinched.

Yeah, that was the man's problem. He'd never had the stomach for field work. Never could handle the darkest of the cases. Most people couldn't.

Golden boy? Bullshit. That wasn't the title he had at the Bureau. But Colby had touched on Oliver's real nickname. The monster hunter. And, yeah, he had job security because he could get in the heads of those bastards who tortured and murdered for sport.

And he wasn't worried about Colby getting mad at him. Oliver had a direct line to the Deputy Director of the FBI. Oliver's position at the Bureau didn't slide into the traditional hierarchy. Which meant...*I don't have to answer to Colby.* The bastard could bitch and moan, but a threat of a reprimand wasn't gonna do jack shit for Oliver. "I'm not looking to jeopardize the case."

"Then let someone else guard your precious Lark."

She is very precious. It was good that Colby understood that fact.

"There are plenty of other agents and local cops who can do the job. Hell, we'll even put her up in a safe house for you. That make you feel better?" Colby raked a hand over his face. "Not like I want the woman getting attacked."

"Good to know."

Colby's hand dropped.

"Appreciate the offer of the safe house, but I'll be sticking close to her. After I pay my visit to her brother, I'll be taking a bit of personal time—"

Colby gaped. "You're asking for—"

"Not asking. I'm telling you. I will be taking some personal time while I investigate to see what the hell is happening with Lark. I want to be free to follow the leads wherever they may take me."

Worry flashed on Colby's face. "You...you really think the wrong guy might be locked up?"

He should worry. Because a mistake this major would have the Bureau looking like fools in the press. Colby often worried about the press. By often...*every single day*. The man was image conscious to the extreme. *Narcissist, self-involved, inflated ego.* Oliver could profile Colby in his sleep. And that was why Oliver knew that Colby would go for his plan. "If Lane Lawson is innocent, I'll be the one to take the blame. I was the one who centered in on him, who brought in the evidence...*I'll* take the fall. You can very publicly fire me."

"Shit. You're actually serious about this." More worry.

"And if he is innocent," Oliver continued grimly, "you know I am not going to stop until I have the real murderer locked away. There is no way I will leave him out there so that he can hunt again." *No way in hell.* "That's why I'm taking time off. But, I still want full access to the Bureau's resources. Full access," he emphasized. "I will not be working other cases. I will be off book, and I'll be recruiting some...friends to help me." The Ice Breakers counted as friends, didn't they? Most of them, anyway. He'd use the Ice Breakers, and a few other associates he'd be pulling into the fray.

He'd already called one of those associates on the way to the Bureau's Vegas office. An old buddy that he could count on when things went to hell.

"You sure sound demanding for someone who is already walking on thin ice."

Oliver glanced at the floor. "Don't see any ice." Just some shitty carpeting that needed to be replaced. He looked back at Colby. "I do see a man who might come across as a prick most days, but at your core, you're only half an asshole. You don't want an innocent man locked away any more than I do. You don't want a monster still out on the streets."

Colby's jaw tightened.

"You know I can do the job. Not like it will be the first time I use unorthodox methods." He was the master of those. The whole reason he wasn't technically in the FBI's hierarchy. He did things his own way, and he got results.

"It's on you if he's innocent," Colby said, voice flat. "You admit you fucked up. You take the fall for the press. And when you catch the real killer..."

When, not if. Nice to know the man had some faith in him.

"I'll handle the press conference," Colby concluded.

Of course, he would. Oliver rose from his chair. Automatically, Colby backed up a few steps. "Then I guess we're done here," Oliver said. He turned for the door.

"I know your big deal is that you get into the heads of the killers. You think just like them. Which, honestly, is some scary shit."

Oliver hesitated.

"Lark Lawson is still the key in all this, isn't she? The one that the killer seems focused on. Either her brother was killing women who looked like her or...or the real murderer is now coming after her. Either way, it all goes back to Lark."

Oliver looked over his shoulder. "Your point?"

Colby's hand rose, and he scratched his chin. "Are you using her as bait?"

"Never."

A nod. "Then, next question...are you sure you're the one who wants her? Is your obsession with her real? Or are you just still so linked to the killer that you want the same prey he does?"

"Lark is not prey to me." Anger churned in him, but he didn't let the emotion slip out.

"No? Then what is she?"

Everything. Without another word, he marched for the door.

CHAPTER SIX

Lark's gaze darted around Oliver's office. Small, with a window that overlooked the busy street below. No photos on his desk. Perfectly organized with zero clutter.

She knew that he often traveled around the country with his special team. Hunting the worst predators out there. *Why is he even still in Vegas?* After her brother had been locked up, she'd expected him to leave.

And, he had. But for only a few weeks.

Then he'd come back.

He'd left her in the office while he went to speak with Colby Ballard. A man who always put her on edge. His light blue eyes were so cold when he looked at her.

The door to the office flew open, and Lark gave a start of surprise.

"Boss, the Cadillac Escalade was reported stolen—" Jase Guillory broke off when he saw her. "Oh, I, uh, heard Oliver was here today."

She rose and smoothed her hands over the front of her jeans. "He's in a meeting with the Executive Assistant Director."

Jase winced. "That has to be hell." His gaze darted around the office then slid back to her. "Sorry to bust in. I'll come back later."

But Lark hurried toward him. Her hand flew out and her fingers lightly touched the side of his arm. "What did you find out about the Escalade? It was stolen?"

"Yeah, stolen about four hours before you saw it. It belongs to a high roller in town. He checked in about two days ago, and it was taken right out of the valet lot at his hotel."

"Which hotel?" Lark asked as her stomach seemed to dip.

"Oh, you know the one."

No, she didn't know it. That was why she'd asked. Her brows scrunched.

"It's got all those dancing fountains in front." His hand waved vaguely in the air. "Apparently, it's our high roller's favorite place to stay." Jase rattled off the name of one of the most well-known hotels and casinos in the area. Then he shook his head. "And I just got word the Escalade was found fifteen miles outside of Vegas. Whoever took it must have ditched it. The area where it was found is known for a pretty high crime rate. The officers on scene say the vehicle was heavily stripped down."

"So whoever ditched the Escalade would have *known* it would get stripped out there," Oliver said, his strong voice sounding from behind Jase.

Jase whirled around. "Boss! Didn't realize you were there!"

Lark's hand fell back to her side.

"We need to get video footage from the valet lot," Oliver said. "They've got great security there. Hell, I was in that hotel not too long ago on another case."

His gaze dipped to Lark.

She lifted her chin. She knew exactly what case he was talking about. She'd been at the same location, following up on a lead from a PI that had not panned out. To her surprise, she'd walked straight into Oliver in the hotel's lobby. She'd stumbled into him and right into the case he'd been working. One that had sent the building into lockdown as a killer was hunted.

"I have connections there," Oliver added. "I'll put in a phone call and get us access right away. You head over and start talking to the security personnel and to the valet attendants. I want to know everything they saw."

"Absolutely." Jase started to edge around him.

"I'll be...technically on leave," Oliver said quietly.

Jase stopped his edging. "*What?* No, no, do not tell me that the Executive Assistant Director—"

"My choice. Not his. I have some off-book investigating I want to do. All the intel you collect should still be directed my way." His gaze drifted to Lark. "I'm staying close to her until I'm satisfied we have the right man behind bars."

Her heart slammed hard against her chest.

"You—you think—" Jase stopped and shook his head. "Boss..."

"I think I need to be certain. After I leave here, I'm going to talk to Lane Lawson. You get to the high-priced hotel. Update Theo. You two are going to keep working the attack from last night. That is priority. The local cops aren't in charge. You are, got me?"

Jase nodded quickly before hurrying away. Oliver moved to fully fill the doorway. His broad shoulders took up all the space, and his hooded gaze swept over Lark as she stood there, with her hands loose at her sides.

When the silence stretched a little too long, she licked her dry lips and asked, "We're going to talk to Lane?"

"I am. Alone."

"But—"

"I have to be able to read him, Lark. If you're in the room..." And he advanced into his office and shut the door, sealing them away from the other agents. "His reactions will be different. I tried to interview him before. Many times. He refused. Wouldn't say a word."

"That would be because he hates you." Hard to sugarcoat that fact.

"You told me that my profile was wrong."

"It was. It is." *Because I'm the killer.*

"Then I need to talk with Lane. Face to face. No distractions. I have to see his responses. I need to get past the mask he's put on for the world. I can't do that if you're there."

But she wanted to be there. She didn't want—

"Not worried he'll confess his guilt to me, are you?"

Her shoulders straightened. "Absolutely not."

"Good. Then you'll stay with my friend Midas while I have the little chat with your brother."

"Midas?"

"He's someone I trust." A pause. "And I don't want you going to your apartment. Change of plans. We'll clear out everything later. But don't worry, Theo brought a bag for you earlier. I put it in the guest room closet while you were in the shower. Should last a few days until we can get to your place."

"A few days?"

"I want you in a secure location. Your apartment *isn't* secure."

No, she didn't think it was safe. At all.

"After I finish with Lane, you and I will meet up again and see what the hell has been found out about the Escalade." He lifted his hand, and the sleeve of his black suit coat slid back to reveal his watch. "Maybe we'll hit the high roller's hotel ourselves. I always like to be at a location to get a sense of the scene."

Of the crime. She knew that was what he'd actually meant. *To get a sense of the crime. To feel things that the perp might have felt.* As for the whole her staying with his friend part... "I want to know more about this Midas."

A light rap sounded at the closed door.

"Man is always perfectly on time," Oliver murmured. "Never fails." He turned and swung open the door.

She blinked. Oliver was tall. About six-foot-three. The guy in the doorway had him by about two inches. Maybe three. Tall, no, *big*. With wide shoulders. Arms that stretched his t-shirt.

His dirty blond hair was thick. A short beard covered his powerful jaw.

"You finished up with the pop singer?" Oliver asked.

Lark frowned.

"Security detail is over," Midas said. His voice rumbled like thunder in the distance. The low rumble that tells you when trouble was coming.

Oliver eased back a bit. In his black suit, he looked polished and crisp. Elegantly handsome as always.

As for his friend...

His amber gaze raked over her. "You're the mark."

Lark blinked. "Excuse me?"

"Lark is the woman you guard with your life," Oliver corrected curtly.

Midas grunted.

Oliver waved between them. "Midas Monroe, this is Lark Lawson. Lark, Midas. He's the best bodyguard I know."

"Stop trying to make me blush," Midas rumbled. "You know Wilde is the crew that has the top-notch reputation."

Wilde. The name rang a bell for her. Wilde was an elite protection firm. One that specialized in guarding the rich and famous. It was pretty much *the* best-known protection firm in the United States. And there was no way in the world she'd ever be able to afford their services.

"Wilde is a firm," Midas said as he swept an assessing glance between her and Oliver, "while I'm a one-man army." He made a sweeping bow. "At your service."

Lark wet her lips. Her attention shifted to Oliver. "I don't really think I need a one-man army."

He closed in on her. "The bastard was waiting for you in your car. He threatened to kill you."

Like she could forget.

"You're getting the damn one-man army," Oliver assured her. Then, voice lowering, he added, "Midas and I go way back. There are few people in this world that I trust completely, but he happens to be one of them."

She darted a glance Midas's way. She found him staring straight at her and Oliver. A thoughtful expression filled his eyes.

"I need to know that you're with someone I trust. Stay with him, okay? He'll take you back to my place. I'll meet you after I talk to Lane."

She didn't want to be left out of that talk. But...she actually understood. Her brother would be different when she was with him. Her head moved in a quick nod.

A sigh of relief slipped from Oliver. He started to spin back toward Midas.

Her hand pressed to his arm. Oliver tensed. He glanced down at her fingers.

"Tell Lane I love him," she murmured.

His gaze rose to catch hers. "Trust me," he returned. "Your brother knows."

***

His gun had been taken. Secured. He'd been led into the small interrogation room in the back of the facility. A guard stood inside the little room.

The man waited at stiff attention. Oliver knew the guard would remain in the room during his questioning. Oliver's connections had gotten him inside and those same connections would get the prisoner delivered to this meeting...

But even the monster hunter wouldn't be allowed to interview Lane Lawson without someone else in the room. A slightly problematic situation considering what he needed to discuss. *So the guard will stay.*

But Oliver could deal with most problematic situations. They just took some finesse.

The door swung open. Lane Lawson staggered inside. He had to stagger. Cuffs bound his wrists and ankles, and a long chain connected them. When he saw Oliver waiting for him, Lane immediately stopped his stagger. In fact, he froze completely.

Then the hulking guard behind him pushed Lane forward.

"Fuck this," Lane said, voice flat. A purple bruise lined the side of his jaw. Another bruise— this one darker, fresher—dipped around his right eye. "I'm not talking to him."

That was the reaction that Oliver had expected.

Lane spun toward the guard who'd just pushed him. "Take me back to the cell," Lane ordered. "Take me back to the yard where those assholes like to take turns swinging punches. Take me any-fucking-where but here."

Oliver sighed. "I think you'll want to talk with me."

"I want you to go screw yourself," Lane snapped without looking back.

The guard in front of Lane glanced uncertainly at Oliver.

Oliver smiled at the man. "He wants to talk to me," Oliver assured the guard.

"The hell I—" Lane blasted.

"Your sister was attacked last night."

Lane whirled to face him. Shock and fury flashed on Lane's face. A face that was so very different from Lark's. While Lark was beauty and delicate elegance, Lane was all angles and hard planes. He had Lark's dark hair, and his eyes were green, but the green was different. Harder. Or maybe it was just Lane's glare that made his eye color seem brittle while Lark's eyes were warm and such a deep green.

But, at least Oliver had succeeded in snagging Lane's full attention. So while he had that attention, Oliver said, "The man was waiting in the back of Lark's car. He had a syringe so that he could drug her. The bastard said she'd go to sleep, and when she woke up, she'd be his." *The fuck that will happen.* Oliver rose from his seat. He walked around the table and pulled out the other chair for Lane. "Now, shall we talk?"

***

His stare unnerved her.

Lark shifted uneasily on the couch—Oliver's couch because Midas had driven her back to Oliver's place. Oliver had headed off to meet her brother, and she'd been left with the bodyguard.

A bodyguard who just watched her with his too intent amber gaze. Midas stood near the fireplace mantel, with his arms crossed over his massive chest and with his stare pinning her.

Lark cleared her throat. This business had gone on long enough. "You know it's not polite to stare." It was, in fact, super creepy, and she already had enough going on to creep her out, thank you very much.

"It's also not polite to break my best friend's heart."

Her mouth dropped open. She hurriedly snapped it closed even as she leapt to her feet. "I did no such thing!"

"Sure, you did." A sage nod. "I'm the one who had to pick Oliver's drunk ass up the day after you walked out on him. Man is a sad drunk, by the way. Was moaning about how you were the best thing ever to happen to him."

She shook her head.

"Yeah, I told him that, too. Plenty of fish in the sea and all that. No sense getting broken up so hard over one woman."

Her eyes narrowed. "I don't think I like you."

His mouth hitched into a half-smile that never reached his eyes. "Surprisingly, I get that a lot. Honestly, though, it helps with the job. When clients go falling in love with you, it just makes things complicated as hell."

The man was not serious. *He can't be serious. He's just trying to get a reaction from me. There is no way I broke Oliver's heart.* "Oliver was using me to get information on my brother—"

His deep and loud laughter cut her off.

"I stand by my previous statement," she muttered. *The one where I said I don't think I like you.*

"I was there," Midas informed her with a roll of one big shoulder. "Saw him. Heard him mooning over you. Poor bastard even wanted me to drive by your house like some lovestruck teenager. Thank Christ he got called away to handle some other serial killing freak so he could get some distance from you for a while."

She blinked. "Did you...Wait, are you *thankful* for a serial killer—"

He winced. And one hand rose to rub along his jaw. "Yeah. That probably came out wrong, didn't it?"

"I don't think it came out right," Lark assured him. "I don't know if there was a way in which that statement could sound right."

He shrugged. "It was good for him to get away. Stand by that. He needed to put some distance between the two of you. Especially seeing as how you had broken his heart."

Enough. She strode toward him. Put her hands on her hips. Tilted back her head. "I was the one who told *him* that I loved him. Your *best friend* never said those words back to me. As far as I know, it's because he never loved me. He was using me all along. Oliver had no real interest in me whatsoever."

Midas's brows rose. "You tell yourself that a lot or something?"

Yes, actually, she did.

"You did hear Oliver when he said I was supposed to guard you with my life?"

"Yes, obviously, I heard him say that. I was standing right beside the man," she muttered. "And you guarding me with your life—that's an expression."

"Not for Oliver. Not when it comes to you. For him, it was an actual order." His stare swept over her. "When it comes to you, he meant every word. Why else would he call me in? Why not just use one of those Feds that were running around the Bureau like crazy?"

She opened her mouth to reply.

"I'll tell you why," he said before she could speak. "It's because you matter. And what matters to Oliver—even if I am mad as hell at you for breaking his heart—well, it matters to me."

She could only shake her head.

"So I'll protect you with my life. He is my best friend, after all. I also owe him more than I can ever repay." Another shrug. "It is what it is."

She didn't know what anything was with this giant of a man. "Why do you owe him?"

His expression changed. Hardened. Small changes...but...

Okay, he is super intimidating.

Because staring into his amber eyes right then was like staring into the fires of hell.

"I owe him because he didn't give up. He didn't give up on me, and he won't give up on you." Both of his hands fell to his sides. "Now let's go see what's in his kitchen. I'm hungry as hell." He brushed by her.

Frowning, Lark peered after him.

But right before Midas reached the kitchen, he tossed a glance over his shoulder. "But just so we are clear, if your brother is guilty, Oliver is never going to let him see the light of day."

"That's...for a judge and jury to decide."

Midas stared back at her.

"He's not guilty," she fired back. Maybe that should have been the first thing she said. Dammit, was this guy *testing* her? She felt as if he was.

"For your sake," Midas returned, voice lower than it had been a moment before, "I hope that's the case. But I've seen it over and over again—and I know Oliver has, too. People think their family members are freaking saints. But they aren't. Sometimes, you're just too close to realize the truth. You don't see the evil that is right in front of you. You don't see it standing there because it's hiding behind a smile and a face you know too well."

"I see what's in front of me." Her vision was 20/20.

"I didn't," he told her with a slightly cruel twist of his lips that maybe should have been a mocking smile. "Sure as hell didn't see it when my own father was killing people. And when I was the one being blamed for the crimes? When I was the one about to be locked away? Oliver is the person who cleared me. He didn't give up, even when my own flesh and blood set me up to take the rap for his crimes."

Her breath rushed out in shock.

"I think there's a reason Oliver wanted me to be the one guarding you. I suspect you understand that reason now, too." He turned his head away from her. "Sometimes, the people you need to fear the most are the ones you love the deepest."

"Your father?" And her own father's image flashed into her mind. For an instant, Lark could feel his hands reaching for her. She could see the flash of the knife. *Boom*. The madness had faded from his eyes as he fell...

"Yeah, and unlike your dear old dad, my father didn't have a brain tumor or some illness making him do the things he did. He was just a straight-up psycho killer. And lucky me, I'm his only son." Midas shoved open the kitchen door.

CHAPTER SEVEN

"You've got a lot of bruises," Oliver noted as he sat in the chair across the table from Lane. The guard who'd brought Lane into the room had left, but the other man still maintained his watchful position near the wall on the left.

As for Lane, he'd been secured at the table. His ferocious glare burned hotter as he bit out, "Aren't you the fucking observant one?"

Oliver exhaled on a long sigh. "I try to be. But even I miss things."

Lane's eyes widened dramatically. "You don't say?"

"You should drop the dick act so that we can get down to business. I don't want to be away from your sister for longer than is necessary."

Lane lunged at him. Instantly, the guard sprang from the wall and clamped his hands on Lane's shoulders and shoved him back into the seat. Not like Lane would have been able to actually attack Oliver. His chain had been hooked to the floor before his "escort" had left the room.

Oliver just watched the byplay between Lane and the guard with one slowly raising eyebrow.

Lane kept glaring.

The guard didn't move back.

"Gonna stop lunging?" Oliver asked quietly.

"I want you the hell away from my sister!"

"I'll take that as a yes." He waved toward the guard. "He's good now."

Lane snorted. Clearly, he was not good.

But the guard removed his hold and stepped back.

"Your sister is in danger," Oliver informed Lane. "You want her unprotected?"

"There are plenty of bodyguards out there. Plenty of other Feds. She doesn't need *you.*" Disgust tightened Lane's lips. "You broke her heart already. What the hell do you want? To do damage a second time?"

You broke her heart already. "I want to fix what's broken." The truth slipped from him. But when it came to Lark, that was all he wanted.

"Not gonna happen." Lane seemed certain on this point. "She doesn't trust easily. She doesn't give second chances. Neither of us do." He leaned forward. A lean, not a lunge, so the guard didn't have to pounce again. "You know what sucks? When you trust someone completely, and they shatter that trust."

"Are you talking about me..." Oliver tilted his head as he watched for Lane's reaction. "Or your father?"

Lane's lashes flickered. He cleared his throat. "You here to analyze me?"

Absolutely, I am. He did have a Ph.D. in psychology. Abnormal psych had been his specialty and the reason he'd wound up hunting killers. Someone had to get them off the streets.

"Lark and I recently talked about the night your father died."

Lane's stare dipped toward the silent guard before returning to Oliver. "So what? Everyone knows about that night." His voice roughened as he added, "I had to stop him. He would have killed my sister." His Adam's apple bobbed as he swallowed. "I had no idea he was sick. No one knew. No one could have known. He'd just gotten meaner and meaner, and the man I used to know? The man who'd come to my football games and cheer...he turned into a bastard who'd punch me as soon as I walked into the house." His lashes flickered. "I was supposed to protect my sister. My mother was on the floor, not moving at all. She was covered in blood, and my old man was going after *Lark*." A rasping breath. His chin lifted. "I was supposed to protect her."

"So you shot your father."

"That's already been established, hasn't it?"

"You pulled the trigger?" Oliver pushed.

"Self-defense," Lane snapped back. "Ruled that way years ago. I don't get the point in this twisted walk to the past that you're making me take."

He won't actually confess to killing his father. Interesting. "Lark walked me through the past already. Told me everything about that night." He paused. Stared straight into Lane's eyes. "*Everything*."

Lane swallowed again. Another quick bob of his Adam's apple. "My sister would say anything to protect me."

"Would she?" Now they were getting somewhere. "Would she lie and say that the package I discovered—the one with the dead women's jewelry—it had actually been sent to her and not to you?"

Surprise flashed in Lane's eyes but was quickly concealed.

"Lark said the package came to her florist shop. She took it home, forgot about it, and then I found it." He waited for a response.

Lane's breathing seemed a bit faster.

"If that story is true, then this really didn't have much to do with you, did it? If we're buying the tale Lark is spinning, then the killer was contacting her." Not that Oliver wasn't doing more investigating. He was. Or rather, he'd given orders for Jase to track down Katya. *Did that before I left the crime scene in that parking lot last night.*

But this chat was not about the work Jase was doing. It was about Lane.

Lane wet his lips.

Oliver carefully continued, "The killer is attacking women who look like Lark. And...well, Lark does have the florist shop. And flowers were left with the dead women. Almost like they were brides holding bouquets. Isn't that why people in the press call you the Bridal Killer?"

"I'm not—" he stopped.

"Not a killer?" Oliver finished for him.

Once more, Lane swallowed. The click seemed extra loud.

"Let's go back to Lark, shall we?" Oliver mused. "As I was saying, she has the florist shop—

or rather, had since she was forced to sell it." Rage churned in him because he knew how much the shop had meant to her. *I'll get it back for you.* But now wasn't the time to lose focus. He cleared his throat, then said, "She looks like the other women...or maybe the other women look like *her.*"

Lane partially turned toward the watchful guard. "I don't want to be here. Take me back to my cell."

Fuck. He couldn't let Lane leave yet. "She was attacked last night. If you didn't kill the other women, then that would mean the man who attacked her last night...maybe he's finally going after the bride he really wanted all along?"

Lane's head whipped toward Oliver. "No one hurts my sister."

"She's got bruises on her from the attack last night." He hated those bruises. "But don't worry, I plan to stay close to her."

Lane didn't lunge at him even though the words had been a taunt. Instead, he gave a jerky nod. "You had freaking better."

Oliver blinked, deliberately. "I thought you didn't want me—"

"I don't want you breaking her heart again. Lark deserves some happiness. She shouldn't be used and discarded by some jerk who just wants to lock me away."

"Lark thinks you're innocent."

"Because I am." Simple. "I didn't hurt those women. I wouldn't have." His jaw tightened. "He killed my mother. I was holding her when she died. You think...you think I would *ever* hurt a woman? *Ever?*"

Oliver didn't respond.

"Lark was taken to the hospital after my dad's shooting. I confessed." A nod. "Nothing was going to hurt Lark again. I swore to it."

So you took the fall. You wanted to protect her. Hell, your father's actions...

They'd made Lane hyper protective of his sister. Of all women? Of anyone who he thought was weak? Oliver's mind churned with possibilities as he realigned his—

"Hey, asshole!"

Oliver frowned. He blinked and realized Lane was glaring at him.

"You got more questions or you just looking to piss away more of my time and stare off into space?"

He had a million questions, especially since Lane was finally talking to him. "Your lawyer isn't going to like that you're suddenly so eager to chat with me."

"If my sister is in trouble, I don't care what my lawyer likes or doesn't like. I'll tell you anything you want to hear." He exhaled. "It's...Lark can't wind up like those others. She *can't*. Not cold and dead and clutching those flowers." A shudder worked over him.

The reaction seemed real. But Oliver had met plenty of monsters who were good at faking their emotions. "You ever notice anyone who had too much of an interest in your sister?"

"Yeah, I'm staring at the bastard." Lane sent him a cold smile.

Right. "Anyone *other* than me?"

"Lark doesn't give most guys the time of day. She doesn't get close to people. Doesn't trust easily."

Wonderful. Keep making me feel like even more of a jackass. "So there was no one who stood out for you?"

"Lots of guys want to date my sister. None of them seemed like crazy killers. Like I said, she didn't get close to them. The only guy she ever really talked to me about was your sorry ass. Otherwise, she would date a man for a few nights, then move on. She never trusted anyone but me, you see. I got the same damn problem. The only one I can count on is my sister. As far as the rest of the world is concerned? If you trust too much, you set yourself up for one colossal nightmare just waiting to happen."

Because the people you trusted—the people you loved—would turn on you.

Lark isn't going to take me back. That certainty seeped through him. She wasn't going to give him a second chance. He'd been hoping but...

"Why don't you just ask my sister about her exes?" Lane smiled, and the big bruise near his eye crinkled. "Gonna interview them all? I'm sure that will be fun for you."

No, it would not be. *Fucking bastards.* "When you were in foster care, did anyone ever show too much attention to Lark?"

That question wiped the smile off Lane's face.

Someone had. Oliver knew he'd hit paydirt. "Who?" he demanded.

"Years ago...second home we were in...no, third." Lane's voice roughened with anger. "The Montgomery family. Nice enough husband and wife. They had a teenage son who stared at Lark—too much." A hard shake of his head. "At school, he was always two steps behind her. He tried to peek at Lark in the shower once. I had to teach him some manners. Would have thought he learned...he didn't. A few days later, her scream woke me up. He'd snuck in her room and was watching her sleep or some weird shit like that."

Oliver realized his hands had fisted.

"That make you mad?" Lane asked, voice casual.

Lane's gaze had fallen to the fisted hand that Oliver had on top of the table. One fist was on top of the table. One under it.

Slowly, Oliver unclenched his fists. "I don't want anyone hurting her."

"Careful, Mr. FBI Profiler. You keep saying stuff like that, and I'll think you weren't just using my sister. I'll think that you were actually falling for her."

"Think what you want."

"I generally do."

"What was the teenager's name?"

"Blain. But that was years ago. After the night I found him in her room, well, the mom and dad didn't exactly take kindly to me breaking his hand."

"Can't imagine why they didn't appreciate the gesture."

"Right?" His lips pulled down. "So strange. Even odder when the parents called and had our case worker on the doorstep the next morning. They wanted me taken away, but they wanted to keep Lark. They thought she'd stay with them and their creepy-ass kid."

"But Lark would never leave you."

Lane blinked. "No, Lark would never leave me."

"She'd stay with you no matter what you did. See, I actually read your old case worker's files. This isn't the time to bullshit me. I've read everything about you that I possibly can."

"Sure, you did. Building that profile. Good for you. I'd clap but I'm cuffed and chained."

"Blain Montgomery is a now state representative in Nevada. Never had a hint of scandal in his life."

"Some people are really good at hiding their true selves."

Yes, they were. "You got into quite a few fights at foster homes. Were all those people doing things to Lark that you didn't like?"

"I only fight when there's a reason."

"Some would say there's never a reason for violence."

"Then those people have obviously never been on the receiving end of a fist. *I am not easy prey*. Won't ever be again. If I saw someone weak being attacked, then I stepped in."

Oliver motioned toward Lane's face. And the bruises there. "Been seeing some weak people get attacked?"

Lane's gaze hardened even more. "Others here are making the mistake of thinking *I'm* weak. I'm correcting that wrong assumption."

"I don't think you're weak." He knew he was staring straight at a predator.

"You just think I'm a killer."

"I think anyone can kill, under the right circumstances."

Lane's eyes lit with sudden interest. "Have you killed, Mr. FBI Profiler?"

Yes. But this wasn't about him. "Would you kill to protect your sister?"

"In a heartbeat." Lane paused, for just the barest of moments. "Would you kill to protect her?"

In a heartbeat. Oliver rose. "I think we're done here."

***

"You need to go grocery shopping."

Oliver paused just inside the doorway of his home and frowned at Midas. "What?"

"Your cupboards are bare, man. Bare. Now I'm hungry as hell and you know I get grumpy when I'm hungry." Midas folded his arms over his chest. "I did order some takeout so your lady wouldn't starve but that little bit was barely the tip of the iceberg for me. Get more food the next time you want me pulling babysitting duty."

Oliver kicked the door closed behind him. "It's not babysitting duty. It's bodyguard duty. You know, that thing you do professionally?" He craned to look around Midas, a hard task considering just how huge his friend was. "Where is she?"

"Sleeping. Avoiding me in the guest room. Same thing. I...*might* have made her a bit uncomfortable."

Great. "Do I want to know what you did?"

"I told her about my freak of a father. Not real surprised when she went running after that. Most people do," Midas said flatly, as if it didn't matter but...

It mattered. It always did. Oliver knew the truth. So he craned a little more and finally saw behind Midas. "That the reason you went running?" he asked a silently watching Lark.

Midas stiffened. Cursed creatively—he was always extra creative with his curses. Said something about fucking fish flying in the air—and he spun to face Lark. "You snuck up on me!" he accused and sounded a little bit impressed.

"I walked out of the guest room. Came in when I heard Oliver's car in the drive."

Midas pointed down at her bare feet. "You didn't put on shoes. You wanted to be sneaky."

"I didn't stop to put them on. I took my boots off before I tried to nap." Her head tilted. "I wasn't avoiding you because of your father. If that's what you thought, you're wrong. Of all people, I understand that we are not our fathers."

Midas...backed up a step. One, then another.

Odd, because Midas didn't usually retreat from anyone or anything.

But he was retreating from Lark.

"If that's not why you ducked out..." Midas's brow furrowed. "Why'd you get so quiet when the food arrived? Why'd you run as soon as you were finished eating?"

"Because you said I broke his heart." Her attention shifted to Oliver. "Painting me as the villain in the piece, are you?"

Never, sweetheart, never. "Nah," he answered easily. "Just telling my buddy the truth."

"You need to have a heart in order for it to be broken."

Midas whistled. "Damn. That is cold."

I have a heart. It will always belong to you, Lark.

Her chin notched up. "Did you get to grill my brother?"

"We talked. Don't know if I'd call it a grilling, but..."

She surged forward, then seemed to catch herself. Lark drove her hands into the back pockets of her jeans. "Did you do your magical profiling thing? Did you peer into his soul to see if he was telling you the truth or not?"

Would you kill to protect your sister? "I think I got the truth from him." *In a heartbeat.* "And what I do isn't magical." Not by a long shot.

"So...you don't think he's the killer?"

He realized she was holding her breath. Staring up at him with her emerald eyes as she waited and hoped that he no longer believed her brother was a killer.

"Yeah..." Midas grimaced. "I think I should probably go clear out my hotel space. I was staying next to the pop star, and now that my business with her is done, I don't think I'll be needing that connecting suite much longer." He inclined his head to Oliver. "I'm assuming you'll be staying close to Lark for a while."

"We have some leads to run down. Lark and I will be heading out soon, and, yes, I'll be close."

"Good to know." Midas walked toward him and clapped a hand on Oliver's shoulder. He leaned in close and whispered, "Don't let her break your heart again."

Like I can stop it from happening.

Then Midas threw a glance at Lark. "Interesting meeting you. You weren't at all like the wicked witch that I expected."

"Thank...you?"

"And I'm not the son of the devil, either. Or maybe I am. Who the hell knows?" He lifted his hand in a wave. The door shut behind him moments later.

The silence grew thick. Heavy.

The big foyer with its fifteen-foot ceiling suddenly seemed too small.

"That's an...unusual friend you have." Her hands were still tucked in the back pockets of her jeans.

"That's the only kind of friend I like to have." Oliver headed for his study. Nervous energy hummed within him. He knew Lark wanted him to say...*No, I don't think your beloved brother is a killer. I'm completely convinced of his innocence now.* And if he said that, maybe she'd throw herself into his arms, just like in the fantasies he'd had so many times. Fantasies where she said she never wanted to be away from him. Where she said she'd choose him, always. That he mattered more to her than anything else.

He turned at his desk, propped his hip against the edge, and watched as she tip-toed in after him.

"Prints are still being run on the Escalade." He'd checked on the way home. "Unlike on TV shows, that kind of thing can take time. Theo is looking at traffic cams, though. So far, he can see the Escalade, but not get a view of the driver. Not one when the driver is not wearing that damn ski mask, anyway."

"What about Jase? Has he turned up anything? Did he talk to the valet staff where the car was stolen?"

Oliver nodded. "He's got video of a man in a black ski mask walking right up to the Escalade. Guy has a key. Doesn't need to pick the lock. Just accesses it and drives away. He must have lifted the key from the valet station or had someone else lift it for him." *And that's why Jase is spending extra time grilling every member of the staff there.* "I want to go over. Take a look myself. But since I'm supposed to be stepping back, I was letting Jase have his run first."

"I don't think you should be stepping back."

His lips twisted. "Not like there's much of a choice. Can't be having you in my bed every night while I'm running a case that involves you. Looks like a major conflict of interest." Hell, like everything with her wasn't a conflict? *My days at the Bureau are numbered.* But he'd known that for a while. Even with the special designation and privileges the Deputy Director had given Oliver, there was still too much red tape. Too many rules that he wanted to break.

And that was why he'd been in talks with the Ice Breakers.

Maybe it was time to go freelance. He could still do consulting work for the Feds, on the side. He'd also been offered several teaching positions at colleges. He could make his own schedule, teach when he wanted, and take the cases with the Ice Breakers when they needed him. Memphis had certainly been making a convincing sell in his arguments to Oliver over the last few weeks.

His phone rang.

Oliver pulled it out and glanced down at the screen. *Speak of the devil.* Well, technically, he hadn't spoken about the devil in question. He'd just *thought* about the Ice Breakers and Memphis Camden. With his eyes on a slowly approaching Lark, Oliver raised the phone to his ear. "Mind if I call you back?"

"Uh, mind if you start keeping my ass in the loop?" Memphis retorted. "Thought we were working together on this thing. Then I catch a news story about how Lark Lawson was attacked last night, by the *same* man who abducted and killed those other women."

"Sounds like the reporter was jumping the gun. Don't have enough evidence to say that with certainty yet."

"Don't give me your FBI public relations bullshit," Memphis huffed right back. "This is me. Was it him?"

Lark stopped just a few feet away.

"Trying to figure that out," he said.

"She's with you?"

"About three feet away, yes, and when I'm not with her, I have someone I trust who will be. Until we catch the guy from last night, she's not going to be staying alone."

"Good. I don't like this shit."

"Can't say I'm a major fan, either."

Lark watched him.

"I've got my team digging into the families of the vics," Memphis informed him. "I know, I know, the Feds already checked them out. I want my own checking done. With *my* people. The first vic, Casey—she came here to get married, right? Only she had a fight with her fiancé. She stormed off into the night."

"Yes. Casey Gallows. The fiancé didn't report her missing right away because the guy believed she was angry with him and that she'd hooked up with someone else." And maybe she had. Maybe she'd gone off and met the wrong man.

The first victim was important. She set the stage. She'd been the first bride. An actual woman who'd come to town to get married, only she'd met a killer instead.

"Did you know her fiancé is in town?" Memphis asked, voice going low and soft. A dangerous thing, that. Because when Memphis got quiet...

Trouble is stirring.

"No." A knot formed at the back of his neck. "Thought he'd gone home to Colorado."

"He *should* have been in Colorado. I learned about ten minutes ago that he's actually supposed to be here in town. Thought I'd call my friendly FBI agent and report about what I discovered."

Oliver's grip on the phone tightened. "Where's he staying?"

"I don't know. Still working on that. But I figured—"

"Call you back," Oliver snapped. He hung up on Memphis and dialed Jase.

The agent answered on the second ring. "Boss? What's up?"

"You at the hotel?"

"Yeah, but—"

"Find out if Nate Quest is staying there. If he is, you call me immediately, got it?" He got the affirmation from Jase that the agent would call him back, and then Oliver ended the call.

"You have a lead," Lark said. Hope lit her eyes.

"I don't know what I have...yet." Not entirely true. He had the memory of Nate Quest, the guy's shock and horror when Nate had ID'd his fiancée's body. And Oliver remembered how quickly that shock and horror had turned to fury.

"I'm...not in your bed."

Oliver shook his head. His mind was on Nate, but those soft words from Lark had just ripped his focus right back to her. "Say again?"

"Before the phone call...you were saying you couldn't have me in your bed every night." She shook her head. "I'm not in your bed."

"I wish the hell that you were." He tossed the phone onto his desk. "Wrong thing to say, wasn't it? You don't want that. You don't want to hear that I'm stepping away from the Bureau because I'm trying to fucking win you back. You don't want to know that I am *desperately* hoping to be wrong about a killer just so that I don't have to see you shatter before me again." His gaze focused on her. Like there was any other place that he wanted to look. "I want you in my bed. I want you back in my life. And I'm breaking every rule I have to get you once more."

She crept toward him. "I'm...am I your conflict of interest? Are you losing your position because of me?"

"I'm choosing to step back. And, baby, you are so much more than a conflict." His hands fisted and released. Fisted. Didn't release. The better to stop himself from grabbing for her. Time for full fucking disclosure. All his dirty secrets exposed. "You're what made my world implode. I lied to you, thought I could get the evidence and walk away, but *you* walked instead, and I've been trying to catch you ever since."

And you had danger all around you. I didn't know it. Someone is trying to hurt you and the hell that will go down.

Only over his dead body would she be hurt. His fucking cold and dead body.

"What am I supposed to say to you?" Lark asked. "What am I supposed to do?"

With him? "Anything you want. Fuck the rules. Fuck everyone else and what they think. Fuck—"

"You?" she whispered. Then, shaking her head, she surged toward him. "Because that's still what I want. *You* are still what I want. I should hate you—I do, dammit, I *do* hate you."

Her words pierced straight to his heart.

"I hate you and I want you and I can't stop." She rose onto her toes. "Why can't I stop?"

She was right there. She wanted him. He'd die for her.

His arms locked around her. His mouth took hers.

CHAPTER EIGHT

Mistake. Mistake. Mistake. The single word blasted through Lark's mind over and over again. Touching Oliver was a mistake. Kissing him was a mistake. Still wanting him so badly?

Such a mistake.

But her heart wasn't listening to her mind. And her body? It clearly had its own agenda. Because she seemed to be igniting. Every cell felt alive. Hungry. Lust poured through her veins. The wild, consuming desire that she only seemed to feel...for him.

His mouth claimed hers with desperate need. His tongue thrust past her lips, and he tasted and he took, and a moan rose in her throat. Her hands had locked around his powerful shoulders, and her nails bit into the fabric of his black suit coat.

His hands were around her waist. Seeming to scorch her right through the shirt she wore. The cotton was no match for him. His touch burned away everything else.

"Fucking missed you," he growled against her mouth. "Every day. Every night. *Missed. You.*" He kissed her again. Deep. Hungrier. Harder.

When they'd been together before, he'd always been so careful with her. Careful with his touches. His kisses. His control. Until the last night when his control had broken.

When she'd deliberately set out to seduce the man who'd captured her heart.

I didn't wear panties. All night long, I was so conscious of every movement of my body. So conscious of him. It had taken all her courage to finally make her move on him. Right in his den. In front of the roaring fire.

She shuddered as the memory of that night blasted through her. Sex had never been that amazing. She hadn't thought it *could* be like that. Good, yes. She'd had good before. But with Oliver? The pleasure had been body quaking. Soul shattering.

Heart breaking.

His mouth tore from hers, and Oliver began to kiss a fiery path down her neck. Her eyes squeezed shut as she tipped back her head. Her neck seemed hypersensitive. Correction, her whole body was hypersensitive.

Mistake. Mistake. Mistake.

But how could a mistake feel so good?

His hands tightened on her waist, and then he lifted her up. The move caught Lark by surprise, and her eyes flared open. "Oliver?"

"Easy." He held her easily and twisted so that he could put her on the edge of his desk. He released her waist, but only so he could push apart her legs and move between them. "I need you."

She needed him. Every traitorous part of her needed him. "Just sex." Was she saying the words for him or herself? Did it even matter? "This isn't about love." A sharp shake of her head sent Lark's hair flying. "We can do just sex." *Just* sex meant no emotions. No world being broken apart again. Just sex meant safety.

Didn't it?

His head whipped up, and his dark eyes locked on her. "That what you want? For me to fuck you without emotion?"

No. She... "Mistake," Lark whispered. Her heart thudded hard against her chest. She perched at the edge of his desk, and her legs were splayed wide now. He stood so close to her. Leaned toward her. And there was definitely no missing the heavy length of his aroused cock as it stretched toward her.

"Sex between us isn't a mistake." His hand curled under her chin and tipped back her head. "It's heaven. It's oblivion. It's more pleasure than should be humanly possible to feel." His mouth pressed to hers once more. A hot, open-mouthed kiss. "Never a mistake," he rasped. "Never."

Could she have sex without emotion? Big, bad brave words she'd spouted, but could she truly hold back with him? Already, her control had snapped or else...or else she wouldn't be doing this. Wouldn't have kissed him. Wouldn't be sitting on his desk. Wouldn't be aching so much for him.

He doesn't love me. Midas was wrong.

But...

"Stop thinking," Oliver ordered roughly. "Just feel. Feel me, baby. Only me." And his left hand slid down her body. His right kept tipping back her chin, but his left hand eased between her legs. Pressed to the juncture of her thighs. Rubbed her through the denim of her jeans. "You want to fuck without emotion? Fine. I'll fuck you any way you want." His hand rubbed harder. She arched against him.

His stroking touch wasn't enough. Her jeans were too thick. She needed them gone. She wanted his fingers on her. In her.

"I'll fuck you until you forget everything else," he promised.

She couldn't forget everything else. Not an option.

But his right hand had released her chin. He unhooked her jeans. Eased down the zipper. A hiss had never seemed louder in her life. Oliver wedged his hand into the opening he'd made, and his fingers maneuvered down to rub over her panties, and she gasped as—

The phone rang.

He'd worked his hand into her jeans. *He got into my pants, literally.* His fingers were slipping under the edge of her panties. He was touching her, and she was already wet and eager for him.

And his phone was ringing.

She thought he'd pull back. Stop caressing her. *Answer the phone.*

But he didn't stop touching her. One hand stayed in her jeans. *Brushing my clit.*

His other hand grabbed for the phone he'd tossed on the desk. He caught it and swiped his finger over the screen before hauling it to his ear. "*Foxx,*" he snarled.

She arched harder toward him.

His fingers stretched and teased—

"Jase?" Oliver bit out. "What did you find for me? What did you—"

Horrified—because reality had just exploded past the passion—she caught his wrist and stilled his hand. Then she shoved his hand away from her.

Jaw locking, Oliver stepped back.

She hopped off the desk. Almost fell because her legs—specifically, her knees—seemed a little weak. Her hands fumbled before snapping and zipping up her jeans. Heat poured in her cheeks.

"It was a hunch."

Her head snapped around at Oliver's flat words. He'd turned his back to her.

"I'll be there as fast as I can. No, no, I'm not coming back on officially. Not yet. You run this thing. Report to Executive Assistant Director Ballard what you find, but you damn well keep me in the loop."

He talked a bit more, and she strained to hear him over the booming of her heartbeat as it echoed in her ears. There was something said about finding out how long Nate Quest had been in town. Why he was in Vegas.

And...

"Get his alibi," Oliver directed. "For last night. We need to know exactly where he was." He ended the call and spun to look at her once more.

His expression...

Her breath caught.

There was need, lust, fury—they all flashed on his face as he stared at her. Then, everything vanished. He blinked, and it was like a mask slid into place. The change was so sudden and so eerie that she shivered.

"That got...intense." No emotion entered his voice. He seemed to simply be stating a fact.

And he was right. Things had certainly gotten intense.

"Why'd you kiss me, Lark?" Again, no emotion.

Her gaze swept over him.

"Oh, yes, sweetheart, I'm still aroused. Absolutely."

She felt her flush deepen.

"Hardly surprising when I'm around you, though. You breathe and I want you. You smile at me, and I nearly go nuclear."

Her brow scrunched. "Don't lie to me."

Oliver's head inclined toward her. "Trying really hard not to do so again."

She backed up. "How do you do that?"

"Do what?"

"Sound so...calm. Controlled." While her whole body was still in overdrive. "And you changed your expression in a blink. You're staring at me like..." Her words trailed away.

He advanced on her. Slow, determined steps. "I'm trying not to scare you."

"You're doing the opposite job of it. Seeing you close down *everything* that fast unnerved the hell out of me." Total truth. Because she was also trying really hard not to lie to him again. There had been enough lies.

"I didn't close down." He stopped right in front of her. As she stared up into his eyes, she saw the heat blazing in the darkness. "I jerked back on my control. Didn't want to look like a man possessed. A man who would do *anything* to have his fingers dipping inside of you again. A man who would rip apart the world if it meant he got to fuck *you* again."

Her head shook.

His mask fell away. The lust and need and stark hunger were clear to see once more. So was the possessive gleam in his eyes. *Primal.* He looked at her as if...as if...

I'm his.

"Does this work better?" he rumbled. "Me looking at you like you're the only thing that matters? The only thing I want? You are. Be clear on that. I want you so much I would have fucked you and let the world burn down around us."

Not true. He'd answered the phone—

But he hadn't stopped touching her. He'd kept his hand stroking her and had nearly made her come for him while he'd been taking the call.

"I can fuck you without emotion, Lark. If that's what you want, I can make it happen. As you just saw, I can close it all down."

"But...but you said that was a mask." And just because you masked something, it didn't mean you didn't *feel*.

"I can make the sex so good you won't care if it's a mask or not."

She knew he wasn't just bragging. Sex with him was so incredible that she lost track of everything but the pleasure she felt with him. "We should go." Breathy. That was how she sounded. Breathy and uncertain. "If Nate Quest is at that hotel, if you think he's some kind of lead to follow, we should go." She vividly remembered Nate Quest. He'd been engaged to the first victim. In interviews on the news, he'd looked...broken.

"I'm not in official FBI capacity, remember? Nate doesn't have to talk with me. That's why I told Jase to have a run at him first. But, yeah, we'll be going. Because I want to see how he reacts to you."

She blinked. "What?"

His hand raked through his thick hair. "You get that it's possible the person who came after you last night just came after *you?* As in, you were his one and only target? That he isn't the same man who killed those other three women?"

She didn't speak. *Yes, I get that.* But she also knew...*It is possible he is the same man who hurt those other women.* The Bridal Killer was out there. "What did you learn from my brother?" Oliver hadn't said he believed in her brother's innocence. Despite her hope that he'd rush back and suddenly be convinced Lane didn't belong in a cell.

"You should put on your boots. We need to go."

She didn't move.

"Unless you want to fuck," he added, voice raw. "Because we can do that right here and right now. I can sit you on the desk and you'll be coming for me within two minutes."

"You're such a bastard." She spun and marched away. A double-time march.

"I know." Soft. His words drifted after her. "But what I don't know...is why you kissed me."

Lark stilled. "I told you why already." She didn't look back at him.

"Because you hate me, but still want me?"

Nothing seemed to kill the desire she felt for him. Maybe nothing could kill it. Did that mean something was wrong with them? Or that something was just wrong with her? "It's not natural. I shouldn't want you. It should have ended long ago." The dark need that would whisper through her. The desire that would even have her touching herself late at night as she thought of him.

"What do you want us to do? Fuck until we get each other out of our systems?"

Was that even a possibility? Could you fuck someone out of your life? "What I want..." She inhaled. "I want to catch a killer." With that, Lark left him.

She didn't look back but...

I also want you, Oliver. And I can't seem to stop.

***

The hotel, as always, buzzed with activity. One of the biggest and most visited hotels-slash-casinos in Vegas, the place attracted tourists from around the world. The fountains outside twisted and danced, and when you stepped foot into the elegantly decorated lobby, you were transported into another world.

As soon as Oliver entered, he caught sight of a familiar figure working the concierge desk. Kurt Sasser. The guy chatted with a guest as he gestured animatedly toward the ceiling. Or rather, toward the enormous art display that made up the ceiling. Hand-blown flowers of every shape and size filled that display. Over two thousand of them. A masterpiece for every guest to enjoy.

Oliver wrapped his fingers around Lark's hand and pulled her toward the concierge desk just as Kurt finished his discussion and the silver-haired man in front of him departed. And as Oliver and Lark approached and Kurt got a look at Oliver's face...

"No." A weak gasp—and plea—from Kurt. "Please, no. Anyone but you. Anyone..." He hurried from behind the desk and stepped into Oliver's path. "Why are you here? Do you want to ruin my life?"

Oliver smiled at the concierge manager. "Is that any way to greet a friend?"

"You are not a friend. You're an FBI agent."

Technically, he was an FBI agent on a *break*. But he didn't clarify the situation for dear old Kurt.

"I've already talked to one of your men today. I don't know how that vehicle got stolen from the valet lot. You can rest assured that our security will be on high alert from here on out." Kurt tugged on his collar. "Tell me there is not any danger to my guests. Tell me this hotel is completely safe."

"Gonna need a favor from you, Kurt," Oliver began. Poor Kurt. The man had been working the last time Oliver had needed to storm the place during a hunt for a killer. Over the course of that hunt, he'd learned that Kurt didn't exactly excel under pressure.

Instead, Kurt tended to panic.

"What do you need?" Kurt's voice emerged as a whisper even as he cast a nervous glance around his beloved lobby.

Oliver also glanced around the lobby and— "Never mind," he told Kurt. "Found him." And he started to immediately advance toward the man who'd just stepped foot off the elevator. Talk about your perfect timing.

Nate Quest.

Tall, a little leaner than he'd been the last time their paths had crossed, and with close-cropped, black hair, Nate stormed off the elevator like a man on a mission. He bulldozed straight ahead.

Only to come to a jarring halt when he caught sight of Oliver. Or, rather...of Lark as she stood beside Oliver.

Rage ignited on Nate's face. A hot, heavy rage mixed with hatred. And the man made no move to conceal his feelings.

Oliver automatically took a step forward in order to partially put his body in front of Lark. The urge to protect her was as natural as breathing, and when Nate started surging toward them, Oliver knew things were going to get ugly.

But he still sent the other man a smile in an effort to disarm and confuse him. "Nate Quest!" Oliver called. "I had no idea you'd be back in town, and you are—"

"You are still fucking her?" Nate snarled. A very loud snarl that no doubt carried quite the distance in the lobby. "Couldn't believe it when I got the call...you've been fucking her all along and now you are actively helping her to prove her brother's innocence? What the hell?"

So, the gloves were off. Fair enough. Oliver took a step to the side so that the guy couldn't even look at Lark any longer. Forget partially shielding her with his body. He now blocked her completely. "First, lower your voice." A flat command. He waved his left hand toward a watchful and sweaty Kurt even as his right maintained his hold on Lark. "This is a fine establishment, and the families in the lobby don't need to hear you being an ass."

Nate's face mottled with his fury.

So not good. This guy is boiling for an explosion. Oliver released a slow breath even as he kept his body battle ready. "Second...what call?" That bit had certainly caught his attention. "What are you talking about?"

Nate jabbed an index finger into Oliver's chest.

Oh, don't do that. Not unless you want me to break that finger.

"The call I got telling me that you were screwing things to hell and back on the Lane Lawson case!" Spittle flew from Nate's mouth. "You want in her pants so badly that you're going to let a killer walk and you are—"

"Lower your voice." Cold and hard. "And don't say another negative word about Lark. My patience is razor thin when it comes to people insulting her."

"She's the sister of a killer!"

The heavy scent of booze surrounded Nate and had Oliver's nostrils flaring.

"Her brother killed my Casey!" Nate's voice cracked. "He killed her, but Lark is standing right there. She's walking around. Freaking holding hands with you."

Lark jerked her hand from Oliver's hold.

"Why does she get to live?" Nate demanded. "But Casey doesn't? My bride is cold in the ground, and that bitch is out free."

"I want you to get your hand off my chest, and don't you *ever* call her a bitch again." He got that grief could twist a man into madness. Oh, he more than got it. But Nate wasn't going to insult Lark while Oliver stood there. "I want you to step the hell back. I want you to—"

"She shouldn't live! You can't let her brother go free! You can't!" Nate yanked his hand back but...

He immediately balled it into a fist. That fist came swinging at Oliver's jaw in a wild, fast attack.

Was he supposed to just let this prick take a hit? Screw that. Oliver threw up his hand and used his forearm to deflect the blow.

"Boss!" A shout from nearby.

He ignored the shout and plowed his own fist into Nate's stomach.

A heavy *oomph* burst from Nate as he staggered back. Oliver followed swiftly and delivered a powerful, second punch. *That one is for calling Lark a bitch.* Oliver drew back his hand to punch again.

"Freeze!" Jase's slightly breathless voice ordered. He rushed forward and glared at Nate. "You just attacked a federal agent!"

Technically, a federal agent on a *break*. But, semantics.

"Sorry," Jase muttered to Oliver. "I was across the lobby. Ran over as fast as I could."

Nate crumpled on the floor. Tears leaked down his face. "Why is Casey in the ground? She's supposed to be my wife. We were going to have kids. We were going to have a life together." His body shuddered. "Why is she in the ground?"

Wringing his hands, Kurt crept toward Oliver. "Can we *please* take this out of my lobby?"

"Why is she in the ground?"

CHAPTER NINE

"How much have you been drinking?"

Lark rubbed her arms to try and chase the chill from her body. They weren't in the lobby any longer. Their little group had moved into a small conference room on the hotel's second floor. Kurt had been too eager to get them out of sight and into a private location.

Nate Quest sat at a table and cradled a cup of steaming coffee in his shaking hands. The coffee had come courtesy of Jase. As for Oliver? He stood and watched his attacker with a cold, dark gaze.

I can't believe Nate swung a punch at Oliver.

And Oliver hadn't hesitated to strike back.

"How much?" Oliver pressed.

Nate blinked his bleary eyes. "I don't...I don't know."

"You attacked me. You get that I could press charges against you, right?"

Nate glanced toward Lark—

"Nope." Oliver immediately stepped into the other man's line of sight. "I don't want your eyes on her. Lark was nearly abducted last night. You know anything about that?"

"I...what?"

"Where were you last night?" Rapid-fire.

"Am I...am I being charged with something? Punching you?"

Lark craned to see around Oliver. Tilting to the left, she was able to get a glimpse of Nate.

He rubbed his red eyes. "I don't think my hit landed on you. Can you charge me if it didn't land?"

Jase pulled out the chair next to Nate. "When did you get into town, Mr. Quest?"

Nate just rubbed his eyes harder.

"I can ask the concierge," Oliver snapped. "We can get the truth from him. Just thought you might want to tell us yourself first. You know, thought you might want to *cooperate.*"

Nate's hand dropped from his eyes. "Yesterday. I-I arrived yesterday." He blinked. "No...day before. After I got the call...one telling me that you were going to help her. I left as fast as I could after that." His voice hardened. *"You can't let him out."*

Oliver stalked forward to tower over Nate. "Who called you?"

"Don't know...Didn't recognize the number." Nate started to look at Lark.

Only to catch himself. His gaze shot back to Oliver.

"Where were you last night?" Oliver demanded to know.

"Uh, boss?" Jase rose. "Can we step outside?"

Oliver didn't look like he intended to step anywhere.

"Out drinking," Nate mumbled. "Wandering the city. Trying to retrace Casey's steps." His shoulders slumped. "I should have gone after her that night. So stupid...it was such a dumb fight. My ex texted me. I-I sent her a quick note back. Casey got jealous. I told her it was *nothing*. I was marrying her. *Her*. That was why I was in Vegas. I didn't have cold feet. Wasn't thinking about someone else." His eyes squeezed closed. "She saw my phone. Freaked out. Said if I was gonna have a last fling, she was, too." A rough shake of his head. "*There was no last fling for me. I loved her.*" His eyes opened. "*I loved her.*"

Lark wrapped her arms around her body.

"I still see her...cold and too pale on that stupid metal table. The bruises around her throat..." Nate's hand rose to touch his own throat. "She must have been so scared. It wouldn't have been instantaneous. She would have struggled. Fought. My Casey would have known that she was dying. And he—he probably looked right into her eyes when he killed her."

Nate's pain seemed to fill the room.

"I miss her every single day. She's everywhere and nowhere. *Everywhere and nowhere.*" His hand flew away from his throat and fisted right before it slammed into the table. His head jerked toward Lark. "Why do you get to live?" he suddenly bellowed as he jumped to his feet. His chair tipped over and fell onto the floor. "*You will die, too!*"

He lunged for her.

But Jase caught him. Jase grabbed Nate's arms, twisted, and slammed Nate's upper body down onto the table. "Get her out of here, boss," he huffed. *"Out."*

Oliver reached for Lark. He pushed her toward the door.

She glanced back. Lark expected to see Nate struggling in Jase's hold, but instead...

He'd slumped forward and started crying.

***

"You think it was him." Lark stood outside of the hotel and watched the guests come and go in a blur. "You think Nate was the one who waited in my car and attacked me."

"I think Nate Quest is wrecked by grief. I think rage burns through him all the time. And I think when he looks at you?" A muscle flexed along Oliver's hard jaw. "I think he sees an outlet for his rage. *He said the same fucking words.*"

Her brow furrowed in confusion. "What?"

"'You will die, too,'" he repeated. "Those were the words spray-painted on the wall of your apartment. Am I supposed to buy that it's some massive coincidence that the guy just spouted that same BS? Even if he wasn't the one in your car—and he damn well could have been—think he was in your home. One hundred percent, I believe that. He broke inside. He left that message for you." Oliver moved in closer to her. So close their bodies almost brushed as he stared down at her with an expression gone tight with his own fury. "He wants to hurt you, Lark. That's not going to happen." Oliver shook his head. "I shouldn't have brought you here."

"Y-you wanted to see his reaction to me." Damn that stutter. But she was feeling more than a bit nervous. *More like completely shaken.* So it was no surprise it had slipped out.

"I saw it, all right. Now I never want him near you again." He blew out a rough breath. "Where the hell is he?"

"Who? Nate?" He was inside with Jase. They'd just left him—

"No, Memphis. While you were getting your boots at my place, I contacted Memphis to let him know which hotel Nate was using." Impatience and what could have been a hint of worry slid into his voice as he added, "And then when we were grilling Nate, I sent Memphis a text so he'd know how much time he had here. Memphis had better be done."

Done with what?

But, as if on cue, Memphis bounded up. He seemingly just appeared from nowhere.

Lark blinked at him.

"The Feds are definitely gonna want to search Nate's room," Memphis said as he closed in. His low voice only carried to them. "The man is going over the edge. Got rope in his room, two knives, and her home address written on a notepad right next to his freaking bed."

Her jaw dropped in shock.

Oliver didn't say a word, but his whole expression changed. His eyes glittered. His cheeks seemed to sharpen. His jaw tightened, and he spun on his heel. He took a step back toward the doors that led to the hotel's lobby.

Her hands flew out and curled around his arm to stop him. "Oliver!"

"He's fucking dead," Oliver swore.

Memphis coughed. "Uh, buddy, don't think that is the way an FBI agent is supposed to talk—"

"Not acting as an FBI agent now, am I?" He fired a glance toward Memphis. "He came here to kill her. Instead, he'll be the one who dies." A flat promise.

Her chest shook with her heartbeat. "Oliver, this...this isn't who you are."

His head leaned in close to her. His lips came near her ear, and, for her alone, he whispered, "Maybe you never knew who I really was."

She did...didn't she?

He started to pull away.

She tightened her hold even as her stare jumped to Memphis. "How did you even know what Nate has in his room?" But she had a twisting suspicion. And Oliver's words of *"Memphis had better be done"* took on an ominous significance.

Had Memphis broken into Nate's hotel room? Sure seemed that way to her.

Memphis pursed his lips. "I think you can connect the dots without me making a confession. Actually, judging by your expression, I'd say you are connecting them right now. So, how about you let your boyfriend go so he can kick the jerk's ass, we can wrap up things here, and we can—"

The sliding doors that led to the lobby opened, and Jase rushed out. Red mottled the right side of his face. "He got away!" Jase shouted.

"What?" Oliver leapt toward him.

"Bastard sucker punched me." Jase glanced to the left. To the right. "Knocked my ass flat. One minute, he's sobbing his eyes out. The next he's swinging. Sonofabitch." His hand rubbed over his cheek. "Locked me in that stupid room—had to kick open the door to get out. *Where the hell is he?*"

Oliver spun back to Lark and Memphis. "Get her out of here," he told Memphis. "Get her back to my place, *now*."

Memphis curled an arm around her shoulders. "On it."

She elbowed him. "You are not on anything!"

Jase had his phone up and was calling someone. Backup?

"Get hotel security on the search," Oliver instructed Jase. "Get an APB out for Nate Quest. He assaulted you. You also need to check his room right away. Could be hiding in there."

"Nice," Memphis murmured as his head bent near Lark. "That gets the Feds in the SOB's room so they can see that twisted shit in there."

She shuddered.

"You should really come with me now," Memphis added, his voice quiet. "Otherwise, Oliver is gonna lose his shit and not be able to concentrate. He seems pretty...emotional to me right now."

"*Get her to safety, Memphis!* It's too open out here! I should never have brought Lark to this hotel. This shit is on me." Oliver's hands fisted. "Go with him, Lark. Please."

Wait, had he seriously just said—

"I'll have Midas meet you both at my house."

Memphis's fingers steered her to the right.

She didn't want to go with him.

But already, security guards were swarming. And even though Oliver wasn't supposed to be in charge, he was busy snapping orders left and right. She glanced around.

"He could be anywhere," Memphis muttered. "Stay on alert. I sure as hell will."

"H-he was drunk. Crying. Slurring some of his words. He hardly seemed capable of making some grand escape."

Oliver rushed to her. "Unless it was an act. He could have poured the booze on his clothes. Could have pretended to be drunk. Just like he pretended to be grief-stricken before he swung at Jase." His eyes glittered. "I need you away from the scene. I get that you want to help, but that man wants you dead. I trust Memphis—"

"Aw, thanks, man, that's so sweet of you to say, I really appreciate it—"

"—to get you home," he finished with a growl. "And Midas will be waiting there for you. I'll come as soon as I can. I need to help hunt this bastard first. But you have to be secure. I *need* you to be out of danger. Please, Lark."

He'd just used the P-word once more.

"*Go home.*"

She nodded.

And he—

Oliver grabbed her. Hauled her close. He kissed her. Right there. In front of Memphis. Jase. The security guards who rushed left and right.

Then he let her go. Yelling order, Oliver strode away.

Without a word, Memphis led her from the scene. He put her in his ride, a vehicle that waited just a few feet away. He zipped away from the hotel even as he cast a quick glance in the rearview mirror.

Her hands twisted in her lap. "He's...Nate Quest isn't the first person to hate me."

"You haven't done anything to him, Lark. The guy is mad with rage and grief. None of this is your fault."

Wasn't it? She'd gone on the news. Told the world that she was going to find the real killer. Had that been like waving a flag in front of Nate? "I wanted to find the man who murdered those women."

"Yeah, I know." He turned to the right.

"Do you...do you have Oliver's address?"

"I know where his rental house is, don't worry."

She was worried. About a million things. Mostly... "Oliver isn't going to kill him."

Silence.

Pulling against her seatbelt, she twisted in her seat. "He's not."

Memphis braked at a light. "If it makes you feel better, sure, keep telling yourself that."

"He'll arrest Nate. He and Jase will find Nate and arrest him, and we can go back to hunting and—" Tears pricked at her eyes. "Nate...came to Vegas to kill me?"

"Sure seemed that way when I was searching his room. I mean...when the FBI agents go inside room seven-oh-nine, they will probably connect the dots and realize that Nate needs to stay far, far away from you for, oh, say the rest of his life."

He had to stay far away...

Because he came to Vegas to kill me.

***

"How the hell did you let him get the drop on you?" Oliver raged. He glared at Jase, then switched his attention back to the security monitors. The guards were busy searching the hotel, but he'd gone straight to Kurt and gotten the man to give them access to the hotel's video feeds. Now he huddled in the main security office as the footage played.

Unfortunately, there had been no camera in the room Jase had used with Nate during their little interrogation. No camera right outside of it, either.

As for the rest of the feeds? *Nate isn't on here.* So where was the bastard?

"He was crying," Jase mumbled. "Saying how badly he missed his girl. I felt..." He stopped.

But Oliver knew what the other man had been about to say. "You felt sorry for him. So you lowered your guard." Amateur mistake. But Jase was still new. Still seeing victims everywhere and not realizing that a victim could also be a perp.

He should realize it, though. He dealt with criminals for years as a lawyer. He's seen plenty of their tricks.

"He elbowed me in the ribs. Slammed his fist into my cheek." Jase winced as he touched the still red skin. "I fell back. Hit my head."

Oliver's jaw clenched. "You need to get checked out."

"No, no, I'm *fine!*" His hand dropped. "I'm the agent in charge here. You're on break, remember, boss? You shouldn't even be here. I shouldn't have let you ask him those questions. Shouldn't have let you in the room with him in the first place."

"The man spoke freely. His choice if he wanted to bury himself." Oliver pointed to one of the monitors. "Rewind that footage. I thought I saw him."

Obligingly, the young guard seated at the bank of monitors did.

The footage rolled back, then played again. Exterior scene. Near the loading bay. A delivery truck arrived and—

Nate Quest raced past the truck.

"Dammit!" Jase exclaimed. "He's gone off property. We have to get a citywide search going. We have to get—"

I have to get Lark secured. Because Oliver had no doubt about just where Nate would go. He'd fled the hotel, and he would be heading for the person he seemed to hate.

My Lark.

Oliver backed away. "You're right. I shouldn't be here. You take care of things. I'll check in with you later." He turned and brushed past a nervously sweating Kurt.

His steps picked up speed. Faster and faster. *Get to Lark.* He'd thought sending her away with Memphis was the smart plan. He *still* knew it had been the correct call to get her out of the open. And Memphis would protect her. As for Midas? *I know I can count on him.* But Oliver still wanted to be with her.

He double-timed it out the hotel's sliding doors and found Special Agent Theo Tutweiler racing toward him. They damn near collided.

"What's happening?" Theo demanded as he staggered to a stop. "Got the text from Jase and came as fast as I could! I was already on the way over, and—"

Oliver jerked his thumb over his shoulder. "Jase is inside. He needs you. The team has to hunt down Nate Quest."

"Quest?' Theo's eyes widened. "What has he done?"

So far...*he just assaulted Jase Guillory and tried to assault me.* But it wasn't so much what Nate had *done* that had ice snaking through Oliver's veins. It was what Oliver feared Nate would do that chilled him.

He's going after Lark. The man's obsession had been clear as day. All of his rage and pain had been channeled onto one person. *My Lark.* When Nate saw Lark, he saw his chance for revenge. He saw the killer's sister. He saw punishment.

An eye for an eye.

Nate thought he was going to get vengeance by hurting Lark. *You are so wrong.* The only thing he would get when he came after her...

It's a one-way trip to hell. Because I will send you there myself.

Oliver hurried past a limo that had just slowed to a stop near the hotel's entrance. An attendant quickly opened the side door of the long, black ride. Oliver didn't glance back to see which high roller spilled out. He was too busy scanning in front of him so that he could look for Nate Quest. *The bastard left on foot. But he could have jumped into a taxi. Could have hopped on a bus. Theo and Jase will need to check—*

"Representative Montgomery, so glad to have you back with us," a man's voice said from behind Oliver. A voice that kicked with excitement as the guy added, "Hope your meetings were successful."

Representative Montgomery? As in, Blain Montgomery? The jerk who'd once received a broken hand courtesy of Lane Lawson because the prick had been creeping on Lark?

Oliver had halted at the mention of the state representative's name, and now he turned slowly toward the limo. As he watched, a man climbed from the rear. Carefully styled hair. Super white smile. Expensive clothes.

Blain fucking Montgomery.

Right there.

What were the odds of that?

Blain's head turned. He met Oliver's stare.

And damn if the man's smile didn't widen even more.

He knows who I am.

Oliver advanced on him. "Representative Montgomery?" Like he didn't already know. *And I should be giving chase after Nate. I should be getting to Lark.* But his instincts were screaming, and he knew better than to ignore those screams. Oliver took a deep breath and schooled his expression.

Memphis is with her. Lark is protected. She'll have Memphis and Midas. They are better protection than an army of Feds. She is safe.

Knowing all that, though, didn't change the way he felt. Oliver still wanted to be with Lark. But...

Blain Montgomery eased away from the limo. "You're FBI Special Agent Oliver Foxx." He inclined his head toward Oliver even as he closed the remaining distance between them. "I must confess, I recognized you on sight." He extended his hand toward Oliver. "I have to say, I'm a fan."

Oliver looked at the man's hand. Then back at his face. "A fan?" He shook the representative's hand. A soft hand. A little sweaty. Weak grip. Oliver let him go.

"My platform is law and order. You keep the streets safe. I admire the work you do." Blain glanced around the area. "Seems to be a lot of activity happening. Is everything okay?"

Not exactly. "Didn't realize you were in town."

"Here for some meetings. Looking to buy up some property. Actually, I'm in Vegas all the time for my business interests." His stare returned to Oliver. "I was so relieved when I heard that you'd locked up Lane Lawson." The fingers of his right hand curled, then flexed. Curled, then flexed.

That's the hand Lane broke.

"A man like that should never be allowed out again. The death penalty was invented for cases just like his." A sad sigh slipped from the representative. "Those poor victims. At least their families will soon have justice."

So, he didn't have time to bullshit and play mini-political games. "You know Lane, don't you?"

"Excuse me?" An owlish blink.

"You know Lane—personally—and his sister Lark. They lived with your family once upon a time."

Blain's brow furrowed. "I...yes?" A question.

Why was the response a question?

But Blain rallied and added, "My family often took in foster children. We wanted to help others." He smiled. That bright, artificially white smile. "I'm proud to say that I have followed in the footsteps of my parents. I've dedicated my life to service. To helping others." He turned away.

"Good to know," Oliver muttered. Then, because he was all about watching reactions, he just had to say... "So you're not still into slipping into the bedrooms of teenage girls? You gave up that habit?"

Blain whirled to face him. Red patches appeared on his cheeks. "How dare you!"

How dare you, asshole. Oliver shrugged. "Sorry." He wasn't. "It's been a bitch of a day, and I've got a stalker to catch. But then you just dropped into my path, like a gift from above." He edged closer to Blain. "It's so interesting to me that you're in town. When did you arrive?"

"Late last night," Blain gritted out. "Not that it is any concern of yours—"

"It is, though. My concern. Because Lark Lawson is *my* concern. She was attacked...late last night. And I'm looking at a man who has a history with her. A man who—once upon a time—seemed to have stalkerish tendencies of his own where she was concerned."

"Lower your voice."

"I actually thought it was low." No, he hadn't.

"I will have your badge!" Blain threatened. "I will have you benched from the FBI!"

Cool. Do that. Should be easy since I benched myself already. "Odd reaction," Oliver noted. "You know, for someone who is such a fan."

Blain's eyes narrowed into small slits of fury.

"Relax, Representative Montgomery. I was just making friendly conversation." Bullshit. He was always profiling. Always analyzing. Every single second. And there was nothing friendly about this conversation.

"Sounds more like an interrogation to me."

The man was not wrong. Points for him.

Blain's neck craned forward in a turtle-like move. "I was a kid back then. A dumb kid who got hung up on a pretty girl. And her insane brother—who had anger issues then and is a *killer* now—broke my hand. He came out of nowhere and attacked me without a word." A slow exhale. Some of the red faded from his cheeks. "My parents shipped him off the next day."

You just lost control, but you got it back, fast. Blain Montgomery had an anger issue. What other issues did the representative have? Oliver pushed a bit more and questioned, "They shipped him off, but you tried to keep her, didn't you?"

Blain searched Oliver's gaze. "She's told you about me."

And, yeah, creepy...because Blain seemed *pleased* about that fact. "Nope. It was her brother who did the telling. I just have to ask...what were you planning to do when you were in her bedroom? I mean, if Lark hadn't woken up and screamed because she saw you? What were your intentions?"

"I was confused," Blain answered smoothly. His neck retracted. His smile slid back into place. He blinked once. "I used to do a bit of sleepwalking when I was younger. Must have wandered in there during my dazed state." The fingers of his right hand curled. Then flexed. His stare didn't waver from Oliver's. "It was all a big misunderstanding. If her brother hadn't attacked, I could have explained everything. I always wanted to apologize to Lark. Not like I want her to go around thinking I'm a monster."

"Course not. No one *wants* to be the monster." But someone still always had to be.

Blain's mouth tightened. "Perhaps I can meet with Lark. Finally bury the past."

Oliver squinted at him. "You want to meet with a serial killer's sister? With your law-and-order platform? How will that play for you, PR-wise?"

"Lark isn't guilty. I bare no ill will to her."

Huh. "Did you happen to miss the news segment she did recently? Lark is convinced someone else is behind the murders. She's fighting to prove her brother's innocence." No way did Oliver think this man had missed that news story.

"It's *your* job to make sure she doesn't succeed in that quest, isn't it?" Blain swept an assessing stare over Oliver. "You put him in jail. Now I expect you to keep him there."

"Or what? You gonna threaten to take my badge again?" *I'm so scared.* No, he wasn't.

Before the representative could answer, someone called his name. An older couple waved excitedly toward him and asked if they could take a picture.

"My constituents," Blain murmured. "Can't very well have them waiting." His smile was wide. His expression friendly. And with that friendly expression in place, he leaned toward Oliver and rasped, "The next time you want to interrogate me, you better have fucking good cause. It will damn well *not* be in public. But just know, if you come at me again, my lawyers will be ripping you apart. And that badge? I won't have to threaten to take it. I *will* take it. You need to remember exactly who I am." He slapped Oliver on the shoulder. "Great to meet you," he declared loudly. "Keep up the good work."

The representative walked to meet the couple. Even posed for a selfie with them.

Oliver unclenched his back teeth. *Don't worry. I know exactly who you are.*

And he wouldn't be forgetting. Oliver yanked out his phone and rushed for his car. Midas answered him on the second ring. "Are you at my house yet?" Oliver asked. "Do you have eyes on her?"

"Dude. Settle the fuck down. I am on my way. I am—"

"Nate Quest is in the wind. Memphis found knives and rope and Lark's address in his hotel room. There is no settling the fuck down." What he *was* going to do? Cuff Lark to his side. This time, he wouldn't be bluffing. If the cops and Feds didn't find Nate...

I will be cuffing her to me. Because there was no way Nate could hurt her. Not Nate. Not Blain Montgomery. Not anyone.

It can't happen.

CHAPTER TEN

Lark sat on the couch. She'd been sitting there for the last hour. Memphis Camden lounged to her right. Midas Monroe paced like a caged tiger to her left. She cleared her throat. "Do you both really need to be here?"

"Yes."

"Yes."

Two instantly growled responses.

Her breath blew out. "What is it that Oliver thinks is going to happen? That Nate Quest is going to burst through the front door and come gunning for me?"

The front door flew open. She flinched at the sound even as Memphis leapt to his feet and Midas lunged forward.

"Lark!" Oliver rushed into the den. He shoved past a glowering Midas and went straight to her. His hands locked around her shoulders. He hauled her off the couch and into his arms.

His hug was tight. Fierce.

And she didn't know what to do. Hug him back? *Never let him go?* Her hands fluttered in the air and skimmed his shoulders.

"Shit," he muttered. "I'm not supposed to be hugging you, am I?" He eased back but didn't fully release her. His stare raked her face. "Nate got away. Security camera picked him up fleeing near the loading bay. There's an APB out for him. Authorities are searching the city."

Nate got away. She swallowed the lump that had risen in her throat. "Figured he'd slipped from the hotel when both Midas and Memphis pulled guard duty and refused to budge." She doubted the two huge, dangerous-looking men would enjoy knowing she'd been calling them the M&M duo in her head. *Midas and Memphis*. That hour had really, really ticked slowly past. And the men hadn't exactly been talkative with her so time had gone past in extra slow motion. "I thought...you were gone a while so I *hoped* Nate had been found, but when those two just kept glaring at me—"

"We weren't glaring," Memphis corrected with a sniff. "We were protecting you. Huge difference."

"I was protecting you with my very life," Midas declared righteously. "Just like Oliver asked me to do."

Uh, huh. "When they kept glaring and protecting, I figured Nate must be on the loose."

"I wanted to come straight back to you." His fingers caressed her shoulders. Did he realize he was doing that? She did. And his touch made her body tense. Tense and yearn.

Swearing, he let her go. "I wanted to come straight back, then I ran into one of your old *friends*."

She had zero clue what friend he meant.

Her confused expression must have indicated as much because he said, "State Representative Blain Montgomery. And are you ready for one hell of a coincidence?" He paced toward the fireplace. No fire danced. He turned his back on it and focused on her. "He's checked into the same hotel we just left. Arrived in town late last night."

At the mention of Blain's name, Lark had sucked in a sharp breath.

Oliver's stare sharpened as he added, "Oh, did I not mention that your brother told me about Blain? When we had our cozy chat as your brother tried to decide if he wanted to cooperate with me or attack me. Luckily, he chose the first option."

Lark shook her head. "Y-you didn't mention Blain."

"Probably because we were busy rushing out...only to discover that Nate Quest came to town gunning for you." Anger beat in his voice. "I tried to find the sonofabitch. Got a tip from Theo that Nate had been spotted near the Ferris wheel. Hauled ass over there just to discover that beat cops had taken the wrong man into custody."

Do not let the fear take over. "He'll turn up," she said, voice determined. She forced determination into every word as she added, "He'll have to use a credit card. Have to buy food. Have to get on some sort of transportation where he'll be spotted. The cops or your agent friends will find him. It's just a matter of time."

"I'll help on that hunt," Memphis offered.

Her attention slid to him.

He rolled one powerful shoulder in a shrug. "Bounty hunting is my bit. Or, it used to be. I'm really good at tracking down the people who like to run. And by really good, I mean I'm the best. I've got lots of connections in this town. I'll start beating the ground and see what shakes loose." He quirked a brow toward Midas. "Assuming you'll be watching their six?"

"I am the bodyguard," Midas returned with a shrug. "It's my bit."

"Really? That's all you're gonna act like you are?" Memphis laughed. A mocking sound. "Nice try, but I've heard plenty about you."

Midas's face darkened. "Don't believe everything you hear."

"Fine. Be secretive. Do you, bro." Memphis sauntered over to stand near Oliver. He swept a considering stare at Lark. "We can always put her in a safe house. I'd be willing to wager the powers that be at the Bureau have already made such an offer to you."

"No," Lark responded before Oliver could confirm or deny such an offer. "I don't want to be locked away."

But, if anything, her response just had Oliver's expression hardening even more. "Sweetheart, you might not have a choice." Then he nodded to Memphis. "Thanks for the help. Beat the ground extra hard, will you?"

"Always." Memphis saluted Oliver and headed for the door.

Midas immediately turned to follow him. "Got a place staked out nearby so I can watch the perimeter."

That news caught her off guard. "You already have a place?" Like, what did he mean? He was just going to sit in a car or—

"Indeed, I do. I believe in being prepared. In case I needed to be close but out of sight, I took the liberty of contacting the rental agent who is in charge of the property across the street. It will give me the perfect vantage point to keep watch."

When had he contacted the rental agent? Not while he'd been in Oliver's house with her. Before? If so, the man sure worked fast because that hadn't exactly given him a lot of time.

"Lucky it was available," he rumbled. "But then, the Feds keep a few houses on this street open. Use them for agents who have to come to town. Feds like Oliver working special cases. I *might* have used Oliver's name to get access to the rental. I'm a name-dropper like that. Between Oliver's name and the pop star I just finished protecting, well, those two names were golden for me."

So this was like...a Fed block? Shouldn't that make her feel safer?

"Figured you'd be pulling duty inside with her," Midas said to Oliver. "Knew I'd be taking the exterior watch. Count on me. No one will slip past and get in your home."

"Thanks, man," Oliver replied. "I owe you."

Midas paused on his way out. "No. We both know you damn well *don't*." Then he, too, headed for the front door.

Her gaze darted to Oliver. A million questions spun through her mind, and she had no idea which one to ask first. Her lips parted.

"Stay here," Oliver said. "We need to talk, but first, I'm making sure the doors are locked, the alarms are set, and this place is as secure as it can be."

Okay, so that was where they'd start. Securing the perimeter. *Step one.* And step two? *Find out what he knows about Blain.* Because that was a blast from her past that Lark hadn't expected. One she'd hoped to keep buried.

As for step three... *What are we going to do about Nate?* Find him. Arrest him. *Stop him from hurting me.*

While Oliver hurried away, she wrapped her arms around her stomach. *Nate Quest wants me dead.* And considering she had zero plans to be dead, that meant Nate had to be apprehended, ASAP.

Her gaze darted around the den. *Stay here.* Oliver's order. An unnecessary one because where was she supposed to go? Was her apartment still considered a crime scene? Her right hand rose to rub her temples. She couldn't go to her apartment. Definitely not an option. In her mind, she could still see the spray paint on the wall. *You will die, too.*

If she left Oliver, maybe she could get a hotel room for the night. Not like she had a ton of friends in the city who would help her. All of her "close" friends had vanished when her brother was arrested.

I'm supposed to be proving his innocence.

Instead, she'd been forced into hiding. How was that going to help Lane?

"Secure," Oliver announced as he came back into the room.

She spun to face him. "Oliver—"

He stalked straight to her. His hands lifted. Curled under her jaw. And he kissed her. Not some soft and delicate kiss. Not the gentlemanly kind of kiss he'd given her so often when they'd first met.

Deep. Hard. Desperate. With a voracious need that rocked through her. With a demand that pierced right to her soul. And she...

Kissed him back. Her hands rose and curled around his powerful forearms. She didn't pull his arms away. She held on tight. She opened her mouth wider. Lust poured through her body. She ached. Needed. Wanted.

All the steps she'd just plotted? Her precious lists?

They vanished. Only Oliver remained.

Then his mouth tore from hers. "I can't fuck you without emotion."

She blinked. *What is happening right now?* He couldn't kiss her senseless and then—then—

"That was what you wanted, wasn't it? A fuck but no emotion?"

Her breath sawed out. What she wanted...*I'm looking at him.*

"I can't give you that." He backed up. Caught her hand and pressed it to his chest. "My heart is about to break out of my chest right now. Every moment I was away from you, I was scared. I don't get fucking *scared.* Or at least, I didn't. Not until you."

Lark wasn't sure what to say. She did get scared. All of the time, but she refused to let that fear stop her. With him, right in this moment, she was terrified. *He can break me all over again.* Or they could break each other.

That terrified her.

And what else terrified her? *Never being with Oliver again.*

"I left the Bureau for you. Executive Assistant Director Ballard wanted me to send you to a safe house after your attack last night. Hell, maybe that's what I should have done."

Back up. Had he just said that he'd left the Bureau for *her?*

"But I didn't want to be separated from you. I don't want some random agent making sure you're safe. I want to protect you. More than that, I *need* to protect you."

His heart raced beneath her hand. A powerful, driving beat.

"I will kill to protect you."

She could feel her eyes widening.

"I know how monsters think, Lark. When I saw the way Nate reacted to you...*every bit of his fury and pain and grief is locked on you.* He blames you. Hates you for living. Hates you because you're Lane Lawson's twin sister. Nate wants revenge, and he thinks he's gonna get it by hurting you. If he kills you, he'll take out the only person Lane loves."

Goose bumps rose on her arms.

"You thought the real Bridal Killer was in your car last night. But Theo called me right before I pulled into my drive just moments ago." A muscle flexed along his clenched jaw. "During the search of Nate's hotel room, Jase turned up a syringe. One loaded and ready to go. Don't know what is inside that syringe yet, but we will soon." A long pause. "Considering you were attacked by a bastard holding a syringe while you were in your car, this find seems pretty freaking important, don't you think?"

Important. Horrifying.

"Nate isn't the Bridal Killer," he said with certainty. "Nate was in Colorado when Susan Peters and Amelia Wayne were abducted and murdered. I checked his alibis myself. And when Casey went missing? He was drinking in a hotel bar—on camera—until nearly three a.m. Casey was last seen a little after one. *He isn't the killer you're after. You didn't lure the real Bridal Killer out with your story on the news.*"

She couldn't move.

"Maybe you didn't lure him out because the real killer is already in jail."

No. Lane can't be the killer.

"But you do have Nate's attention. He came to this town to find you. To hurt you. To kill you. When he saw the news story, it could have fueled his rage even more. And now he's in the wind."

A fist seemed to squeeze her heart.

"I swear to you, *I will keep you safe.* I might have to cuff you to my side, but I'll do it. He isn't going to get to you. Hate me. Go right ahead and do that. Just know that I will protect you. I will do whatever it takes no matter how you feel about me." Grim.

"Why?" The question was torn from her.

"I told you. Nate is coming after you because you're the only person Lane cares about in this world. The only way to hurt him is by hurting you. But that's not going to happen. I won't let it. I'll see Nate in the ground first."

He kept...kept saying things like that. "You don't sound like a Fed."

"What do I sound like?" His lips twisted. "A killer? Maybe that's what you need." He backed away from her.

Her hand fell to her side.

"Executive Assistant Director Ballard told me—hell, the bastard basically said he thought I was obsessed with you because I'd gotten so wrapped up with the Bridal Killer that I couldn't stop thinking like him. According to Ballard, the Bridal Killer wants you, so I do, too."

Her feet had become rooted to the spot. "That's not true."

He looked toward the fireplace. "It's cold. I'll start the fire." He walked close to the fireplace. Hit a little button and the fire flared to life.

"It's not true," she said again. "Tell me—tell me it's not."

Oliver glanced back at her. "I've been inside the minds of killers for so long that sometimes, I worry I can't think like a normal man any longer."

Okay, those weren't exactly the words she'd wanted him to give her. *Exactly? How about not even close?* "That's not what you were supposed to say."

"I know." Low. "I'm supposed to say something reassuring. Something that makes you stop looking at me with fear in your eyes."

Did she have fear in her eyes? "I'm not afraid of you." Plenty of other things, yes. But she wasn't scared *of* Oliver.

"Liar." He turned his back on the fireplace and returned to her. Stopped only when they were nearly touching. "You're so scared of me that you're practically shaking right now."

"Y-you just told me that Nate Quest wants me dead. Knowing someone is hunting you—that would scare anyone." Her chin lifted. "But I'm not scared of *you.*"

"No?"

"*No.*"

He bent toward her. Brought his mouth temptingly close once again and whispered, "Liar." Oliver breathed the word like a caress. Then he started to back away once more.

Her hands grabbed for his suit coat. Clenched around the fabric. "You aren't a normal man."

Pain flashed on his face.

"Normal would be too boring for you. You court danger every chance you get. You take risks. You track people who truly do terrify me." She tightened her grip. "And despite everything that has happened between us, I can promise you, *I am not afraid of you.* You wouldn't ever physically hurt me."

His head moved in a slow shake. "No."

"You don't want me because of the Bridal Killer."

His jaw tensed.

"You want me for the same reason I want you—because when we touch, need explodes. Because there's a charge between us that just burns hotter and hotter even as we fight to stop it. I *tried* to stop wanting you. I can't." The full, humiliating truth for her? "Despite everything, I need you as much now as I ever have before."

"You have me."

No, she didn't.

"I will protect you, Lark. I told you that. I'm right here, and Midas is camped out in a house close to us. Of all the people in the world, he's the one I want watching my back the most. He's a good friend, and I'm lucky to have him. We will both make sure you're secure."

"You cleared him."

A furrow appeared between Oliver's brows.

"Midas told me about his father. About how he was being set up. Midas said you didn't stop until you'd cleared him. And you *are* helping me. If there is evidence to exonerate my brother, you'll find it." *If.* God, that hurt to say. *If.* But, no, there *had* to be evidence. She couldn't believe that Lane was guilty.

Not Lane.

"Midas doesn't typically talk about his past." His lashes flickered. "Surprised he got so chatty with you."

"I think he was mad," she responded. "Guy seemed pretty upset. He kept telling me I'd broken your heart."

Oliver's gaze cut away from her. "Can't happen when you don't have a heart to break."

She'd had her hand over his heart just moments before. She'd felt the fierce pounding. A wild beat, for her. "You can't fuck me without emotion." His words.

He stared into the fire.

"You said that—you can't fuck me without emotion."

"Lark..."

She moved to stand in front of him. He didn't need to look at the fire. She wanted him looking at her. *See me, Oliver.* "The first time we had sex—it was right here in this room."

"I remember. Hell, not like I can ever forget."

Good to know because neither could she. "I told you that I loved you the next day. You never said the words to me."

"Nope. I was too busy arresting your brother."

That hit went straight to her heart. "I thought you didn't care about me."

He'd been staring just over her shoulder. Still looking at the fire. But now, his gaze jerked to latch onto hers. "I care more than you will ever know."

Oh, really? "Then fuck me like I matter." Her eyes widened. Wait. Hold on...had she just said...

"You do matter. Always have. Always will." With that, he kissed her.

And this time, she knew there would be no stopping. She didn't want to stop. Didn't want to think of the reasons why this shouldn't be happening.

She just wanted him.

Always have. Always will.

CHAPTER ELEVEN

Adrenaline. Fury. Fear.

Lust.

His blood beat with the vicious combination, and Oliver knew, he *knew* that he should take his hands and his mouth off Lark.

He also knew that unless she told him no, then he wasn't stopping because he wanted her far too badly. Desperation had filled him as he'd raced back to her side. Adrenaline spiked in his blood. And fear? After barely knowing that emotion for years, it was now a too familiar acquaintance because when it came to Lark, terror kept lurking in his heart.

She could have been abducted last night.

Could have been killed while I was just feet away.

The bastard is hunting her.

Lark had thought that she'd be the one hunting a killer. But a predator was clearly hunting her.

As for the lust blasting through Oliver's body? Hell, it was always stirred by Lark. He looked at her, and he lusted. Normally, that lust could stay under control. But this was no normal situation.

There is no normal with her any longer.

His mouth opened wider. He kissed her harder. His hands slid around her hips. Pressed to her ass and lifted her up against the hard cock that just wanted to plunge into her. She'd lived in his fantasies every night since she'd left him.

Only this was no fantasy.

He needed her naked.

He needed her coming for him. Screaming his name in pleasure? Yes, that would be great.

A moan slipped from her, and his greedy mouth swallowed it, but then he pulled back, just long enough to say, "If you don't want this, want *me*, say it now."

Her breath panted out.

"I can't have you hating me even more after this." Hell, was it possible for her to hate him more?

Her long, dark lashes swept to cover her stare. "I want you."

That was it. All he needed to hear. He kissed her again. Took her into his arms and carried her back to the couch. Everything felt familiar but also different. When he stretched her out on the cushions, when he yanked off her boots and dragged down her jeans...

I tasted her here that last night we had together, with the fire flaring.

Her panties were still on. She hadn't worn panties before. He'd nearly exploded when he saw her bare sex. This time, his fingers reached for the silk of her underwear. He stroked her though the panties, thinking that he could take his time and—

She caught his hand. "Harder," Lark urged. "Don't hold back with me."

He heard his control shred. Or maybe that was her panties shredding. Because he'd just jerked them and the delicate fabric had ripped and now, he was shoving her thighs apart and putting his mouth on her. Tasting every delicious inch of her. Lashing with his tongue and taking her with no restraint. His fingers rubbed over her clit. His tongue thrust into her. Not some slow build-up.

He went straight to the full-on feast.

Her hips jerked and bucked, and Oliver used his other hand to hold her in place because he was just getting started. And she was—

Coming against his mouth. Coming for him already. She cried out his name, and he tasted her as the orgasm shook her body. When the trembles eased, his head lifted.

She still wore her shirt. Her hands gripped the cushions of the couch. Her eyes had closed, but they slowly opened, and she met his gaze. Her left hand freed the cushion. Reached up and touched his face.

An oddly tender moment when all he wanted to do was fuck without restraint. Fuck them both into oblivion. Fuck her like...

She's the only thing that matters in my world.

He eased away from her. Rose to stand by the couch.

Lark blinked up at him. "Oliver?"

"There's a perfectly good bed in my room. Let's see if we can make it there." To the bed and to the condoms that waited in the nightstand. He scooped her into his arms.

She began to kiss his neck. Soft, hesitant kisses. Then little, sensual licks of her tongue.

His hold tightened on her. "Lark..." A warning growl.

"I missed you," she confessed.

He'd been in hell without her.

Those soft words had sealed her fate. Did she get that? He wouldn't let her go again. Whatever he had to do in order to keep her, he would. *Whoever I have to become, I'll do it.*

Oliver made it to his bedroom. Took her right to the bed and lowered her onto the mattress. He backed up to strip. While he ditched his clothes, she rose to her knees and watched him.

He kicked out of his shoes. Tossed the suit coat. Yanked at the buttons on his dress shirt.

"Let me help," Lark offered, voice a husky temptation. She reached for him. Unhooked the buttons with fingers that trembled then pushed open his shirt. She leaned forward more, and her mouth pressed to his chest. Right over his heart. One kiss. Then another. Her mouth went to his nipple. Licked. Teased.

He wasn't in the mood to tease.

Her mouth dipped down. Beneath his heart. She scattered tender kisses over the scar that a killer had left on him long ago. The SOB had been trying to take Oliver's heart.

Bastard made a mistake. I didn't have a heart then. He didn't feel like he'd gotten a heart until he'd found Lark. Found her. Lost her. Had his freaking heart broken.

Her hand darted down his body. Undid his belt. Unhooked the button at the top of his pants and eased down his zipper. Her soft fingers moved to stroke him through his boxers.

"That whole night we had before," Lark murmured, "and I didn't get to taste all of you."

His eyes closed. His hands fisted.

If she wanted to taste him...

Go the hell for it, sweetheart. I'll hold on as long as I can. Which would probably not be very long at all.

Her hair slid over his chest. Then down his abs as her head dipped lower. She pushed his boxers out of the way.

He had to watch her. His eyes opened. Oliver stared down at the curtain of her dark hair. And he felt her soft lips close over the head of his cock.

He nearly exploded in her mouth. Right then. Right there.

Every muscle locked down. Well, his eager cock didn't lock down. It hardened even more as she licked him, sucked him, and stroked him with her tight hand. Her hand pumped him. Her lips caressed him, and—*no more. Can't hold back much longer or I will be exploding in her mouth.*

He hauled her up. Tumbled Lark back onto the bed. Kissed her with desperation and madness because he had nothing else left in him. Fully ditched his pants and his boxers and didn't let her go. He couldn't. Ferocious and consuming hunger filled him. All he wanted was to drive into her.

He did. He sank into her hot, tight, wet core and a ragged groan burst from him because she felt so incredible. He wouldn't last long.

Oliver withdrew. Thrust deep again. She clutched him so tightly. His dick was surrounded by her heat and—

No condom.

He froze. He was looming over the side of the bed. Hadn't even made it fully *into* the bed. He still stood, and he was fucking her from that position. Her legs dangled over the edge of the mattress.

And there was no condom between them.

All he wanted was to drive into her. Over and over. To explode. *And if she gets pregnant, she'll stay with me. We'll be linked forever. I can have Lark forever. I can—*

No, he could not be that much of a bastard where she was concerned. *I'm trying to be someone different with her.* Not a monster. More like a hero.

Maybe both a monster and a hero. Maybe that's what she wants.

Jaw locking, every cell in his body protesting, Oliver withdrew from her.

"Oliver!"

"Condom, baby, condom." Guttural. He grabbed a condom from the nightstand. Ripped the foil packet and rolled on the condom in record time. His gaze never left her. She sprawled on the bed. Legs open. Body waiting.

For him.

Only for me.

"There wasn't anyone else," he gritted.

Her head shook. "Only you."

He'd meant...*There couldn't have been anyone else for me, sweetheart. No other woman was you.* But her confession...that she'd waited... *Only you.*

So fucking good. Because now he didn't have to go find some random bastard and kick his ass. Not something an upright Fed would do?

He'd tried to warn her he had a dark side.

When it came to Lark, he also had one major possessive side.

His hands curled around her thighs. He pulled her closer to the edge of the mattress. Positioned his cock and drove deep into her. She gasped and arched her hips. Her hands grabbed for the arms he'd just braced on either side of her delectable body.

"You...I, ah..." She squirmed beneath him. Her tight, inner muscles clamped harder around him. "I thought you wanted the bed. You're not *in—*"

"I'm in you." That was all he wanted. To be in her. Not in the bed. He'd taken her to the bedroom so she could have the mattress. So he wasn't fucking her up against a hard bookshelf or a wall.

She squirmed again.

Fuck me. He withdrew. Slammed deep. Over and over. And there wasn't any more talking. He was too far gone. All he could do was drive into her. Feel her creamy core all around him. Feel his sanity fading as the release grew closer and closer. But he wasn't going over that edge alone. Oh, hell, no.

Ladies came first. *His* lady would always come first.

His right hand slid between them. Went to her clit. Not for some gentle stroking. Fast, rough. The way he knew she liked it. Over and over as he plunged into her and, this time, she screamed when she came.

Just what he'd wanted.

He let go. The climax consumed him as Oliver sank deeply into Lark once more.

***

Some sick sonofabitch is targeting my sister. Lane walked into the small yard, highly conscious of the guards' stares as they watched the small group of prisoners who'd been let out. Ten minutes. That was all the time they'd been given. Ten fucking minutes of sunshine and fresh air that day.

But Lane didn't give a shit about the sunshine. What was left of it anyway. *They brought us out damn late today.* His mind was on Lark. And the fact that someone had targeted her. *If I wasn't in this hellhole, I'd find him. I'd stop him.*

Because Lark was the only thing that mattered in his world. They'd been watching out for each other their whole lives.

Lark stopped our father, and she did it for me. A part of the story that he doubted she'd told freaking Special Agent Foxx. Though, hell, he still couldn't quite believe that she'd confessed to killing their father. Lane had told her—time and time again—to keep that secret. He'd taken the fall.

Everyone had looked at him like he'd been a monster when he was a teenager. They'd looked at Lark with sympathy. She'd had a chance at a decent life. A normal life. Like the BS you saw on TV.

But she wouldn't leave me. She'd always stood by him.

And now, when she needed him the most, he wasn't there for her.

"Hey, asshole..."

He stiffened at the growling voice. Immediately, he glanced to the left.

A big, hulking jerk with too many bad prison tats glowered at him. "You broke my buddy Ronnie's hand."

Yeah, that sounded about right. The guy who'd given Lane the black eye? Lane had broken the bastard's hand. *Ronnie the rat.* What else should he have done? "He's got two hands. He'll be fine."

Bad Tats grunted at him. "You won't be." And he came in fast, gripping something in his fist.

A shiv. Wonderful. What had the guy done, spent too many freaking hours honing that nasty-ass spoon for this big moment? Lane caught the man's wrist and prepared to break the prick's hand, too. He and Ronnie could be a matching set but then...

Then an idea struck.

Instead of disarming his attacker, Lane just jerked the shiv to the left. A good two inches to the left. Pain sliced through him—so did the shiv—and a low hiss escaped Lane.

Shouts filled the air.

The guards had noticed the attack. Finally. *So much for actually watching our asses.* What had they been doing? Surfing on their phones? They always seemed extra slow to notice bad shit when it happened to Lane.

"That's what you deserve," his attacker snarled as he was hauled away. He spat on Lane.

Oh, gross, asshole, I will remember that.

Lane fell to the ground. His hand went over the wound. One bleeding very, very nicely.

"Dammit, dammit, dammit!" A guard glared down at Lane. "He's bleeding like a stuck pig!"

Good of the man to notice.

"We need to get him to an infirmary, now!" Hands grabbed Lane. Not very gentle hands considering he was...ah...*bleeding like a stuck pig.*

"Do we?" Low. Growling. From another guard.

Lane tensed, wondering if he'd made a serious miscalculation and he was about to—

More shouts. More guards. More footsteps rushing toward him.

And more hands hauling him toward the infirmary. *Too public now, isn't it? Too many eyes.* One of the guards had been ready for Lane to die, but the others were taking him to the infirmary. Lane let out a ragged groan even though nothing vital had been hit. He had made sure of that. He'd done two years in medical school, once upon a time, before he realized that he shouldn't be in the business of saving lives. Not someone like him.

But he'd still learned a few useful bits of info.

Like how to stab someone so the wound will bleed like hell, but your vic will recover.

He wasn't being hauled back to his cell. His chains would be off in the infirmary. People there would think he was weak. Not a threat.

I've never been weak.

Maybe he should be grateful to the shiv-carrying prick. After all, the jerk had just given Lane...a shot at freedom.

No one will hurt my sister.

CHAPTER TWELVE

It wasn't the morning after. It was still daylight. Mostly daylight. Maybe late evening-ish? And she'd just had hot, driving sex with Oliver.

Her enemy.

Her lover.

Twenty-four hours ago, she'd been sure he was still the enemy.

And maybe he was. But he was also the man her body craved. The only man she wanted. He remained inside of her. His hands curled around her. They were both hot and sweaty, and, every now and then, her sex quaked with aftershocks of pleasure. No one had ever given her as much pleasure as he did.

Maybe because she only let down her guard with him? Even knowing he held such power to hurt her, she'd just done it yet again. Given herself fully to him.

Because maybe I do hate him, but I think I still love him, too. Perhaps I always will.

His head lifted. His dark eyes gleamed as he stared down at her. His expression—possessive. Primitive.

Satisfied.

She tensed.

He began to slowly slide out of her. A gasp broke from Lark because she was so sensitive and the withdrawal sent off another little aftershock within her.

His eyes narrowed. "I want to fuck you again."

Evening-ish. Not the morning after. He wanted to fuck her again. With, oh, jeez...with Midas keeping guard from a nearby location. A flush rose in her cheeks. She could feel the heat building. *I forgot Midas was watching the house.*

"Is that a no?" He'd pulled out completely, but he still stood between her legs as they dangled off the side of the bed. She couldn't very well clamp them closed when he was right there.

As for his question... "I haven't said no yet."

His jaw hardened. He turned away. Disappeared into the bathroom.

She did use that opportunity to clamp her legs closed. And, wow, awkward, she still wore her blouse. Should she ditch it? And her bra? Or should she be grabbing her jeans and her ripped underwear and trying to put herself back to rights? Sitting up, her hands went to the hem of the shirt.

"You're beautiful."

He was back. Standing just a few feet away.

"I remember the first time I saw you in person. You were behind the counter at your shop. I walked in, and the whole place smelled so good. There were flowers everywhere and...you. You smiled when you saw me. Your eyes were the greenest eyes I'd ever seen. Your lips were full and sexy, and for a moment, I couldn't move at all."

Their first meeting. When he'd come to her and lied about needing flowers for his mother. "You said...that was the first time you saw me in person." A telling phrase. *In person.*

He advanced.

She kept sitting on the side of the bed. She'd pushed the hem of the blouse down so that the tops of her thighs—and her sex—were covered. Modesty at this point seemed ridiculous, but being completely naked? *Too vulnerable.*

"I'd seen your photo before that day. I'd already worked up a profile on your brother." A tight pause. "And on you."

This was not the after-sex talk most women dreamed of hearing. "You had created a profile so that you could seduce me."

"I created a profile so I knew what you wanted." He didn't look away. "And I became that man."

Her lips pressed together. *Do not dare cry.*

"You wanted someone upstanding. Someone you believed was the true-blue type." A roll of one big shoulder. Oliver was completely naked and didn't seem to care at all. No vulnerability for him. Just power. Muscles. Strength.

A giant cock.

Her gaze whipped up and off said cock.

"With your past, I knew trust would be an issue for you. By telling you I was a Fed from the first moment, I was cementing the idea of me being one of the *good* guys in your head. By saying I was there to get flowers for my mother, I was indicating that I was a family man. That I had close ties to my mother. That I was the reliable sort. A good son."

Her breath choked out. She really, really should reach for her jeans.

"But in reality, I was none of those things." He put his hands on the mattress, settling them on either side of her and caging her in. "Want to know why I hunt monsters?"

"Because you're good at it." *Except with my brother. With Lane, you made a—*

"I could think like them long before I entered the Bureau. I studied abnormal psych so much in college and grad school. I did it not because I was preparing for my career with the Feds, but because I was trying to figure out my own damn self. My past. My future." His stare bored into hers. "I come from a line of killers, Lark."

What? She shook her head. "No, no, I read about you. You're the only son of Esme and Doug Foxx. They were a sweet couple from Kansas City who worked for a charitable organization to help former prisoners to—"

"They adopted me when I was three days old. My father was in prison when I was born. He died in prison. That's what happens when you go on a shooting spree and you take out four innocent people." He swallowed. His Adam's apple rose and fell. "My mother was with him during that spree. A demented Bonnie and Clyde. She never got out of prison, either. Took her own life when she found out my dad passed." The words were cold. So emotionless. "My dad's father was just like him. Went up for murder when he was twenty-four years old and never saw the light of a free day again. They are in my blood. They are in me. And I *never* wanted to end up like them."

She had to touch him. He seemed too cold and distant, but he was right there. Her arms curled around his neck. "You're not like them."

"I'm a predator, Lark. I see prey everywhere I look. I always have. I wanted to channel myself. Get focus. Learn *control.*"

"You have control." Even when they'd just been fucking like mad, he'd been careful. Never hurting her. Never being too rough.

"I hunt the killers because I could always think like them. I learned as much as I needed in school so that I could pass any psych test given to me. So I'd always know the right things to say and the right things to do."

She shook her head and refused to let go of him. "You *are* right. You're not pretending." Is that what he was trying to say? That he was one of the monsters just hiding beneath the guise of an FBI agent? "Bullshit."

He blinked.

"You're not your father. You're not your mother. Or your grandfather or whoever else you've got in your family tree that did bad things. You're *Oliver Foxx.* The famous FBI agent who puts the killers in jail and keeps people safe."

"Lark..."

"You keep people safe," she said again, voice firmer. "You're keeping me safe right now. You're not bad. I wouldn't want you so much if you were." *I wouldn't love you so much.*

He dipped his head forward and pressed a kiss to her mouth. "This is the part," he rasped against her lips, "where you were supposed to run from me."

Not happening. "I don't have on jeans or panties. Running now isn't a possibility." She tried to lighten a mood that had turned so very dark.

No humor lit his face. His gaze seemed deeper than ever before. "I'd just hunt you if you ran. I don't think letting you go again is a possibility for me."

His words seemed like a warning. "Do you want me to be afraid of you?"

"No. I don't want you afraid of anything or anyone. And if something or somebody does scare you, I want to eliminate that threat by any means necessary." His eyes narrowed. "I *will* eliminate any threat to you."

She sucked in a breath. "Why are you telling me all of this now?" So many secrets he'd kept.

"Because I want you to know who I really am. If you fall in love with me again, I don't want you to be falling for the illusion. I want you to need *me.*"

She did need him. She slid her hips a little closer to the edge of the bed. There was one surefire way to prove that he was the one she wanted. "You're still naked."

"Didn't seem a point in putting on clothes when all I want is to get balls deep in you again."

Lark licked her lips. "No, ah, not much point in that."

"But you need to know who you're fucking."

Her hands were still locked behind his head. His mouth still kissably close. "I know." Utter certainty.

"You still want me?" A rumble.

"I never stopped." *Not when Lane was arrested. Not when my world collapsed. And certainly not now.* This time, she kissed him. Hotly. Wildly. Freely. No reservations. Nothing held back.

Just need.

A desire that wouldn't end.

They fell back onto the bed. Twisted and turned and somehow got close to the center of the bed as their mouths met in hungry bursts. He rolled with her once more, and suddenly, she was on top of him. Her legs on either side of his hips. His cock pushed against her, and she rode him. Her folds rocked against him. She was slick and the friction of their bodies pressing together had her aching. She didn't take his cock into her. Not yet. Just rubbed. Stroked.

"Don't tease," he bit out. His hands flew up and curled around her hips. "And why are you still wearing this damn thing?"

The blouse. Right.

Before she could pull it off, he did the job for her. The blouse flew and landed somewhere on the other side of the bed. Then his big, warm hands were going behind her back. Unhooking her bra. Sending it sailing away, too.

Completely naked now, she straddled him. His hands went to her breasts. Held them. Cradled. Teased her nipples with his callus-tipped fingers. She kept rocking against him. Sliding over the thick length of his cock. If she just arched forward a little, if she angled her hips, she could take the head of his dick inside of her.

"Condom," he said.

Her head lifted. Her eyes met his.

"Condom...then I'm *in* you."

"I'm on birth control." He'd felt so good sliding into her before. With nothing between them. "I've never..." She stopped. Had to stop because he'd lifted up and his mouth had closed around one nipple and speaking had become impossible.

He licked. He bit lightly.

She shuddered.

He let her go.

Her knees pressed into the mattress. "I've used a condom with every other man—"

His rough growl broke through her words. "Don't want to hear—*ever*—about you with another man." His hands tightened on her. "You are mine."

Just as he was hers. She knew it, in her soul. Maybe that was why his betrayal had shattered her so deeply. "I don't want anything between us."

He didn't ease his grip.

"I'm clean. Healthy as can be." Her breath shuddered out.

"So am I."

She caught one of his hands. Pulled it from her hip. Eased it down until his fingers were over her clit. "Touch me the way I like." The way he did so perfectly.

His fingers went to work.

Her mouth opened on a gasp even as she pushed up a bit on her knees. She tilted up her hips, and, this time, she curled her hand around his cock as she positioned him.

The head slipped inside of her.

Then he sank all the way in.

At first, she didn't move at all. Just savored the fullness of him filling every single inch of her. Then she clamped her inner muscles around him as tightly as she could.

"*Lark*." His fingers rubbed her clit faster. Harder.

She lifted up, then rocked down. He stroked her. She lifted up. Rocked down.

His fingers worked her feverishly. Frantically. There was no stopping the release. It barreled through her at breakneck speed and all she could do was cry out as her body seemed to spasm with the waves of release that blasted through her.

Again and again and again.

He surged up. Tumbled her back onto the bedding. Caught her legs and lifted them over his shoulders. Then he pounded into her. So deep. Felt deeper than ever before. Nothing was between them. Just body to body. Sex to sex.

He consumed her.

She craved him.

Her nails raked down his back because another orgasm was building. Or maybe the last one hadn't stopped. She couldn't slow down. Couldn't catch a breath. All she could do was feel. Him. Everywhere. Inside. Out. Surrounding her. Taking her.

"*Lark!*"

Exploding within her.

She bucked beneath him and let the pleasure take them both.

***

Too possessive.

He'd come off too strong.

He'd taken her too hard. There'd been no restraint. No control.

And he wanted to do it all over again. Endlessly. For now, though, he should probably lift his heavy-ass body off her. Oliver knew his weight had to be crushing Lark. He heaved up and stared down at her. Worry filled him.

With her eyes closed, she smiled for him. "You don't have to worry about anyone else."

She'd better damn well not be talking about another man—

"No one could ever compare to you." Her lashes lifted. Her green gaze gleamed. "Sex never felt this way—this amazing—until you. I could never let go so completely, until you."

Satisfaction pulsed through him. "I plan to wreck you for anyone else." An asshole thing to say? So what? He was an asshole. "Forget that. *There can be no one else*. I meant it, Lark. You're mine." She had been from the day that he'd walked into that florist shop and gotten lost in a pair of incredible, emerald eyes.

"Does that mean you're mine, too?"

Always have been. Didn't she get it? She owned him, body and soul. He'd do whatever it took to get her back. She came first. She—

His phone was ringing.

Ignore the damn thing. The first instinct he had. But Nate Quest was loose in the city and maybe that call was Jase or Theo saying the bastard had been spotted. Or, better yet, maybe one of the agents was calling to say he'd caught Nate.

His phone rang again. "Hold the thought," he rumbled. Then he withdrew.

A little gasp slipped from her when he slid out.

I'm still aroused for her. Want her again and again.

The phone wouldn't stop its damn ringing. He jumped from the bed and fished the phone from the pocket of his suit coat. When he saw the caller ID...*hell.* Not Jase or Theo. But it still could be related to Nate. His finger slid over the screen right before he put the phone to his ear. "Executive Assistant Director Ballard. To what do I owe this seriously untimely—"

"Is Lark Lawson with you?"

He stared straight at her. "Absolutely. I'm assuming you've been briefed on the situation with Nate Quest?" Jase would have updated him ASAP. "I am guarding Lark, and she will not be let out of my sight."

"This isn't about freaking Nate Quest. It's about Lane Lawson."

Do not change expression. He kept gazing at Lark. "What about him?"

"He was stabbed in the yard and taken to the infirmary—"

*Her brother has to be okay. If Colby Ballard is calling to tell me that Lane died in some inmate fight and I have to give Lark that news...*No, no, he could not.

"Docs thought he was unconscious. Let down their guard and the sonofabitch broke out."

"I'll need you to say that again."

"The sonofabitch broke out. He's loose. Forget the hunt for Nate Quest. I'm directing all of our resources to focus on finding the freaking escaped serial killer who is out roaming in Vegas."

Oh, this was not good.

"The same day you visit him, and Lane Lawson breaks out. The very same day." Colby's rage poured across the line. "You know how this looks?"

Bad. Very bad. "I had nothing to do with the escape."

The escape.

Lark had pulled the covers over her body, but at that word, she jerked. Hard. Then she flew out of the bed and surged toward him.

"You'd better not have," Colby snarled. "Because if I found out you helped the prick, your ass will be the one behind bars. You hear me?"

"The connection is perfect. I hear you quite clearly." He was also pretty sure that Lark had heard those booming words.

"Get to my office. Bring Lark with you. If she knows anything about this mess, I *will* be finding out. If she doesn't know, hell, we both understand that her brother will be coming for her. No way he leaves town without his sister. So that means *Lark* doesn't leave. If she tries to get away from you, if she refuses to come in—hell, refusal is not an option. You arrest her ass if you have to do it but *bring her to me.*"

His jaw had clenched. With an effort, Oliver loosened it, a bit. Then he snapped, "She's not getting arrested."

"She is if she had something to do with her brother's escape! I can't believe this shit! *Get her here.*" Colby hung up.

He gripped the phone. Thought about smashing it into a million pieces. But, no, that wasn't what a good, upstanding FBI agent would do.

I took a break from the Bureau. I'm ready to stop pretending to be someone I'm not.

"I didn't catch all of that." She'd wrapped a sheet around her body. One hand clasped it to her chest. "Sounded like Executive Assistant Director Ballard was angry."

"Angry is an understatement." Dammit. If Oliver didn't take Lark to the Bureau office, then Colby would just send someone after her. And that someone? The agent who came for her would arrest Lark if she didn't cooperate. Make up some BS charge about obstruction.

She'd be taken to Colby Ballard's office, one way or another.

"What's happening?" She inched forward. The sheet trailed behind her.

"Your brother escaped."

Her mouth opened. Her eyes widened. Then she—she shook her head. Instant denial. "No."

"Yes, sweetheart, he did." *While I was fucking you, your brother broke out of jail.* "He was injured during an attack from another inmate." *We'll have to see if that attack was planned. Maybe the other inmate was in on the escape.* "Lane was transferred to the infirmary. I'm guessing the staff there didn't have him properly restrained. They thought he wasn't a threat. They were wrong."

"No." Another shake of her head. Her mouth snapped closed.

"He's on the run. A full manhunt is about to take place." If it wasn't already taking place. He put the phone onto the nightstand and grabbed his boxers. Oliver hauled them on. Then dragged up his pants. "You have to get dressed."

"No."

"Colby wants you in his office. I'm sorry but he...he wants to question you."

"Lane didn't break out of jail. He's waiting for his trial."

No, he wasn't.

Oliver yanked on his shirt. Buttoned it with quick flicks of his fingers.

"He didn't break out," Lark insisted.

"Yes, baby, he did. And Colby basically gave me two options. I bring you in—or he has a team come and get you." He tucked in his shirt with angry shoves of his hands. "I'm not being separated from you. I will stay with you every moment. I will *not* let agents haul you off in handcuffs."

"Innocent people don't run."

His hands fell to his sides.

"He was waiting for his day in court. He was..." She wet her lips. "I was going to prove his innocence. Lane can't—he can't run."

He would run if he thought you were in danger. And I told him you were. I should have seen this coming. Dammit.

"The cops will hunt him." Her hand fisted around the sheet section she clutched to her chest. "Everyone will hunt him. They won't care about bringing him back in alive."

She wasn't wrong. Not with the stories that had spread about Lane Lawson. The man would be considered extremely dangerous.

"They'll kill him," she said. Her eyes filled with tears. "They'll kill my brother."

He wanted to tell her that wouldn't happen. But he didn't want any more lies.

When her knees started to buckle, he caught her under her arms and held her upright.

***

This was one major cluster. Oliver gripped his phone as his eyes remained on the closed bathroom door. Behind that door, Lark was dressing. He'd brought her fresh clothes from the suitcase in the guest room closet.

He feared she was also crying behind the closed door.

"Yo," Memphis answered on the second ring. "You good? Your girl safe? You—"

"Things are far from good," he shot back in a low growl. "Lane Lawson just escaped."

"What?"

"Executive Assistant Director Ballard is demanding I bring Lark in for questioning."

"Does she have something to do with—"

"No," Oliver cut through Memphis's question, voice firm. "Not a damn thing. The escape just happened. She was with you and Midas, then she was with me." *Fucking me*. His breath shuddered out. "I need you on this. We both know you're the best bounty hunter that pretty much ever breathed."

"Flattery will get you everywhere." But his voice was just as grim as Oliver's had been moments before. "If I'm hunting Lane, you know I can't focus on Nate Quest."

Yes, he did. And he hated pulling Memphis off the search for Nate. "I'm staying with her. I'm also going to make sure that Midas is in the shadows." He'd already texted his friend and updated him on everything. Midas would be trailing them and making sure not to be spotted. Not unless he was needed. Then Midas would come in with a fury. "I need you to find Lane. If someone else does…" He stopped. Had he just heard a sob from the bathroom?

"If someone else does, you think they'll shoot first and screw any plans to bring Lark's brother back to a cell?"

That was exactly what he thought. "I'm worried he won't surrender easily."

"They never do, man. They never do."

The bathroom door opened. Smudges lined Lark's eyes, and her skin seemed far too pale.

"I need you to do this for me," Oliver said to Memphis. "I'll pay any price."

"We'll work that shit out later. Right now, just know I'm on it." Memphis ended the call.

Oliver lowered his phone. "Are you okay?" he asked Lark.

"I didn't help him escape."

"I know, sweetheart." All he wanted was to pull her into his arms.

"It makes him look even guiltier, doesn't it? Running?"

Yeah. It did. And they both knew it.

Guilty as sin.

CHAPTER THIRTEEN

"Where is Lane Lawson?" Executive Assistant Director Colby Ballard leaned aggressively over the small conference room table. Both of his palms were flat on that table, and the wedding ring on his left hand gleamed dully in the light. "Where the hell is your brother right now, Lark?"

She kept her spine straight. Her chin up. She *hated* that she'd almost fallen before Oliver in the bedroom. Her knees had just gotten too weak. She'd had a terrible image of Lane.

Dead Lane. A bullet straight to the heart. Just like our dad.

"Lark, *answer me.* You visit your brother all the time. You planned this with him, didn't you? You know where he is. You know—"

"Lark didn't plan anything with him," Oliver cut through Colby's words to say. "I've told you that already. Settle down. She's cooperating. You don't need to terrorize her." He advanced from the watchful position he'd taken near the left wall.

Colby immediately whirled toward him. "Did you just tell your supervisor to 'settle down'—did I hear that shit correctly?"

"You absolutely heard correctly. Good for you."

Colby's body stiffened even more.

"Don't berate her. Ease the hell up," Oliver ordered, seemingly unintimated by the man who was his supervisor. "What do you want, for her to lawyer up and tell you nothing?" His gaze slid to Lark. Lingered. There was a clear message in his eyes.

He's telling me to lawyer up and say nothing.

"The longer her brother is out there, the more dangerous this situation becomes! Law enforcement personnel are hunting him as we speak." Colby spun toward her. His hands slammed onto the table again. "Do you want your brother brought back in a body bag?"

"N-no." That was the last thing she wanted and the very thing that she feared the most.

"Then tell me what you know. Tell me what you planned. Tell me—"

"I planned to prove his innocence." Her sweaty palms rolled over her jean-covered thighs. "I was going to get him out. Find evidence to exonerate him." That had been her whole plan. From day one. *Prove he's innocent. Free Lane.*

Ever since she'd been a teen, she'd made lists. They helped her to stay organized. To stay focused. When life was chaos, her lists were the map she used for navigating. So when her brother had been taken from her, she'd started a new list.

Step one: Get proof that Lane is innocent.

Step two: Find someone to help you— someone who has expertise in hunting killers.

She'd tried hiring two PIs. They'd turned up nothing.

Step three: Don't give up. Ever.

So she hadn't.

Step four: Do whatever is necessary to free Lane.

Whatever was necessary.

The *whatever was necessary* part had led her to the Ice Breakers. To Memphis. Back to Oliver.

Step five: Sometimes, lies are the only weapons we have.

Her breath shuddered out. And her hands curled into fists. Her nails bit into her palms.

"Innocent people don't run," Colby announced.

She flinched. She'd said those exact words to Oliver.

"You know who does run? People who are guilty. People who don't want to face the punishment for their crimes—they are the ones who run." He glared at her. "The last time you went to see your brother, what did you talk about?"

She could speak the truth. "The Ice Breakers."

"What?"

She glanced toward Oliver. Found his eyes on her. Staring straight at him, she said, "I talked to Lane about the Ice Breakers. I wanted them to help with his case." A slow exhale. "I told Lane not to give up. He was going to get out." *Just wait, Lane. You'll be free soon.*

Only her brother hadn't waited.

"Well, he damn well did get out, didn't he?" Colby threw his hands into the air. "Bastard stole a car that belonged to one of the nurses in the infirmary. He put on green scrubs, took the dumbass's ID and keys and was able to sneak right out of a high-security facility like it was freaking child's play." His eyes shot fire at her. "You expect me to believe he did that all on his own?"

"I don't expect you to believe anything I tell you." Again, that was the truth. "You've never believed me before when I said that Lane was innocent. You're not going to believe me now when I say that I wasn't involved in his escape." She wasn't sure what he hoped to gain from this interrogation. "I can't help you. I don't know where my brother is."

"He's never far from you." A shake of Colby's head. "That's been your life story. Where you go, he goes. First with foster families, then with colleges. Hell, he had the chance to set up his business in France, but instead, he sold his house and moved in with you."

"That was just temporary. He was buying a bigger place. Getting architectural plans drawn up—"

"You're a liar, Lark."

She sucked in a breath.

"Watch it," Oliver warned.

"You're a liar," Colby claimed again, apparently not in the mood to watch anything. "And your brother is a killer."

"No, he isn't." Fine. She'd confess all. She'd tell him about her father's shooting. She'd tell him—

"Didn't you lie to Special Agent Oliver Foxx?" Colby waved to Oliver.

Her breath seemed to freeze.

"Didn't you lie to Memphis Camden? Your lie is what convinced the Ice Breakers to help you in your quest to find that so-called 'real' Bridal Killer, isn't it?" A brief pause. "See, I already knew about the Ice Breakers. Just like I already knew you were a liar."

She had to pull in another breath. Had to do it. *I'm frozen. So cold.*

"Oliver suspected you were lying, too, of course."

She didn't look at Oliver. Couldn't. But she felt his stare on her.

"So right after that meeting he had with you and Memphis at Side Strip, Oliver asked his team at the Bureau to do a little digging. Your assistant, Katya, I believe is her name?"

"There was no need to dig." Her nails bit deeper into her palms. Yes, Katya had been her assistant at the florist shop.

"She's visiting family in Russia right now, isn't she?" Colby pressed as he studied her. She had the feeling he was a snake poised to strike.

Lark wet her dry lips. "Her family left Russia about five years ago. They live in England now. *That's* where she's visiting."

"Thanks so much for that clarification," he murmured. "But I actually knew that, as well."

If he knew so much, why the games?

"My agents do understand how to do their jobs. Jase tracked her down in a very fast amount of time. That happens when you're a federal agent with incredible resources. He interviewed her over the phone earlier today. He was able to question her and see if the story you fed the Ice Breakers and Oliver was true."

She could feel the blood draining from her face.

"It was a lie, of course. She said there was no video footage recovered. Didn't remember anything about a mysterious package arriving at your florist shop."

Lark would *not* look at Oliver right then. *Had he known this? Had he realized—*

"Oliver is on a *break* from the Bureau. So that means that Jase has been reporting to me before telling Oliver anything of import. When he found out that you'd lied to Oliver and to Memphis, he informed me of the discovery." Colby crooked an eyebrow at her. "Want to tell me that I'm wrong? That Jase is wrong? That you didn't *lie to a federal agent about evidence?*"

No words came out. She just didn't know what to say.

Then she felt a touch on her shoulder.

Lark jerked even as her head whipped to the side. And up.

Oliver stared down at her. She hadn't even heard his footsteps close the last bit of distance between them. But he was beside her. No judgment appeared in his eyes.

There was plenty of judgment in Colby's voice as he informed her, "The Ice Breakers will stop helping you when they learn the truth. As for Special Agent Oliver Foxx...do you really want to see his career crash and burn because of you?"

No, that was the last thing she wanted. Lark mouthed *I'm sorry* to Oliver.

He gave a barely perceptible shake of his head.

"Cooperate with me, and we can make a deal," Colby offered, voice all magnanimous. "Tell me where your brother is."

"I don't *know* where he is." She searched Oliver's eyes. He had his mask on again. No emotion at all showed in his expression. Was he furious with her? If so, why had he just crossed to stand by her? Almost as if...as if he'd shown where his loyalty rested.

With me.

Even though she'd lied to him?

"We've got a team going to his lawyer's home." Colby's words had her focusing on him once again. "She's been pretty close with him, too. Lots of visits. He'll be frantic and looking for a safe place to crash...tell us his safe places, Lark. You know him better than anyone else. Tell me where he'd go."

To me. Lane would come to me.

"We're watching your apartment, of course," Colby added as his fingers tapped across the table's edge. "If he shows up there, we'll have him. But where else would he turn?"

Her lips parted.

"This bullshit is getting old," Oliver said curtly. "Everyone in this room knows that Lane isn't going to cut town. He isn't going to vanish. He broke out because he was worried about Lark."

"Oh?" Interest stirred in Colby's voice. "So you know his thoughts. You two talked about what he would do—"

"When I questioned him, I told him about the attack on Lark. And now, bam, he's out. Doesn't take a profiling genius to connect the dots. Does make me wonder though..."

And that was it. Oliver just stopped and didn't tell them what he was wondering.

"Uh, gonna share with the rest of the damn group?" Colby snapped.

Oliver rubbed a hand over his jaw. The stubble seemed to scrape beneath his fingers. "Makes me wonder if he had an idea of who might be going after her. Maybe he felt like it was someone he had to handle himself."

"And who the hell might that be?" An explosion from Colby.

"Well, the person who came up in our conversation was Blain Montgomery."

A chair leg screeched. Colby had whipped back from the table so quickly that he'd kicked a chair that had been behind him.

"*State Representative Montgomery?*" Colby gaped. "You can't be serious."

"Don't feel like I'm joking, so, yeah, I'm serious. The man has a past with Lane and with Lark. And he happens to be in town. Staying at the very place where the Escalade that was used in an attempt to run down me and Lark—he's staying at the same damn place where it was stolen. Lots of coincidences, don't you think? Too many."

Colby took a step back. Hit the chair again. "You're saying Lane Lawson broke out of jail to go after Blain Montgomery?"

Her thundering heartbeat echoed in Lark's ears.

"I'm saying why not put a tail on the representative?" Oliver's question seemed all calm and reasonable. "Wouldn't you rather be safe than sorry?"

The air thickened. Colby's glare grew angrier. And then... "Sonofabitch." He whirled and stormed from the small interrogation room. The door slammed shut behind him.

Lark's shoulders sagged. Not that she was relaxing. More like collapsing and—

Oliver hauled her out of the chair and into his arms. A tight, hard hug. Her hands fluttered around him because she didn't know what was happening.

"Eyes are on us. Agents watching through the one-way mirror on the right," he whispered into her ear. His breath slid over the shell of her ear and sent a shiver chasing down her spine. "Do you just hate lawyers? You must. Get over that. Because the next time I throw you a hint about bringing in one, take it."

She didn't know what to say. Or maybe she wasn't supposed to say anything. Not if eyes were watching. Maybe she was just supposed to listen.

"Trust me. I am on your side. Always."

Even with the lie she'd told? *The box didn't come to my shop. I have no idea how it got into my basement. Just...Dear God, please, don't let my brother have put it there.* Her arms wrapped around Oliver, and she held him as tightly as he held her.

"And stop digging your nails into your palms. You're making yourself bleed, sweetheart." He squeezed her once more, then let her go. Eased back. Swept his stare over her. "Feel better?" Louder.

She shook her head. "No." Honest. "I want out of here."

The door flew open and bounced against the wall. "I have agents going to meet with the representative. They'll keep him safe." Colby pointed his index finger at Lark. "You want—"

"You can't keep me here." She didn't think he could. A lawyer would be able to tell her. Yes, she should definitely take more hints from Oliver. But...

She blinked. Inspiration had just struck. Inspiration and a bit of hope. "My brother is out there, and if you want him found, then let me hunt for him."

Colby laughed.

Anger spiked inside of her and erupted as she blasted, "You're the one saying I know him better than anyone else. If you truly believe that, then stop wasting my time! Let me go out there and find him. I don't want Lane getting shot—"

"And I don't want your brother killing again." Colby's nostrils flared. "You think I just will let you waltz out of here on your own? For all I know, you go out and you will disappear. Maybe you have plans to meet up with your brother and vanish into the sunset together."

"That is *not* the plan. I want to find him. I can't do that locked in this room!" Her head moved in a jerky nod. "I do know him better than anyone else. If I'm out on the streets, I can visit all the places that he loved."

"You can give us a list of those places..."

Yes, and they'd leave her behind. Maybe even lock her away some place while they hunted for Lane. "If he sees the cops or the Feds, he'll vanish. But if he sees me...if *I* am there, then he'll come out. You've said it yourself—he'll come to me. I just have to be there." *Do not leave me behind.*

Interest shone on Colby's round face. "You're offering to let the Feds use you in order to catch your brother?"

"I'm offering to help bring my brother in safely. I don't want anyone getting hurt. I never wanted that."

His lips twisted. "Seems funny, doesn't it? One day, you're working so hard to prove his innocence and get him out of jail and now...now you're all too eager to send your brother right back there."

She bounded toward him. Her chin jutted into the air. "I don't want him *dead*. I don't want people shooting at my brother because they think he's a killer. I want him safe, and I'll help you to keep him safe. That's my deal." The Executive Assistant Director had spoken so easily of a deal earlier. Well, this was her deal. "Use me, but I'm there. Every moment." Because she could help Lane. Protect him.

"You realize, of course, that if you're present and things go to shit...and the officers are given no choice but to employ deadly force in order to contain an escapee..." His head cocked. "You will quite possibly watch your brother die right in front of your eyes?"

Oliver swore.

"Saw that happen to my father," she returned woodenly. "It won't happen to my brother."

Oliver stepped into Colby's path. "We need to talk."

"Damn straight we do."

They barreled out, and, once more, the door slammed closed.

Her arms curled around her body.

Lane, what have you done?

***

"Did you know she was lying?" Colby asked. Then, before Oliver could respond, Colby's hands waved wildly in the air. "I want everyone else *out* of here! Now! Everyone but me and Agent Foxx!"

The other two agents in the observation room rushed out. One pulled the door shut behind him. Oliver barely spared the fleeing agents a glance. Instead, he was too busy looking through the one-way mirror. His eyes were on Lark.

As he watched, she hugged herself. Rocked a little.

"Now...let me ask again...*did you know she was lying?*"

"About Katya?" He'd seen the tells. The biggest one? Lark hurt herself when she lied. A terrible habit that they would be breaking. *Bleeding palms.* "I suspected it was the case. Why else would I have told Jase to dig so fast and hard?"

"There is no evidence to prove her brother's innocence."

No, there never had been.

"And now he's escaped. And that woman in there..." Colby moved closer to the glass. "She just offered to use herself as bait so that we could lock her brother up again."

Oliver also moved closer to the glass.

Lark's head turned. She stared straight at him. Not that she could actually see him. Sure, he could see her. But when Lark looked at the one-way mirror, she'd just see her own reflection. But he'd warned her people were watching in the observation room.

Does she know I'm one of the people watching now?

"Is she starting to realize he's guilty?" Gruff. Maybe even laced with what could have possibly been a hint of sympathy. "Had to happen sooner or later, didn't it?"

"She doesn't want her brother dead. Better in a cell than dead."

Lark had moved to stand right in front of the mirror. And still, her gaze seemingly looked straight through it. Right at him.

"Do you think she can find him?" Colby asked. "Or is this some scheme so that they can both run away and never look back?"

Her stare didn't waver. Neither did Oliver's as he drank her in. "Her whole life, she never left him. She had the opportunity, again and again, to start over without him. She didn't do it. He's her only family." *She will always side with him.*

"So she'll run." A long sigh. "Shit. Makes things complicated as hell. I *need* to use her to draw him out."

"I won't let her run." *I won't let Lark turn into a wanted criminal.* "I'll keep her at my side. You can have Feds with us the whole time. There will be no way for her to give us the slip." Would she hate him even more if she knew what he was saying? Probably. But Lark wouldn't live the rest of her life looking over her shoulder.

"You sure about that?" Colby's doubt was clear. "The woman seems to have you wrapped around her finger. How do I know that you won't let her do anything she wants?"

Lark turned away from the mirror.

So Oliver finally looked at Colby. "I am in complete control when it comes to Lark."

Colby's brow furrowed. He searched Oliver's face. "You're...holy shit, man, have you been *working the case* all along?" His mouth formed a giant O before he snapped his lips closed and got himself together enough to ask, "You been working her this whole time? Trying to get more evidence?" Another hard exhale. "Trying to shut down this nonsense about her brother being innocent by sealing all the holes in his coffin? You—you let her think you were working with her, but you were really working *her* all along?"

The Executive Assistant Director talked far too much. He also asked the wrong questions. "She won't run. If she finds her brother, I'll be there. I'll arrest him. Then you can have one of your press conferences and let the city know it's safe again."

A slow smile spread over Colby's face. "Guess your break is over, huh?"

"What break?" Oliver returned.

Colby slapped a hand on his shoulder. "That's what I thought. You tricky bastard...*go bring that asshole down.*"

CHAPTER FOURTEEN

Lark had always believed that when darkness swept over Vegas, the city truly came alive. Maybe that was why she'd been so drawn to the city. Right after college, she'd moved to Vegas and never left. There was light in the darkness of Vegas. So much light.

"We should go back to my place," Oliver said. Quiet, intense Oliver. He'd been that way during the hours of their search as the darkness stretched and stretched. "It's getting beyond late—"

"And we've turned up nothing so far," Special Agent Shannon Steele finished. Shannon had been with them ever since they left the Bureau. Tall, with short, black hair styled in a modern pixie cut and sporting a no-nonsense attitude, the agent had been on high alert every moment.

Oliver had been on one side of Lark. Shannon on the other. Guarding her? Or keeping her prisoner?

Did Oliver truly think that she might run?

And what about the big lie? He'd clearly suspected from the beginning that she had made up the story about the package being delivered to her store. What was he thinking now that the lie had been proven? She was desperate to ask him all the questions tumbling through her mind, but she couldn't exactly do it with an audience watching.

Lark was sure Shannon wasn't the only FBI agent on guard duty for her. She'd caught glimpses of Everett Callen, another member of Oliver's team. Everett seemed to be busy skulking in the shadows. *Skulk all you like, I still know you're watching.*

She'd first met him months before so when she'd caught a glimpse of him at their second stop—an old gym Lane had frequented—she'd known that he'd been brought along to keep watch.

Oliver's gang is getting back together. The team she'd first met? Oliver, Shannon, Everett, Theo, and Jase. Theo and Jase weren't beating the streets with them. No doubt, they'd been sent off by Colby Ballard in another direction.

But as for Oliver, Everett and Shannon? They were in hunting mode. The elite agents were needed to bring out a monster once again. Her brother.

"After we check inside, we can go back to your place," Lark offered. They'd sleep and try again at first light. But she didn't want to turn back now. After all, they were just steps away from their final destination.

They'd searched so much already.

Lane hadn't been at his lawyer's—not her office or at her home.

He hadn't been at his gym. None of his favorite bars or coffee spots.

Lane's business had been shuttered and empty. The warehouse he owned locked up.

Lane had never been exactly tight with any friends, but Lark had still taken the agents to the homes of his closest acquaintances. People who had *not* been pleased to see her on their doorsteps as the hour grew later and later.

And now—now she was down to her last hope.

She looked up at the FOR RENT sign on the side of the building. The new owner of the building hadn't yet succeeded in renting the place out. The front window was empty and dark. In the past, she'd always tried to put in fun and creative displays in that window—displays usually themed around whatever holiday approached.

It wasn't just the window that was dark. The whole store was dark. There would be no bright and beautiful flowers inside. She'd sold them all long ago. Sold all of her equipment. Nothing would be left.

"Why would he come here?" Shannon asked as she leaned forward to peer in the front window.

"Why not?" Oliver returned. "It's abandoned, and he'd know that. Lark would have told him that she'd sold the place."

Yes, she had told her brother. She'd told him that it sold to a new owner. One who was trying—but failing—to rent it out to a tenant.

"It would be a good place for him to hide," Oliver continued. "Street is quiet. Deserted at this time. He could lay low and come up with a plan. Stay out of sight here."

"We're gonna need a warrant to get inside." Shannon kept peering through the window.

"Since she doesn't own it. Not like she can give us permission and hey—I see a light in there! Small, bobbing—a flashlight!" Shannon raced for the front door. She grabbed the knob and twisted but the door didn't open.

"Two heavy locks are on the front door," Lark told her as she hurried after the agent. "You won't be getting in that way. But the back...the lock there is—"

Shannon had already taken off. The agent had drawn her gun. Lark surged after her.

"*Behind* me. Behind the people with guns, got it?" Oliver hauled her back. Then he rushed off behind Shannon.

As fast as she could, Lark followed suit. They raced around the building, and she saw that the back door had been thrown wide open. Getting inside wouldn't be a problem. Someone else had already beaten them to breaking the weaker lock in the back.

Shannon ran inside.

So did Oliver.

Shannon saw a flashlight. She saw someone moving in there. "Lane!" Lark called out. "Lane, they are federal agents!" She hurried into her old shop.

Flashlights bounced off the walls. Lights that came from Shannon and Oliver. They were quickly sweeping around the scene. Ducking into and out of the rooms that snaked from the main area of the old shop as they searched.

Lark could have sworn the scent of flowers teased her nose. Lilies.

She'd kept so many lilies there once upon a time.

Lights flooded on overhead. For a moment, she just blinked against the blinding illumination. Then she realized Shannon had hit the switch. The female agent was turning on all the lights in the building.

"Nothing! No one!" Shannon whirled. "Maybe he ran out back. I *know* that I saw him! Or, dammit, a light. And someone had to be attached to the light!"

Just then, footsteps rushed from the back of the store, from the door they'd just entered.

Oliver grabbed Lark and shoved her behind him—

"Did you find him?" Everett Callen's hard voice demanded.

Oliver shook his head. "Place seems clear. Go check the perimeter with Shannon. She swears that she saw someone inside, and the perp could have fled through the back door while we were rushing around the building."

The two agents hurried to obey him.

That left Lark alone—for the first time since her interrogation—with Oliver.

He swung toward her. "Did you see him?"

Her head shook. "I-I never even saw the light that Shannon mentioned." Speaking of light...she looked up. "Good thing the new owner is still paying the power bill, huh?" Her nose twitched. The scent of flowers drifted in the air. Not some memory. A real scent. She was *sure* that she'd just caught the sweet fragrance again.

But her flowers had been gone for months.

"Why did you bring us here last?" Oliver wanted to know. "Were you trying to give him time to clear out?"

Her attention snapped to Oliver. "What?"

"Did you have extra clothes stashed somewhere in here?" He stormed around the shop. "Maybe a disguise for him to use?"

He couldn't be serious. "There is nothing here. Everything was sold." Extra clothes? What—"I thought you believed me." A fist squeezed her heart. "I thought you knew I hadn't helped Lane."

His back stiffened. As usual, he was in his suit. Black coat. White dress shirt. Black pants. And a gun gripped in his hand. Slowly, he faced her again. "Maybe you and your brother talked about possibilities."

"Excuse me?"

"If he ever did find himself on the outside...where would he go? What would he do? Maybe you came up with a hypothetical plan, just in case."

"I *didn't*." They'd never talked about escape. Just about proving his innocence.

"You can't run with him, Lark."

What? Run with him? Where? "I don't know what you're talking about. I'm here to help you find him." Shannon had said that she'd seen a light. Maybe whoever had been inside had left something useful behind. "If you aren't searching, then I will." She hurried toward the red door that still had *STAFF* written across the top in a whimsical script. She'd done that, her second day in the building. In an attempt to make the place her own.

"Shannon looked in there already. She cleared the room," Oliver said from behind her.

The door hung partially open. Lark's fingers shoved against the wood to open it fully.

Her nose twitched. The scent of flowers was everywhere in this building. Ever since she'd been a child, Lark had loved the smell of fresh flowers. Flowers were fragile but so beautiful. And they made people happy. People always smiled when they were given flowers. Joy would slide on their faces, even in times of grief. Flowers brought joy, and the joy took the place of sadness, if only for a little while.

There had been so many flowers at my mom's funeral.

But there had been hardly any at her father's.

"He's not in there, Lark."

Her desk was gone. Her filing cabinets. The workspace where she'd carefully prepared bouquets with ribbon and twine sat empty when once she'd been snipping and shaping the flowers and...

Flowers.

There were flowers in her old workspace. Flowers—

Where there shouldn't be any.

"We need to go outside," Oliver said. "If it's your brother, if Shannon and Everett run him down..."

Her steps stumbled forward.

"*You* want to be there, right, Lark? To tell him to stop. To tell him not to run."

Her head shook.

"You don't want to tell him to stop?" Oliver's voice deepened. "Thought that was the whole point in you coming along? Or were you just saying that to get away from Executive Assistant Director Ballard? Because you thought if you didn't act like you were helping to find Lane, then you'd get locked away. You couldn't meet up with him if—"

"*White bouquet.*" She surged toward it. From the doorway, it had just looked like old flowers, tossed onto the floor.

But the flowers shouldn't be there. She'd carefully cleaned out every single inch of the building. She'd made a list.

1. *Donate flowers. Don't let them die.*
2. *Sell equipment. Make as much profit as you can.*
3. *Floor to ceiling clean. The building has to be in top-notch shape.*
4. *Get a realtor to—*

"What the hell is that doing here?" Oliver's voice snapped out from behind her. But he was only behind her for a moment. In the next instant, he'd hurried around her. Easy to do since she was frozen in place.

"I donated all my flowers. *No flowers should be here.*" But a fresh bouquet *was* there. Right where her desk had been. White flowers. Tied with...what was that wrapped around the bouquet?

Oliver crouched next to the flowers.

Rope. A white rope had been bound around the base of the bouquet. Just like the rope used on those three poor women who'd been murdered.

Her hand rose to her mouth.

Lilies. Hydrangeas. Peonies.

Oliver's head snapped up. "We need to get you out of here, now."

"But—" She didn't get to finish because a guttural scream broke through her words. A scream that came from behind her. From the door that they'd left open. She turned around at the scream, but the movement felt oddly slow. A turn that seemed to take forever. It shouldn't have taken so long. She knew it. But every single inch took such a long time to—

Nate.

Nate Quest stood in the doorway with his shoulders heaving and his face twisted with rage. He had a flashlight gripped in one hand and a rope in the other. Another guttural cry erupted from him even as he lunged for her.

"Lark! Get out of the way!" Oliver roared.

She didn't have a chance to get out of the way. Nate swung the flashlight, and it clipped her on the side of the head. The powerful blow had her falling to the floor, and he was on her. She raised her hands because she thought he'd hit her again. But he came at her with the rope. He locked it around her throat and he—

Boom.

The gunshot slammed into Nate. The blast hit his shoulder, and he flew backward.

She grabbed the rope and jerked it from her neck even as she scuttled backward. Oliver locked his hands on her shoulders and pulled her up against him.

"Lark?"

Her breath heaved. Her temple pounded painfully. Nausea twisted and churned with the terror in her.

"You're always protecting her!" A yell from Nate.

Her head swung toward him. The pounding in her head grew worse. The nausea rose.

Nate gripped his shoulder. Blood pulsed from the bullet wound and soaked his fingers. "She doesn't get to live while my Casey is in the ground!"

"Nate, you need to calm down." Oliver let go of Lark to fully face him. Oliver raised his weapon and pointed it at Nate. "We're all going to keep living, you understand me? Now I want you to freeze."

Nate didn't freeze. He took a gliding step toward them. "I'm not living without her. Tried it. But I see her everywhere and nowhere."

The other agents must have heard the boom of the gunshot. They would be coming. They had to come.

"What will it be like for you, Special Agent Foxx, when you see *her* everywhere...and nowhere?"

Lark gripped the rope in her hand.

"You broke into Lark's apartment," Oliver accused. "You spray-painted the threat on her wall."

She craned to see around him.

Fury twisted Nate's face. "So easy to get to her." Another gliding step. "But you came home with her. Had to rush out."

"You were in her car. Waiting to attack her. We found the syringe in your room at the hotel."

Nate's brow furrowed. "What car?"

"Hands in the air!" Midas blasted as he erupted into the room.

So someone had heard the gunshot. Midas. She had thought he might be trailing them but, unlike Everett, she hadn't been able to spot Midas no matter how hard she tried.

Until now. Now it was pretty hard to miss him.

Lark's breath rushed out. Nate was surrounded. Midas behind him. Oliver in front of him. Nate had to surrender.

He—

"Gun!" Midas shouted.

And Lark saw that Nate had just shoved his hand into his coat and he was pulling out a gun. Aiming it at—

"Everywhere," Nate breathed.

Oliver rushed toward him. He lunged fast and he—

"Nowhere," Nate finished. He pulled the trigger just as Oliver slammed into him. The bullet exploded from the gun, but it didn't go into Nate's head.

He'd been planning to shoot himself. He'd brought the barrel of the gun right under his chin.

The bullet blasted into the ceiling and a broken chunk of plaster fell to the floor.

Oliver wrenched the gun from Nate's hand and tossed it aside. "That's not how you're going out."

Lark crept forward. Blood covered the left side of Nate's face.

"Get an ambulance!" Oliver snarled at Midas. "Bullet cut straight across his cheek on its way up, but he is one lucky bastard."

Nate turned his head toward her.

She could hear Midas calling the ambulance.

Everett and Shannon had just rushed into the work room, too. Shannon was—maybe reading Nate his rights?

Oliver put his hand over the wound on Nate's shoulder.

And Nate just kept staring at her. An unblinking gaze. "You will..." He barely breathed the words. It was more her just seeing the movement of his lips and knowing what he meant... "Die, too."

"Only over *my* fucking dead body," Oliver swore right back. "And you will never, ever get near her again."

CHAPTER FIFTEEN

"I don't need to be here." Lark glowered at Oliver. "I can't believe you made me ride in an ambulance."

She couldn't believe it? He put his hands on the exam table—the table she was currently sitting on—and leaned in close. His fingers brushed against the thin hospital gown she wore. "The prick slammed his flashlight into the side of your head. You could have a concussion." Those moments kept replaying in his head.

Right there. For the second time, I was right there. The bastard had slammed the heavy flashlight into Lark's temple, and she'd gone down. Just crumpled. Oliver had roared her name even as Nate wrapped a freaking rope around her neck.

His fingers rose to touch her neck. "Already bruising."

She flinched. "It...doesn't hurt."

"The hell it doesn't." Nate had tightened that rope around her neck as hard as he could.

Her hand lifted and curled around his wrist. "You saved him."

Maybe I should have let him shoot himself. One less threat to Lark in the world. "He's not saved. He'll go to jail once he gets patched up." *But I have a few questions for him first.* And wasn't that why he'd really saved the prick?

Instinct. Unease.

There is a piece that doesn't fit.

"You *saved* him," Lark insisted. "He was going to kill himself. Right there, right in front of us all."

Nate's voice slithered through his mind. *What will it be like for you, Special Agent Foxx, when you see her everywhere...and nowhere?*

The sonofabitch. He'd put a rope around her throat. Around her throat. *No one is taking Lark from me.* "I was right there," he muttered. "You were attacked again, with me—"

Her hold tightened on him. "Yes, you were there. Thank God, you were there. You saved me. If I'd been on my own, I-I..." She swallowed. "I didn't have a gun."

Because Colby had made that one of his conditions before they'd left the Bureau. No weapons for Lark. *Colby really thinks she will turn on anyone when it comes to her brother.* But Lark wasn't some monster.

She was...

Everything.

His thumb lightly brushed over her bruise. "The doctor wants you to stay twenty-four hours for observation."

"No." An immediate denial. "I don't want to stay here. It's too open. Too many people. Too many strangers."

"You are *hurt.*"

"I was just...dazed," she corrected. "For a moment. To tell you the truth, I can barely remember even falling to the floor. I-I do remember the rope around me. Then you shooting Nate in the shoulder to get him off me." Her lips pressed together.

I remember everything. Every second had been burned into his mind in vivid color. "What you've just described, sweetheart? Classic concussion symptoms. Being dazed, not being able to recall what happened right after the attack..."

"I can heal from a concussion just as well at your place as I can here."

His place. He wanted her at his place. He wanted to scoop her into his arms and rush away with her. Absolutely at the top of his to-do list.

A quick knock sounded on the exam room door. He turned because he expected to see the doctor coming in to talk more with them. But instead, Colby poked his head inside. First his head, then his whole body.

"Lark." Colby's gaze slid over her. Lingered on her throat. The throat that Oliver still touched.

Slowly, Oliver let his hand fall away from her.

Colby's attention shifted to him. "Heard that Nate Quest is still breathing because of you."

"I took down the perp."

"You stopped the perp from blowing his brains out."

Lark sucked in a sharp breath.

I have questions for Nate. Death wasn't taking him. Not...yet.

"Cops just searched his place in Colorado. They found a manifesto of sorts on his computer. Manifesto, suicide note. Whatever you want to call it." Colby advanced, but his steps seemed a little uncertain. "I know he told you that he'd received a phone call telling him to come down here. Saying that he knew Lark was going to use you to prove her brother's innocence. Jase briefed me on all that. Said the guy kept going on and on about the call before Nate surprised him with that sucker punch at the hotel."

Lark shivered.

"That gown is too damn thin," Oliver groused. Why the hell did people always have to wear those BS paper gowns in hospitals? Hospitals were freaking *cold*. Oliver shouldered out of his coat and put it around Lark's shoulders.

"Nate wanted people to know what he was doing. He even left a note telling his parents that he was going to be with Casey again." Colby's lips pulled down. "Seems to me that the man was planning to kill himself before he came to town. Just wanted to...take someone else with him first."

"Me," Lark said. "He came all the way here to kill me."

Colby nodded. "Only he's still breathing. And so are you."

"Because of Oliver," Lark added instantly. "Without him, I-I would be dead."

Without me, you never would have been in that shop.

"He's a real hero," Colby murmured.

Oliver's jaw locked. *Not in the mood for your sarcastic BS right now. And if you tell Lark I was trying to use her—*

"Guess Nate was hiding out in the shop after he ran from the hotel. Cops at his home said he had all kinds of recon work on you there. The address of your apartment. The location of your shop. Your car tag number. All signs indicated he'd been doing some serious stalking for a while."

"I want to talk to him." There were questions that Oliver had to ask. *Isn't that why I let the sonofabitch live?* The dead didn't talk.

"Not happening." Colby shook his head. "The man's in surgery now getting that bullet cut out of his shoulder. And as he was being driven in on the ambulance, he kept screaming for a lawyer. Hate when they do that." He thrust back his shoulders. "So don't expect him to be cooperating with you anytime soon. Doesn't matter. We've got enough evidence to lock him away for a long, long time." His gaze drifted once more to the darkening bruise on Lark's neck. "Glad you're safe."

"I didn't find my brother."

His eyelashes flickered. "We will find him. Count on it."

Oliver felt like the unspoken words of *one way or another* lingered in the air.

But Colby projected concern as he told Lark, "It's been one monster of a night. You need to rest."

"I'm trying to convince her to rest *here*," Oliver groused. "The doc wanted her kept for observation." Concussions were tricky. He'd seen the hell they created firsthand with other agents who'd been injured. The vic would seem fine at first, and then later, the person would start vomiting or having seizures.

As if on cue, the doctor darted inside the room. When she saw Lark, the woman smiled. "Are you feeling better?"

"Feeling like I just survived a murder attempt," Lark returned. "Don't know if 'better' is the right word, but I am incredibly happy to be alive right now." She reached out and absolutely shocked Oliver by taking his hand in hers. Her fingers squeezed his. "Thank you."

He looked at her hand. So fragile compared to his. And she was *thanking him?* He hadn't moved fast enough. Hadn't seen the threat. Hadn't been able to take down the perp until the bastard already had a rope around her throat.

"The flowers." Oliver swallowed. Cleared his throat. He was pretty much just growling and snarling, and he needed to do better. "We need to find out where he got the flowers."

"That will be another nail in his coffin," Colby agreed. "We'll have agents track them down. Sure appears to me like the guy was doing his best to repeat the pattern of the murders. The flowers, the rope..."

And the victim who looks just like the others.

Oliver brought Lark's hand to his mouth. Pressed a kiss to her knuckles.

"I'm not running." A whisper from her. "You understand that, don't you? I'm not looking for Lane in order to run away with him. That was never my plan." Lark looked right at him. *Right into my soul.* "I'm not leaving you," she said.

"Well, I'm afraid he has to leave *you*," the doctor informed her.

Oliver sent her a glower. Why the hell did he need to leave Lark?

"Just for a moment," the doctor reassured. "You can stand right outside of the door. *Both* of you gentleman." She waved to Colby. Actually, more like a shooing motion than a wave. "I need a few moments to examine my patient, and I'd like to do that without you two adding any additional stress to the situation."

Lark tensed.

"Right outside of the door," the doctor—Monique Coleman—repeated. "You will be perfectly safe in here, Lark, and I'm quite certain these gentlemen will make sure no one else gets inside."

Lark nodded. "It's all right, Oliver. Go."

Oliver squeezed her hand. "Call my name if you need me." Simple as that. Would be from here on out. If she needed him, all Lark had to do was call. He pressed another kiss to her knuckles and then let her go.

Oliver made sure that Colby left the room first, then Oliver followed him. He pulled the door *almost* shut, then took up a position right in front of it. Damn straight no one was getting in there. "As soon as possible, I want a crack at Nate Quest."

A long-suffering sigh escaped Colby. "I told you already, that is not happening. He's in surgery. Apparently, that bullet nipped the

subclavian artery and vein. Don't look at me like
that. I'm just repeating what a doc told me a few
minutes ago. I didn't suddenly gain massive
amounts of medical knowledge."

The subclavian artery and vein? "That's why
the bastard bled so much." Blood had soaked
Nate.

"His surgeon said he could have permanent
disability in the arm. Something about the
brachial plexus? Yeah, he lost me after that. And
I'm sure you'll cry plenty over the bastard having
trouble moving the arm he used to strangle Lark."

Oliver would shed zero tears. "You're...too
happy." Something was off with the guy.

"Is this my happy face?" Colby pointed to
himself. To his face.

It wasn't his pissed-off face, so, yes. "You have
a plan."

Now Colby smiled. A chilling sight. "I do have
a plan. Since you and Lark weren't able to turn up
her brother—"

"Sorry, we were busy stopping the man who
was trying to *kill* her. Can only do so much at one
time."

"Uh, huh. Well, you tried things your way.
Now it's my turn. Oh, don't get me wrong. I still
think Lark is the key to drawing Lane out. But we
need a different technique."

A nurse bustled down the hallway. Oliver
followed her progress and saw the two orderlies
who waited near the nurse's station. Two
orderlies who were familiar. *Because they are
Feds.* "Shit." Understanding dawned. "You're
setting up a trap."

"The news may have gotten the idea that Lark Lawson was severely injured tonight. They're running with that story. Already put it on social media." Colby lifted his wrist and glanced at his watch. "So late. Too late to correct that false impression."

The false impression you gave them.

"Never fear. I'll hold a news conference tomorrow around noon to update everyone and dispel rumors that are circulating."

Sure. Noon. By that time... "You think Lane will come to the hospital."

"If *you* were told Lark was in a hospital and fighting for survival, wouldn't you rush to her side?"

Fuck. Maybe Colby was better at profiling than he'd suspected. "I'm not Lane."

"No. He's her twin. And she's the only person in this world who gives two shits about him. Considering that information, I think we can assume his response will be the same as yours. And by the same, I mean he will rush to her side."

"No way Lark is sitting in a hospital bed while this goes down."

"Of course, not! You're taking her out of here. Via a staff exit. I'll have a federal agent in the room assigned to Lark. An agent who—"

"Happens to have dark hair, is approximately Lark's height and build, but will be armed and ready to meet her brother."

Colby shrugged. "Nice plan, isn't it? Have I finally succeeded in impressing you?"

"Do you know how much security is already in place here? It's not like it will be a cakewalk for

Lane to get inside and find the right room for his sister."

"So it's a challenge." He shrugged. "I'm sure it was a challenge for him to break out, too, don't you think? But he succeeded. Now, can you hurry things along and get Lark out of here? I'd rather she not know about the plans in place. The woman has been through enough tonight, don't you think?"

He didn't move. He wasn't hurrying shit along. "Lark wanted to come on the hunt because she was afraid her brother would be killed. She wants him brought in alive."

"And we will make every effort to do just that. Come on, Foxx, this is a hospital. You think I'm gonna have some crazy shootout in a hospital?" He shuddered. "Think of the bad press."

I think you're going too far. You're about to make your career crash and burn. "This is not the right place."

"Rubber bullets. Tasers. I'll have this facility filled with my agents so no civilians are ever in jeopardy, *and* Lane Lawson will be brought in alive. That will play far better on the news than a hospital shootout."

Was it all about how things played on the news?

"I need to go see if the agent taking Lark's place is ready." Colby clamped a hand around Oliver's shoulder.

Oliver frowned at the hand.

"Good job bringing Nate Quest in alive. Actually thought you'd kill the bastard on sight.

Instead, you stopped him from taking his own life."

Oliver looked at Colby.

"No easy way out for him, huh? He'll always have permanent reminders of you now. Maybe even the loss of motion in that arm. No matter what else happens, he'll always remember you did that to him. He can think about those memories plenty when he's behind bars. Good punishment, indeed." Colby gave him a pat.

The prick just gave me a pat on the shoulder?

Colby turned away. Took a few steps—

"Grief has twisted that man. I'm not sure Nate knows right from wrong. All he knows is pain. It consumes him, and he wants it to consume others."

Everywhere and nowhere.

"It wasn't about punishment," Oliver said flatly. Colby hadn't looked back, but Oliver knew the guy was listening. "It was about stopping him from killing Lark. I put the bullet in him because he was not killing her in front of me. And I saved him because I have more questions."

"Uh, huh." Colby's doubt was obvious. "You keep telling yourself that, if it makes you feel better." He fired a glance over his shoulder. "Whatever gets you to sleep at night." Then he sauntered down the hallway.

Oliver kept his guard position at the door. He pulled out his phone and called Memphis. Maybe Memphis had a tip on Lane, and this stupid stakeout plan could be dead in the water. The phone rang once. Twice.

Oliver frowned. No matter the hour, Memphis usually answered quickly.

Three rings.

Four.

And—

"Yo." Memphis's voice.

Oliver exhaled. "Have you heard the shit that went down tonight?"

"Can't really talk now, man. Kinda tied up."

What? *"Lark was almost killed."*

A gasp.

"Yeah, yeah, that's what I'm saying." His left hand shoved through his hair. "Nate Quest was waiting at her old florist shop. She went there, thinking she'd find that bastard brother of hers—"

"Such a bastard," Memphis agreed at once.

"But there was a freaking white bouquet waiting for her. We see the bouquet and the next thing I know, Nate is flying at her. He slammed his flashlight into her head—"

An angry growl vibrated over the phone.

"Then he put a rope around her neck and pulled it as tight as he could." Fury surged in Oliver. "Had to fire a bullet into him. *He wasn't killing her.*"

"Ah...good for you. Ahem. So, is Nate dead?"

"He's in the hospital. Getting the bullet dug out. Apparently, it nicked some veins. Maybe an artery. Don't know for sure." That was all stuff Colby had said. Oliver preferred firsthand info. And speaking of firsthand info... "Walk me back through what you discovered in Nate's hotel room."

"Told you...I'm kinda tied up right now—"

"Look, I get that it's late. And tell your wife I'm sorry for calling in the middle of the night." Hell, they'd probably been sleeping. He knew Eliza had come to town with Memphis. Some national charity planning event for her. Some killer hunting for Memphis. "But I need to know this. What all did you see?"

"Rope. Two knives. A notepad with Lark's address." Clipped. "Good enough for you?"

"How hard did you search? Did you see a syringe?"

"I always search hard. Don't be insulting."

"Did you see a syringe?" he pushed.

"No. I didn't see a damn syringe. Why are you asking?"

His shoulders bumped into the hospital room door. "Because Nate confessed to everything else, but he seemed to have no idea what I was talking about when I accused him of being in her car."

"Yeah, you get that people lie, right? Lie all the time. Hell, I could be lying to you right now. Acting like I'm fine but really I—" Memphis broke off.

Oliver frowned. "Why would he lie? The man was about to kill himself. He was confessing all, but he didn't confess to that. He appeared confused as hell when I brought up the car attack."

"Fascinating. Look, I've got to go. I didn't see a syringe."

Fine. "Have you *seen* Lane? Any leads?"

Silence. Then, "Zero leads."

"Got to give the man credit, he's sure been able to disappear." Oliver heard footsteps behind him. "The doctor is coming. I need to find out what she's got to say about Lark. Colby has some dumbass plan to stakeout the hospital in order to get Lane. Thinks he'll come running to see Lark if he believes she's at death's door."

"Dumbass," Memphis breathed.

"I'm taking her home with me. She'll be far away from any drama that goes down here." He turned because the doctor had just opened the door fully. "Check in with you in the morning—"

Memphis had already hung up.

Frowning, Oliver fired off a text on his phone. His instincts just wouldn't stop screaming at him...

***

The knife pressed hard beneath his chin, but Memphis just smiled. "Happy? Did I give the performance of a lifetime or what? Maybe I should get a shiny, gold trophy?" Casual words even as rage blasted through him.

I can't believe this sonofabitch got the drop on me. Infuriating. And humiliating.

Lane Lawson removed the phone and the knife. He put them both on a nearby table before turning back toward Memphis. "That crack about being tied up was supposed to be funny?"

Memphis strained against the ropes that bound him. A freaking lot of ropes. "My friends always say I'm hilarious."

"My sister was almost killed tonight."

"And she was saved by FBI Special Agent Oliver Foxx. Sounds to me like you owe the man a thank you basket."

Lane's eyes narrowed.

Memphis's stare swept over him. "Don't want to tell you your business but...that wound ripped open again. Your shirt is soaked with blood."

"It ripped open because *you* drove your elbow into it, asshole."

Memphis smiled. He had. "Was that me?" Fighting dirty was his specialty. And when he got out of these ropes...*I am going to mess you up*.

Memphis's phone rang again. Lane looked over at the screen and read the name that had just appeared over the image, "Eliza..."

Memphis stiffened.

"We'll let her go to voicemail. Again." Lane left the phone on the table but picked up the knife once more.

Yeah, let it go to voicemail. My wife is about to track my phone and have SWAT swarming. No way would Eliza buy he'd ever ignore three calls from her. The woman was his freaking life. She was—

Lane stalked closer with the knife gripped in his hand.

Memphis lifted his chin. "Gonna slice open my throat now? Even after I played it so cool for you on the phone call? That's the thanks I'm gonna get?"

The light glinted off the knife. They were in a vacant club, one about five blocks from Side Strip. After digging through some serious corporate red tape, Memphis had found four pieces of property linked to Lane's old company. Places being maintained thanks to a ton of corporate BS. Maintained, but not used. Memphis had been searching each one when he hit paydirt.

Or rather, when paydirt had hit him. *The bastard fights as dirty as I do.*

"Relax, Memphis, you're hardly my type."

Memphis's phone rang again. Eliza's ringtone.

"Now, her, on the other hand...she's got the right hair, the right build, the right—"

Memphis leaned forward and deliberately pressed into the tip of the knife. "I will annihilate you," Memphis promised. "You think of hurting her, you so much as—"

Sighing, Lane pulled the knife away. "I didn't break out to kill anyone. And I was just messing with you. You *did* rip open my wound and now I'm bleeding everywhere."

Memphis snarled at him, "Stay away from—"

"I have places to be. Places that aren't anywhere near your wife. Besides, I figure she'll be tracking your phone soon. Turning up here so time is of the essence." He moved around Memphis. With the knife.

Memphis locked his jaw. Was the bastard about to stab him in the back?

"Here." Lane shoved the knife into Memphis's bound hands. "There's a shit ton of rope there—had to bind you really well—so it will take a few minutes for you to slice your way through. And the angle is shit, so, be careful. You'd hate to cut yourself."

The guy was giving him the knife?

Lane popped back in front of Memphis. "My sister is in danger."

Memphis was already sawing the rope.

"I couldn't stay in there while she was being hunted."

"Nate Quest is in the hospital! You heard—"

"I've been targeted in lockup. Over and over again. The guards always look the other way. The prisoners keep coming even when they shouldn't."

"That *happens* when you kill women." He kept sawing with what he now realized was the dullest knife in the world. What? The guy had gotten him to talk BS on the phone with Oliver by using something barely stronger than a *butter knife*?

"I don't kill women. Don't hurt them at all."

The knife was doing jack and shit.

"Yeah, sorry, I found that knife in the kitchen. It might take a bit to cut anything. Found the ropes there, too. Really don't want to know what they were used for previously." He grimaced. "I suspect this place was a brothel *and* a bar before it came into my possession. So, have fun with all that." His jaw firmed. "But back to the breakout. I had to leave. I know someone was ordering the attacks on me. Attacks that kept getting worse and worse. I heard the guards talking after Oliver Foxx left. One of them said no one would be questioning me soon. You couldn't question the dead."

Memphis stopped sawing with the dull knife. For a brief second. Then he resumed, double-time.

"Someone with power and pull has been getting the guards to look away. Getting the inmates to attack. I think that someone is the same person who set me up all along. The person who wants my sister. I can't let that happen." He swung for the door and wrenched it open. "Oh, almost forgot..." Lane turned back and grabbed the phone. "I'll leave this outside the building for you. No hard feelings, right?"

Then he was gone. The door closed behind him with a slam.

The door to what had been the freaking *freezer room* in the place's old kitchen. No freezer any longer but...*but a good prison for me.*

He sawed and sawed and the freaking knife barely seemed to do anything. He twisted his wrists, strained against the ropes, and put all of his power into the strokes of the knife. Over and over and over.

After what felt like an eternity, the tension snapped. The ropes around his wrist gave way. Memphis went to work on the ropes around his ankles. Ropes that bound him to the stupid chair. Took forever, but he got free. He got free and lunged for the door.

He wrenched the handle. The door wouldn't open.

Sonofabitch. "Hard feelings!" Memphis bellowed. "Extremely hard! I am going to kick your ass when I get out of here!" He pounded his fists into the door.

CHAPTER SIXTEEN

"Theo, I want the crime scene photos."

Lark shifted on the bed as Oliver walked into the room. They'd made it home from the hospital. Her doctor had just insisted that someone stay with Lark for the next twenty-four hours.

Oliver had been only too happy to volunteer.

He was supposed to wake her up every few hours. Ask her some questions to make certain she didn't have memory problems. And Oliver had assured Lark that he was going to keep watch in order to make sure she didn't have any seizures or vomiting or—

"From Nate Quest's hotel room. Yes, I know what time it is. I want them sent over to me immediately. Get them emailed. Get them texted. Just get them." A brief pause. "Yeah, yeah, I tried reaching Jase already. I think he was first on scene, but he's not picking up. Last I heard, he'd been the one assigned guard duty with Blain Montgomery because Colby feared Lane might be going after the representative." Oliver looked up and met her gaze. "I am aware another plan is in motion. So maybe Jase has been reassigned, and I wasn't briefed on it. I should have been. Why?

Because consider me off the *break*. Shortest fucking break on record. Now, just get me those pictures, will you? We both know you had a fling with the guy who takes the photos. Send them to me. STAT." He lowered the phone. His stare swept over her.

Lingered on her neck.

"How are you feeling?" Oliver asked.

She rose from her perch on the side of the bed. "I'm feeling like we need to talk."

His lips twisted. "You should be feeling like you want to crash."

No, she wasn't tired. At all. Her throat felt tender, her temple still ached, but adrenaline pumped through her. Lark knew sleep would not be coming anytime soon.

What was the saying about sleeping? Some rock star had been credited with it ages ago. Maybe Warren Zevon? Something along the lines of... "'I'll sleep when I'm dead,'" she murmured.

He immediately surged toward her. "You're not dying."

"No, thanks to you, I'm not."

He stopped. His hands fisted.

He hadn't come all the way to her, so Lark closed the last few steps between them. "You didn't tell Theo that you were the one who got a guard placed on Blain Montgomery."

He shrugged. "Protecting and serving," he said. "My gig, right?"

"You're not protecting him."

"No?" His eyes narrowed. His hand rose to her throat. Hovered over the bruise. Then touched the line lightly as rage darkened his face.

"You're protecting *me*," she returned with certainty. "You got Colby to put an agent on Blain not because you were worried Lane would go after the guy—"

"Oh, make no mistake, your brother hates Blain and the feeling is mutual."

Yes, she more than suspected it was. But she also suspected... "You tricked Colby into placing a guard on Blain because you're worried he will come after me. You wanted eyes on Blain. Someone following his every move."

Oliver smiled. "Guilty." Then he leaned forward. His mouth pressed a soft kiss to her throat. "I *hate* you were hurt on my watch."

Her eyes closed as she tilted back her head. One soft kiss on her skin. Then another. Featherlight. "I hate that I lied to you." Her hands rose to curl around his arms.

His muscles went tight beneath her touch. His head lifted.

Her eyes opened.

"I'm sorry for lying." This needed to be said. "I was desperate. I just needed the Ice Breakers to help me. I thought...if I can convince them to look at the case, they'll find something. They'll see something..."

"That I missed?" Oliver finished.

"That everyone missed." That she'd missed. Because she'd tried and tried to find evidence to use that would exonerate her brother, and she'd kept turning up nothing. "I knew Memphis would want to see the footage." Footage that didn't exist. "I thought I could delay him a bit, thought that if he just started digging, he and the Ice Breakers would turn up new evidence and by the time they learned the package didn't come to my shop—"

"Sweetheart, Memphis suspected that story was a lie, too. Otherwise, he would have gotten the video footage instantly. He took the case because of you. Because you were fighting for your brother the same way Memphis fought for his own brother."

Her heart ached. "Lane lied to protect me when we were kids. So I lied to protect him now." She didn't let Oliver go.

"Any other lies you've told me? Things you want to clear up now?"

Lark's throat went dry.

His phone dinged.

The crime scene photos that he'd requested? Already? Theo sure moved fast.

Oliver pulled away from her. He glanced down at his phone. The phone had been gripped in his right hand while they talked. His left had been the one to lightly stroke the bruise on her throat. As he looked at his phone, he nodded, once. "I need to respond to this text."

Right. Yes. Respond. Because of the case. The nightmare. The hell that wouldn't end.

My brother.

"Why don't you get changed, Lark? Get comfortable? You might not be tired, but you still need to rest."

They were in the guest room. The room he'd given to her, not his bedroom.

I want to be in his bed. I want him.

"I can help, if you like," he added.

But she shook her head. "Respond to your text. I can manage to put on pajamas by myself." Were there any pajamas in the suitcase in the closet? If not, she'd just use one of Oliver's shirts.

His stare lingered on her.

Such a hot, deep stare. So intense. Swirling with emotions that she couldn't name.

But Oliver turned away from her and walked for the bedroom door.

"There's one thing!" Lark called before she could stop herself. Or maybe...maybe she didn't want to stop herself. Why? Why hold back?

Life can be over too fast. Her temple throbbed. She controlled a wince.

Oliver looked over his shoulder.

Tell him. "I've been saying I hate you."

The faint lines near his mouth deepened. "Yeah, I heard that. More than once."

"I think I've been lying."

His eyes widened.

"To myself. To you. I think I hurt so much that I wanted it to be hate, but it wasn't. Not really. Or maybe hate and love can just get all tangled together, and it's hard to tell them apart when the feelings are so strong." She didn't know. And she was probably doing a crap job of explaining but... "I fell in love with you before." *Before.* Before the world had crashed and burned and she'd broken down in the middle of the street as she watched her brother disappear in a patrol car.

"Lark..."

"You said you were pretending back then. Showing me a guy who would be perfect for me." A shake of her head. "I think that was a lie. Your lie. Because you *are* perfect for me. You fight for me. You help me. You're there for me when everything else is chaos." There in the midst of her hell. "You told me that you were trying not to be a monster. That you weren't really the good FBI guy. That was another lie." More certainty entered her voice. "You saved Nate when I think you wanted to kill him. When your feelings for me made you want to destroy him, yet you let him live."

"I have *questions* for him," Oliver growled.

"Maybe you do. But there's a whole lot more to it than just that. You don't want to be a killer. And you try hard not to be. You fight to be good. That means so much, don't you see that? It means so much that you *choose* to keep doing the right thing."

"I'm not. I'm not right. I'm not good. I took you out earlier to catch your brother. I paraded you around the city to draw him out. I was afraid you'd run with him, and I couldn't let that happen, so I didn't let you out of my sight. I needed you with me—not to hunt him. I needed you with me so *I could stop you from running with him*. I led you right into danger because I thought if I let you out of my sight, I'd lose you. I should have left you someplace safe. Should have surrounded you with guards and not taken you straight into danger."

Lark shook her head. "You aren't losing me. I love you."

Agony flashed on his face. He bounded back toward her. Reached out, but his hands stopped in mid-air and clenched into fists. He kept hesitating to touch her. Why? Didn't he know how much she needed his touch?

"Lark." Pain gleamed in his eyes. "You know why we left the hospital through the back exit."

A weak smile curved her lips. "You and Colby weren't exactly whispering. I could hear you through the door." A door that had been left partially open. At first, she'd thought he hadn't shut the door completely so that he could hear what the doctor said. So he could hear Lark easily if she needed him.

Then I realized Oliver wanted me to hear him.

He swallowed. "I know you could hear. That's why I wasn't whispering. I was talking as loudly as I could without alerting Colby."

Oliver still didn't reach out to hold her.

"When Lane is caught, he will be tossed right back in a cell. There is no evidence that exonerates him. And with the escape now being added to the list of his charges..." A ragged sigh. "He's not going to be free."

Her heart ached. "I understand what can happen."

"You still believe he's innocent."

"Well, clearly not innocent when it comes to the escape. But I don't think he killed those women." She couldn't let herself believe it.

"Why?"

"I lied."

He blinked.

"I'm trying to come clean as much as I can. No more lying to you. No more lying to myself." After taking a bracing breath, she said, "The day my father died? When I shot him?"

Oliver waited.

"My dad *was* attacking me. He'd stabbed my mom. He'd turned on me. All of that is true. I was begging him to stop. Lane begged him. But my father was too far gone. All I saw in his eyes and on his face was rage. I got the gun and I came back but..."

"Sweetheart..."

"Lane took it from me. He shoved me behind him. He aimed the gun to fire. He was going to be the one to pull the trigger." Tears pricked at her eyes. "But my mom cried out. Lane looked at her. And my dad slammed into him. They both hit the floor. My dad got up. Lane didn't. I grabbed for the gun and when my dad—" Her lips pressed together. *Everything else had been just as I described before. Except Lane was the one who tried to shoot first.* "Lane was ready to shoot for me. He was ready to kill our father. He has always been ready to protect me. To do whatever it takes to keep me safe."

"Like break out of jail?"

A nod.

"What's the story with you and Blain Montgomery? What really happened?"

Another ghost from the past. Pain that she'd fought to bury.

"He said he was sleepwalking into your room."

Her hands pressed to her jeans. She'd put them on after ditching that hospital gown and escaping with Oliver. "When you sleepwalk, do you also grope people? Because I woke up to his hand trying to go between my legs."

Fury flew across his face. "Sonofabitch."

Yes, that was how she thought of Blain Montgomery, too. As a sonofabitch. And every time she saw his smug face on TV, the pain and humiliation rolled through her again. "One hand tried to push between my legs. One had covered my mouth. I fought him, and the hand over my mouth moved a little. Then I bit his fingers as hard as I could." She still remembered the bitter taste of his blood. "I screamed. Lane came running. He got in the room first, before Blain's parents. I told him what had happened."

"And he broke Blain's hand."

Yes. *You won't ever touch my sister again.* Low words Lane had said as the bones snapped. "We were gone the next day." She shuddered. She hadn't even wanted to remain there that long. "Lane stayed in my room the rest of the night. Guarding the door. My brother—because of what happened to my mom, because of the things that I went through—if anything, he's extra protective when it comes to women. He would never hurt a woman the way the Bridal Killer did. He just wouldn't."

"But Blain Montgomery doesn't have any problem hurting women."

"Blain doesn't live in Vegas. He's not—"

"He comes here plenty for business. Told me himself he's in town all the time. And you don't just *stop* predatory behavior. If he was doing it with you, as a kid, I don't buy that he just flipped a switch and stopped. We need to dig into his closet and see what skeletons pop out."

Her breath caught. "You really think it could be him?"

"Don't get your hopes up on evidence just tumbling into our laps." His hands had fallen back to his sides. "I keep telling you, your brother may spend the rest of his life in jail. And you don't want to look at my face each day and know I'm the man who put him there." His shoulders squared. "I hate what you've been through. With your father. With Nate. With that bastard Blain. With *me*."

Her brow furrowed.

"If I could, I'd take away all your pain. That's what I wanted to do. Wanted to win you back. Get a second chance. Prove that we could be different under different circumstances." Oliver retreated. "But I'll always be the man who put your brother in a cell. Then..." Grim. "And now."

"W-we haven't even found Lane yet." And she'd said that she *loved* Oliver.

Only, once again, Oliver hadn't said those words back to her.

"I know where your brother is."

Her heartbeat seemed to stutter. "What?"

"You didn't want him killed, so I made sure people I trusted were going after him. I wasn't going to let Colby unleash hell in a hospital and risk lives."

Her head shook. "I don't understand."

"I'm good at reading people. And I know Memphis."

"Memphis? What does he have to do with this?" Her eyes widened. "Wait, you—you sent

Memphis after Lane. Did Memphis find him already? Is that what you're saying? Memphis has my brother?"

"Not exactly. According to the text I just got, I now have confirmation...It's more like your brother has *him*."

***

Memphis slammed his shoulder into the door again. Fuck, fuck, fuck, but the thing wouldn't budge. Made of freaking steel.

I won't give up. I will just make the bitch open. One way or another. He backed up and started to run—

The door swung open.

Memphis stumbled back. Instantly, he grabbed the dull-ass knife he'd dropped because he needed some kind of weapon.

"Aw, really, gonna use that on your hero?"

Memphis squinted, sure that he had to be mistaken. But, no. No mistake. Midas Monroe stood in the doorway. *Filled* the doorway. And grinned at him.

"Guess who just saved the day for you?" Midas boomed.

"Sonofabitch."

Midas's grin stretched. "You're welcome."

A ragged groan came from behind Midas.

"I also captured a prison escapee," Midas continued modestly. "Dragged his sorry ass back inside. Can you believe he tried to run from me?"

"Sonofabitch," Memphis said again.

A lazy shrug from Midas. "What can I say? All I do is win, win, win."

Memphis swiped away blood that had trickled down into his eye.

Midas lifted the phone he held. *My phone.* "Oliver said it would lead us right to you. We just had to track you."

Us? We?

Eliza pushed past Midas and threw herself into Memphis's arms. Sweet, sweet Eliza.

"Who's the hero?" Midas asked again.

Dammit. "You are," Memphis said. "And I owe you."

CHAPTER SEVENTEEN

Oliver's phone rang. The text he'd gotten a few moments before? It had been from Midas, letting Oliver know that he'd closed in on Memphis's location. Midas and Memphis's wife Eliza were on the hunt.

Not that they'd gone alone. Midas had made some fast calls and created his own mini-team. People who would follow his orders completely. People he trusted.

If Midas trusted you, then you were good to go.

"I think this call will confirm—" He broke off. That wasn't Midas calling.

He hadn't assigned any ringtones to his callers. He never did. The caller wasn't Midas.

Jase.

Oliver took the call even as Lark watched him with her stark, but beautiful eyes. "Jase," he rasped. "I've been trying to get hold of you. I've got questions about the crime scene at the hotel—"

"I lost him."

Oliver held Lark's stare. "Say again?"

"Blain Montgomery gave me the slip! And the sonofabitch is twisted, boss. Twisted. Man has all these videos of women who look like Lark Lawson. The women are all tied up and being strangled. *Do you hear me?* Tied up. *Strangled.*" His words rushed out in rapid-fire succession. "Found them when I was looking for him. Guy said he was going to sleep. Heard a loud thump in this big-ass suite of his, and I came running to make sure everything was all right. It wasn't all right. He's in the wind."

You'd better be bullshitting me. "We don't have eyes on Blain?"

"No, no, he left through a connecting door that *should* have been secured and guarded. Only the guard was knocked out. *Blain is gone.* I've been searching and searching, but I can't find him. *Colby is gonna nail my ass to the wall.*"

Talk about a clusterfuck. And, yes, Colby was gonna be far from pleased. Ass nailing would commence.

"He left his laptop behind. The videos were running—*he was watching them before he vanished.* Bastard left a video playing like that was normal shit."

Oliver's heart beat faster. Faster. "How long has he been gone?"

"About...an hour."

Are you serious right now? And you're just alerting me?

"Thought—*hoped* I could find him myself. I reviewed the security feeds just like you and I did before, but he's not on them. I've got a full search running. But, hell, I don't even know if he went willingly. There are signs of a struggle. I'm thinking...Lane could have gotten to him."

Oliver shook his head. Impossible.

"Lane could have forced the guy to leave with him. We could be looking at a hostage situation. I know I need to call Executive Assistant Director Ballard, but I had to report to you first, boss. *Dammit, I wanted to find him!*"

Yes, he was sure that Jase had.

"Either Lane has Blain or Blain is coming after Lark on his own." Jase's breath heaved. "Is Lark safe? I-I heard on the news she was hurt pretty badly. Does Ballard have enough guards on her at the hospital?" He paused to draw another breath after his frantic tumble of words. "Are you close to her right now? If not, can you get to her?"

"She's already with me. We're at my house."

"You're not at the hospital? But—"

"Are there other agents at the hotel?"

"Yes, yes, two more. They're still searching for Blain with the local cops and hotel security, but he's *gone*." Desperation laced each word. "I was actually driving to your house—*almost there*—I was afraid he might try to hide in wait for you or some shit. I'm on the way, boss. I'll give you backup."

Blain was on the move. *Could be heading here.* "If he's coming for her, I'll be ready for him. You go ahead and tell—"

The line went dead.

Tell Colby. Get more agents over here.

His front doorbell started ringing. Over and over and over.

"Oliver?" Fear laced his name as Lark stiffened. "What's happening?"

No time to break gently into this. "Blain Montgomery ditched his guards."

The ringing stopped.

Dead silence.

"Midas isn't watching the house." *Because he's rescuing Memphis right now.* "The Feds are concentrated at the hospital on a stakeout that is going to fail." He should have gotten someone else to watch his house after he'd sent Midas on his mission. Fuck. *My fault.* "I want you to stay in here. Lock the door, understand? Do not open it for anyone but me."

She pulled in a breath. Squared her shoulders. Nodded. "Tell me that you have an extra gun in this house."

Oh, he did. He pulled his backup weapon from his ankle holster. He shoved the backup into Lark's hands.

His main weapon had been taken after the shooting at the florist shop. Bagged and tagged as evidence. But he had another gun in his bedroom. He'd be getting that one.

No more bell ringing. Just a silence he didn't like. He had to check the perimeter. *The alarms are set.* But none had gone off. That meant no one was inside the house, right?

But a man had been in the back of Lark's car in that lot. A killer who might have been able to gain access to all the vics' vehicles without leaving a trace behind.

A man who might be attempting to get into my house at this very moment?

"If anyone but me tries to get through the bedroom door, shoot," he ordered. His fingers tightened around hers. "And for the record, I love you more than anything in this world."

Her eyes widened. "You're telling me *now?*"

Better now than never. "I loved you months ago. Loved you from the first moment I saw you. Will always love you." He kissed her. Whirled for the door. "Do not unlock it unless you hear my voice." He barreled out and yanked the door closed behind him. Then he rushed toward his bedroom. Oliver yanked open the nightstand. Pulled out his weapon and loaded it as—

Gunshots blasted. They came from the front of the house. A fast succession of thunderous blasts that had to be heard by someone else in the neighborhood. Oliver rushed out of the bedroom. Down the hallway.

The front door flew inward.

An alarm shrieked. Loud and piercing.

He shot the door. The lock. That's why the gunfire—

"Federal agent!" Oliver bellowed. "I'm armed and you need to *freeze!*"

Blain Montgomery stumbled forward. From his crouched position near the wall, Oliver could see the man's upper body. Blain stared at him, blinked, then slowly lifted the gun in his hand. His fingers shook and trembled and—

Boom.

The bullet blasted right *through* Blain's chest. Not because Oliver had shot him. He hadn't fired. Someone else had fired from behind Blain, and the bullet tore straight through him and pierced a painting that hung on the wall. Blain's eyes widened, right before he slammed face-first into the floor.

"*Boss!*" Jase yelled. He flew forward and stood over Blain. "Boss, I arrived just as he was busting in!" His frantic gaze found Oliver. "Are you all right?"

"How did you get here so fast?"

"I-I told you, I was just a few minutes away— already on my way here..." He gulped. "Almost didn't get the shot off in time. Jesus, almost *not in time.*"

Oliver kept his weapon pointed at Jase.

Jase inched toward Blain. He kicked the man's leg.

Nothing.

"Oh, God." Jase swallowed. Swayed. "I've never killed anyone before." He put his gun on the entrance table and grabbed for Blain. He caught the guy. Rolled him over. Jase's hand went to his throat. "I-I think I feel a pulse!"

Blood soaked Blain's chest where the bullet had ripped free on its way out of him.

"What do I do?" Panic had Jase's voice breaking. "Stop the bleeding? Apply pressure? How do I stop it?" His hands pressed to Blain's chest. "Boss, help me!"

Oliver stared at the chaos in front of him. Jase's hands pressed desperately to Blain's chest. Blain didn't appear to be moving at all.

"I'm calling an ambulance," Oliver said. He'd left his phone in his bedroom. *Lark is close.* "Stay with him." He whirled and raced down the hallway. "Lark!" Oliver bellowed. "I want you to—"

The door flew open. Lark stood there, aiming her gun. Right at him.

His breath shuddered out.

So did hers. She threw herself against him. Locked her arms around him. "I heard the gunshots. Was scared to death you'd been hit."

He hugged her close, just for a moment. "Not me. Blain. I've got to call for backup and an ambulance." Though judging by what he'd seen, he doubted anyone could help Blain. *I thought for sure that bullet blasted through his heart.* He let her go. "Lark, listen, Jase is here and I don't—"

A gunshot thundered once more. A sound that he seemed to hear only *after* the pain exploded in his lower back. The hit had him staggering forward as it punched hard on his lower, left side. *Sonofabitch.*

"Oliver!" Lark screamed.

She grabbed for him, and he wound up taking her down with him. He fell on top of her. Saw her gun go skittering across the floor. The pain in his back burned and throbbed and he felt the blood soaking his shirt in the back.

When they hit the floor, Lark's head nearly slammed into the hardwood. *No.* His fingers flew under her head even as the movement felt too late. Too slow. He let go of his weapon to cradle her head.

Keep her safe. Always protect Lark. Always.

But his body crushed hers. He tried to push himself up. *Pain.* It poured through him.

A moan slipped from Lark's lips. Her eyelashes fluttered as she stared up at him.

The shooter would attack again. He had to get Lark—

"Not so fast," Jase whispered in his ear right before something soft wrapped around Oliver's neck. "It will work better if you go out this way." And he tightened the *fucking rope* he'd just looped around Oliver's neck.

Bastard. Bastard. Bastard. Oliver's fingers grabbed for the rope.

Lark grabbed the gun. She lifted her hand and fired it right over Oliver's shoulder.

A loud ringing immediately filled his left ear. But the rope fell away. Jase's weight disappeared from Oliver's back as the bastard staggered and screamed.

Oliver shoved off Lark. He took the gun from her hand.

Her eyes were flared wide open. Horrified. And focused just behind him.

He spun—

Jase came at him with a hard tackle. Jase's arms locked around Oliver's stomach, and the man rammed Oliver all the way back until he hit the wall. The gun fell from Oliver's hand even as the wound in his back seemed to erupt in a fury of agony.

Then Jase started pounding him. Punching into his stomach again and again. Blood poured from Jase's ear. Or, from the half of his ear that was still there. *Guess her bullet got you, huh?* And the man was screaming something, but that stupid ringing still filled Oliver's ears and he couldn't quite hear—

"Gonna kill you. Then gonna take her. She'll be mine. I'll put her to sleep, and she'll be—"

A guttural scream broke from Lark, and she jumped up behind Jase. She put the rope around his neck and twisted the edges as tightly as she could with her fists. Jase stumbled back. His hands flew up to swing at Lark. One fist went toward her face.

"The fuck you will," Oliver promised him.

Jase shook her off. Lark fell to the floor. Right beside the backup gun she'd lost earlier when Oliver had taken her down onto the floor with him.

She picked up the weapon. Jase lunged toward her.

Oliver grabbed for the gun that had dropped from his hand moments before. He aimed at Jase. "Freeze, you sonofabitch!"

Jase stilled. Blood dripped from his jagged ear. Lark had her weapon pointed at his head.

Oliver had his weapon centered on the middle of the man's back. "Should have aimed for my spine," Oliver told him. "Maybe would have paralyzed me. I won't make the same mistake. You so much as twitch in her direction, and my bullet shatters your spinal cord. Understand me?"

Shaking, Lark rose to her feet. "You...you were the man in my car."

Yes, he was, and more. "He's the man who set up your brother," Oliver told her. "Who killed those women. Who came here tonight to kill—"

Jase roared. He spun toward Oliver. "You won't take her—"

Boom. Oliver's gun.

Boom. Lark's gun.

Both fired at the same time. Both hit. Jase swayed. "Won't take..." His knees hit the floor. "From...me..." He fell backward and his skull cracked when it hit the hardwood.

Oliver looked across the fallen man. His gaze found Lark. His beautiful Lark. She still had her weapon up. So did he.

Then she took a step toward Jase. Lowered her gun and pointed it at his head. She fired again. Twice more.

Oliver blinked. "Uh, Lark?"

"He's a monster," she said, voice hollow. "I have to make sure he won't come back."

Oliver looked at the bloody mess that was Jase. "He's not coming back. Think you made certain of that." His legs gave way, and Oliver hit the floor. "Sweetheart?"

She rushed toward him.

"Call me an ambulance, would you?" Because the room had started to spin. The pain in his back was stronger, and he was not gonna die next to Jase Guillory. No freaking way.

He wasn't planning to die at all.

"Oliver!" She fell to her knees beside him.

His Lark. No, he wasn't dying. Not when he had so much to live for.

CHAPTER EIGHTEEN

Six weeks later...

"This is bullshit." Lane Lawson glowered at Oliver. "I'm an innocent man, and I'm still locked up."

Oliver settled into the chair across from Lane. These days, Lane agreed readily to meet with him. The guard was still in the room, sure, but Lane didn't have the ankle restraints and handcuffs any longer. He also wasn't free...yet. "You are innocent of murder," Oliver agreed, "but you *did* escape so that makes you guilty of—"

"Not freaking funny," Lane snapped back. "How long is it gonna take for me to get out? Legally get out? Because I have been waiting forever. I thought the Feds were working a deal for me. My lawyer swore to me that I would be out soon."

"The wheels of justice turn slowly." Oliver shrugged. Especially when there were a million miles of red tape to untangle. *Not guilty of murder but guilty of escape, and there is so much shit that had to be handled and smoothed away to deal with that cluster.*

Lane narrowed his eyes. "That supposed to be a joke?"

"I actually find nothing about your situation to be funny." On this, he was dead serious. "You were set up by Jase Guillory. When he found out that you were one of my main suspects, he planted the trophies in Lark's house to frame you."

"Because the bastard was obsessed with my sister. Yes, yes, I *know* this already. My lawyer told me. The prick developed an obsession for Lark long before you did. Saw her at some BS event in Vegas and started stalking her."

Oliver raised one eyebrow. "I like to think I'm in love with her, not that I have an obsession." There was a distinction.

"Yeah, sure, whatever helps you sleep at night."

Why was everyone so concerned with his sleep patterns? First Colby, now Lane. *I sleep just fine, with your sister*. Oliver locked his jaw. He was supposed to be playing nicely with Lane. He'd promised Lark that he would. *Be nice. Don't antagonize him*. "Jase developed an obsession with Lark because she matched his victim profile. She looked exactly like the type of woman he preyed upon. The fact that he was able to set you up for the crimes? That made his link to her even stronger. Every time he saw her, he got a new rush. She seemed perfect to him. Plus, she ran a florist shop. Lark loved flowers, something that fit with his—"

"My lawyer already *told* me," Lane cut in to growl. "His mother died when he was about ten years old. A woman who looked a whole lot like

Lark and the others he killed in Vegas. To hide the smell in the house, he'd steal flowers and put them on his poor, dead mom."

Info that had only just come to light because the guy's past had been buried so deeply. Oliver nodded. "Yes, and when he started killing women in Vegas, he did the same thing. Gave them bouquets just like he gave his mother."

Lane leaned forward. "What I want to know is how did that twisted-as-hell freak get in the FBI? Aren't you guys supposed to have psych tests you pass or something to ward off the nutjobs from getting inside?"

Voice flat, Oliver replied, "Anyone can pass a test, if you know the right answers to give."

Lane's gaze sharpened. "Why do I suddenly feel like you will always know the right answers to give?"

Because I do. "Jase joined the FBI because he wanted to know more about the investigations themselves. He wanted to know how to commit the perfect crime. From what I can tell, he'd seen murderers get convicted over and over at his practice, and he wanted to know how to avoid falling into that trap. The man had the urge to kill. It kept growing and growing inside of him. He joined the Bureau, started watching agents hunt predators and then one night..." Oliver stopped. *So many lives destroyed.* "One night he came across Casey Gallows. She looked like his mother. She flirted with him even as she held white flowers in her hands." A detail they'd only recently learned.

Oliver had thought that the killer gave Casey the flowers. Instead, she'd picked them up from a vendor on the street. The vendor had come forward after Jase's death and made a full statement to the FBI. Apparently, he'd made a statement previously...to Jase. And Jase had made sure that evidence never saw the light of day.

He was sabotaging the case left and right. Destroying evidence. Planting evidence. Telling witnesses what to say and what not to say. The waitress at Side Strip? After Jase's death, she'd come forward, too. And confessed that the "scary FBI agent" had told her to identify Lane Lawson in the photo lineup. There *had* been a dark-haired, Caucasian male buying drinks for the ladies at the bachelorette party that night—just a random stranger. Not Lane.

"You weren't the only one he set up." *I suspected something was off. Just didn't get the facts soon enough.* "Remember Memphis Camden?"

Lane winced. "How can I forget? Pretty sure he's gonna try kicking my ass when I get out of here."

"Oh, there is no pretty sure about it. Memphis holds a grudge. He will kick your ass." That warning only seemed fair to give.

"I didn't want to hurt him," Lane confessed as his gaze cut away. "The man was hunting *me*. I just tried to get to my sister so I could protect her. And I left Memphis with a knife to cut his way out."

According to Memphis, you left him with a sorry-ass butter knife. "You also left him locked in a freezer. So, what you have there would be a kidnapping charge—"

Lane swore. His angry stare returned to Oliver.

"That's what happens when you tie someone up," Oliver informed him. "And lock said person in a freezer, even if the freezer isn't working. Kidnapping and assault. Lucky for you, Memphis doesn't want charges pressed against you. He's calling it all a misunderstanding."

Lane's eyes—green like Lark's but so different at the same time—widened. "I'm going to owe that man my soul."

"Oh, absolutely." Memphis definitely held a grudge, and he also always remembered who owed him anything in this world. "Expect him to collect at the earliest opportunity."

"His buddy Midas already slugged the hell out of me." Lane rubbed his stubble-covered jaw. The bruising there had long since faded. "Felt like a freight train hitting me. Can't we call that even? He hit me a hell of a lot harder than I hit Memphis."

"Don't think that is gonna be equal in Memphis's world." No, he suspected Memphis had plans for Lane.

And, not that he was telling Lane this, not right now, but...Oliver suspected Memphis might even admire Lane a little bit. *The prison break had impressed him.* Memphis always appreciated it when someone could get in and out of a location without being detected. "I had Memphis search

Nate Quest's hotel room. *Before* Nate went off radar and showed up at Lark's old florist shop."

"You had your buddy do an illegal search?" Lane whistled. "That's what you're telling me right now, Mr. FBI hotshot?"

"I'm telling you that Memphis turned up the rope, two knives, and Lark's home address in Nate's room when he happened to be looking there." *Because I told him to look.* "He did *not* turn up a syringe. And yet, a syringe is the smoking gun that Jase told everyone about. Told everyone and even had the crime scene techs photograph it. In the photos I saw, the syringe was right on top of the rope so it would have been utterly impossible for Memphis to miss it." *But Memphis swears the syringe wasn't there.*

Oliver believed Memphis.

"So..." Lane drew out the pause. "Jase framed Nate, too."

"Yes. He framed Nate." An incline of Oliver's head. "Nate wasn't the one who waited for Lark in her car. It was Jase. He planted the syringe because he was just doing his routine of leaving someone else to take the blame." *I think he expected me to kill Nate. If I'd done that, maybe he wouldn't have used Blain at the end. Who the fuck knows? I can't question the dead.*

But he had been able to question the living. Nate Quest had surprised Oliver with the intel he'd revealed. Intel like...*someone had been contacting Nate for months. Taunting him about Lark and Lane and telling him that Lane would go free. Pushing him closer and closer to the edge.*

That someone? It would be the same person who'd urged him to get a room at a very specific hotel in Vegas. The same person who'd framed him. The same person who got off on playing with his vics.

A search of Jase's place had yielded a ton of burner phones. He'd been using those phones to make contact with Nate. Calls that had pushed Nate until he snapped.

Jase gave up his trophies to frame Lane, but Nate Quest was a walking, talking trophy. Pain in human form. Just talking to him or being near him had to remind Jase of Casey's murder. Just as Lark had been another walking, talking trophy. Seeing her had let him relive his twisted moments of triumph over and over again.

But that nightmare had ended now.

"I don't understand." Lane shook his head. "What was the big end game? How did the guy think he was gonna get away with killing you?"

"I believe he forced Blain Montgomery to my house. Probably at gunpoint." They'd found blood in the trunk of Jase's car. Blood that matched to Blain. "He made the man enter my home." He remembered how Blain's hand had trembled when he started to raise his gun. "Jase killed him. I suspect Blain was another guy he was framing. With Nate in police custody, Jase had to move fast. Lucky for him, Blain happened to be in the wrong city at the wrong time."

"And the videos I heard about? Were those really Blain's?"

"The ones with the women being fake strangled during sex acts? No, our techs traced those back to Jase. But there was plenty of other twisted shit on Blain's computer and phone." Blain had still had a preferred type. Underage girls.

Blain was also in the ground. He hadn't survived the bullet wound that had, indeed, shredded most of his heart. Every struggling beat had poured blood out of it. Oliver cleared his throat. "You were right about all of the attacks on you being targeted in here. Someone in a position of power was getting the guards to look away. That same person put a bounty on your head for the prisoners."

Lane's eyes glittered with fury. "*Blain.*"

"Yeah. He held a grudge. With you trapped behind bars, you were helpless. He saw the chance to get some revenge."

"Not exactly gonna mourn for that bastard."

No one was. The guards had been too happy to spill their secrets when Oliver had confronted them. They hadn't exactly been Blain Montgomery fans. *But he had power, and he used it against them.*

"And that's it? The story is over?" Lane demanded. "Seems to me that Jase was just constantly covering his ass."

He had been. "When Nate went down, he picked another fall guy. Probably intended to make it look like Blain went after me."

A confused shake of Lane's head. "But you were alive. You would have said—"

"I don't think I was *supposed* to stay alive." No more bruises lined his throat. They'd faded. As for the wound in his back? Just a new scar. "Jase waited for me to be distracted, and then he slipped down the hallway to attack me. Jase intended to strangle me with his rope. Kill me. Then make it look like he'd arrived and shot Blain as he tried to save the day." *After Blain had supposedly eliminated me.*

Again, Lane shook his head. "My sister would have been there. She would have told everyone that he was lying."

A cold wind seemed to slide over Oliver's skin. "He kept saying he was going to make Lark his." Oliver swallowed. "He made the women his when he killed them. Lark wasn't going to survive. I think he always planned to kill her." *Maybe he would have acted like Blain had killed her. Maybe pinned that on him, too. With me and Blain both dead, he would have seemed like the FBI hero.*

Lane's hands fisted as they rested on top of the table. "You killed him before he could hurt my sister."

Actually, Lark's first shot might have been the one to end Jase's life. "I'm sorry."

Lane scrunched his face. "What?"

"I'm sorry. You were locked up because of me."

"Uh, I was locked up because some freak framed me—"

"I should have seen what he was. He was on my team. I pride myself on being such a damn good profiler, but I didn't see the killer right in front of me." Midas had warned him—time and again—that people often didn't see evil when it was up close and personal.

His friend had been right.

"I didn't believe in your innocence."

Lane snorted. "You don't say?"

"But Lark did. She never gave up on you."

The door to their interrogation room slowly opened. A big, burly guard stood in the entranceway. His narrowed eyes swept to Lane. Hardened even more. He entered the room with a lumbering stride.

"Time to go back already?" Lane sighed. "Great, well, see you next time, FBI Special Agent—"

"Time to go home," Lark said. She stood in the entranceway now. A wide smile curled her lips.

Lane didn't move. Fear flashed on his face. Fear and hope.

Oliver rose. "Paperwork is finally all done. Just thought you might want all the details before you walked out." Those details mattered because... "Fair warning, there is going to be a media firestorm waiting for you. The reporters will be tossing questions at you left and right when you step outside."

Lane kept sitting at the table.

Lark slowly crossed to his side. She extended her hand. Touched his shoulder.

He flinched.

"Do you like it here or something?" Oliver asked deliberately. "Because some people will do anything to escape."

Lane's lashes flickered.

"You're free," Oliver told him again.

Lane erupted from the chair. He grabbed his sister and hauled her close. Lark laughed and cried and held him just as tightly as he held her.

***

"Done." Oliver dropped his badge on Colby's desk.

Colby looked at the badge, then at him. "You can't be serious."

Dead serious. "You've had all your press conferences. Just as promised, you were the star, and I was the agent who put the wrong man in jail. I'm officially falling on my sword."

"Bullshit." Colby stood, and his chair rolled back with a squeak. "You don't fall on jack. You're the man who killed the rogue FBI agent. Who saved the fiancé who'd gone mad with grief. You exonerated the innocent brother." His chin lifted. "The Deputy Director wants you staying. We all know it's just a matter of time until another serial comes out of the dark."

There would always be another one waiting. "'Whoever fights monsters should see to it that in the process he does not become a monster.'"

"What?"

"Nietzsche said that."

"Well, fucking la-di-da for Nietzsche."

Oliver's lips quirked. "I have something important to do."

"Uh, like stopping a killer *isn't* important?"

"I'll still be consulting with the Feds. I'll make sure the Deputy Director knows I'll be available when he needs me. And there are plenty of good agents in the Bureau. Just because we had—"

"We had one twisted sonofabitch of a killer right beneath our noses?"

Yeah. "You do have a way with words. No wonder you enjoy the press conferences so much. Yes, just because we had him, it doesn't mean the whole Bureau is rotten. Good people work here. People like Theo Tutweiler. Give him a chance to lead a team. He's ready." Oliver thought the guy was more than ready.

Colby's eyes narrowed. "You made a mistake, so now you're scared to hunt again? We were all fooled, not just you."

Wow. Was the guy trying to comfort him? Almost sounded like it. "I did make a mistake," Oliver agreed. "One I can't afford to make again." But he wasn't talking about profiling or working with the Bureau. He was talking about the most important person in his life. "Wish me luck?" He turned for the door.

"Hell, no, I'm not wishing you luck. I wish you'd get your ass back here and be sensible about this. The Bureau needs you. We need—"

He looked over his shoulder. "But I need her."

Understanding flashed on Colby's face.

Oliver's gaze dropped to the wedding ring on Colby's hand. The ring Colby wore every single day. "She's dead, but you can't let her go."

Colby's fingers trembled.

"You had ten years with her. Do you regret them?"

"No." Hoarse. "Best ten years of my life."

Oliver nodded. "I want some good years. I really want to see what they will feel like." He wanted more than darkness.

He wanted Lark. Once more, he faced the door. He opened it. Started to step out—

"Good luck," Colby said quietly.

CHAPTER NINETEEN

There were lots of important moments in life. Each of those moments left a mark on you. Kinda like a scar on the inside. But a good scar.

Some people thought scars were bad. Ugly.

It was really all about perspective. Scars shaped you. Changed you. Reminded you of mistakes that you couldn't make again.

I won't make another mistake with her. I can't.

Oliver sat at the table in the posh restaurant and watched Lark walk toward him. She wore a black dress. Pearl earrings. A delicate pearl necklace around her throat.

A white rope, tightening around her neck...

His breath shuddered out. With an effort, he banished that image from his head. Lark was safe. She was alive.

She was also almost at the table. He hurried to stand. His mom would have been appalled at him for not standing sooner.

Lark smiled at him. "Sorry I'm late. Signing the contract for the new shop took longer than I expected."

Because she was going to open her business again. Get her life back again.

Will she let me be part of that life?

The waiter pulled out her chair. She sat down, all elegance and grace. Oliver sort of fell into his chair.

A frown pulled at her brows. "Oliver?"

"Bring us your best bottle of wine, would you?" he asked the waiter. Then Oliver paused because those words felt familiar.

The whole scene is familiar. Different restaurant. Same woman. Same beautiful woman.

Only in the first scene, her heart had been broken at the end of their meeting. Something she might still not understand? So had his.

"Of course, sir. Be right back." The waiter vanished.

Lark glanced around. He'd picked the restaurant deliberately. Quiet. Dark. No reporters. No true-crime fans hungry to hear more of Lark and Lane's story. Lane had been inundated since his release. The guy had headed out of town for a bit...with Memphis.

Like that wasn't trouble waiting to happen. But trouble for another day.

Lark's green stare came back to him. "You seem...extra intense."

Oh, he was.

"Is something wrong?"

He hoped things might finally be right. Her brother was free. The case was no longer between them. Lark might... "Do you still hate me?"

Her long lashes lowered. The flame from the candle on their table danced. Its light flickered and bobbed. "I thought we covered this," Lark said.

"I'm very sorry about your brother." He needed these words spoken. "You never lost faith in him."

Her lashes lifted. Her hands were in her lap. "You think I didn't wonder? In the deepest, darkest part of me, you think I wasn't afraid?"

You didn't let the fear stop you.

"But I just...I had to keep hoping. I know there are people out there—wives, children, *sisters* and brothers—their loved ones had been arrested. They'd committed terrible crimes. I know it happens. I know the ones we love can hurt us. Just like with Midas."

Well, Midas had actually been *framed* by his father and...

"Lane swore to me that he was innocent. I had to fight for him. I had to try."

"He *was* innocent. Now he's free."

Her smile bloomed. So stunning that he almost forgot to breathe.

Don't get lost in her smile. Stay focused. "You...you didn't answer my question. Do you hate me?"

The waiter reappeared. Brought the wine. Poured it with a flourish. Then he said something. Waited.

Shit. What had the guy said? Oliver had been so locked and loaded on Lark that he hadn't even heard the words.

"No appetizers." Lark sent the waiter her sunny smile. "Could you give us just a moment?"

"Absolutely," he replied. "Take your time."

Oliver shoved his hand into the pocket of his coat.

"He thinks we're breaking up," Lark whispered.

Oliver's heart dropped. "What? We're breaking up?" Were they officially a couple? He'd thought so. She stayed in his bed nearly every night. And when she wasn't there...*I want her to be*. Granted, they'd been apart while he recovered from surgery after his attack, but as soon as the doc had given him the all clear...*I went straight to her*.

Why was she talking about breaking up?

"Is that why you asked me here tonight?" Lark's thick, dark hair slid over her shoulder. "For a breakup? The waiter heard the part about hate but..."

Screw this. Oliver jumped out of his seat and hurried to her side of the table. Then he went down on one knee.

"Oliver?"

He pulled the small box from his coat. A box that he'd owned since the second day he'd met her. Foolish? Obsessed? Probably both. But he hadn't lied to her before—not about how he felt. When he'd walked into that florist shop and seen her, everything changed for him. "You changed my world." A spark when everything had seemed so dark for so long. He opened the box. Light hit the diamond. "I love you, Lark. I want to spend the rest of my life with you." He sucked in a breath. *Don't hate me. Don't.* "Will you give me a chance?"

Her gaze never shifted to the diamond. It remained on his face. "No."

The pain hit him harder than any bullet ever could.

"I don't still hate you. Thought we'd been over this. Sometimes love and hate get all confused." Her hand reached out and touched his cheek. "I'm not confused any longer. I love you completely, Oliver Foxx. And, no, I'm not giving you a chance. I'm *taking* forever with you."

His heartbeat drummed in his ears. "That's a yes." For the record.

"That's a yes."

He let out a yell that had their waiter scrambling toward them. Oliver ignored the waiter. He pulled Lark into his arms and kissed her.

***

The ring fit perfectly. Its weight already seemed natural. A part of her.

A low fire flickered in the fireplace. They'd gone back to Oliver's. Forgotten the meal. She hadn't been in the mood for food. *I want him.*

They were alone. In the room where they'd first had sex.

Fucking?

No, even as wild and hot as it gets between us, it was never really fucking. She'd just been too afraid to call the act what it really was. Making love.

She loved him.

She'd nearly lost him. She'd always remember those final moments with Jase. The feel of the gun in her hand. The sweat on her palm. The terror in her heart. A moment so very like another from her past.

The past had been choking her even as she squeezed the trigger. Fighting a nightmare and fighting to save the man she loved, both at the same time.

The past is over. The nightmare has ended.

The future was what waited.

Her future with Oliver. But first... "You surprised me with the ring." Her back was to him, so she turned slowly to face Oliver as he sat on the couch.

She found his eyes on her. Need stamped into the lines of his face. Lust blazed in his stare.

"I had no idea you were planning to move so fast," she added.

"I'd call it slow. Very, very slow. Because I wanted to propose the day I bought the ring."

"And that was when, exactly?"

"Two days after I met you."

Her heart warmed. "But you had a case to close."

A killer to catch.

"I couldn't propose when I was keeping secrets from you." He rose. "When I was pretending to be someone I wasn't."

Ah, not back to that, was he? When he closed the distance between them, she put her hand on his chest. "Tell me that you're not going to try and convince me that you're still a monster on the inside."

"For you, I'd be a monster in a heartbeat. I'd do anything to keep you safe."

"I'd do the same for you." Didn't he get that? Hadn't he seen that?

"I know." He tucked a lock of her hair behind her ear.

A little shiver skated over her. "I have a surprise, too." One she'd planned especially for him. "I think you're going to like it."

"Sweetheart, I love everything about you."

She rose onto her toes. Her mouth went to his ear. She gave a little lick along the lobe and whispered, "Guess what I'm not wearing?"

He stiffened. "Tell me it's—"

She caught his hand. Pulled it down her body. Pushed it between her legs. "Why don't you tell me?" Breathy.

His fingers had caught the bottom of her dress. He shoved it up and out of the way, and then he was touching—her. Her bare sex. Stroking his fingers between her folds, getting her wet and hot, rubbing her clit, and making her moan.

"Baby, what are you trying to do to me?" Oliver rumbled in his deep, dark, and ever-so-sexy voice.

The same thing she'd tried to do so long ago in this room. "Seduce you."

"You do that by breathing." He bent to kiss her neck. And he pushed two fingers inside of her.

Her hands clamped around his shoulders for balance. "My...ah...*yes, just like that*...my wicked plan was to seduce you—" Lark broke off and trembled because his thumb had just raked so deliciously over her clit. "And make you mine forever."

"I already am. Only yours." His teeth scored her in a sensual bite and his wicked, wicked fingers played as they sent her hurtling toward an orgasm. Just touching. Just stroking. Just— "And I want what's mine." He withdrew his hand. Pulled back.

Left her aching. "*Oliver*."

"Bedroom. I want to spread you out and devour every single inch of you."

That sounded fabulous. They'd do that. After.

She tugged him right back to her. Slid her hand down his body. Rubbed over the big cock that thrust out to her even through his pants. "First, make love to me here." No more talk of fucking. That wasn't what they were about. Even as wild as it could get, it was more. Would always be more. "Right here."

"Baby..."

"Shove my dress out of the way. Right—"

He'd hit his knees before her. He shoved her dress out of the way, but not, as she'd intended, for him to then drive his cock into her. His hands yanked her toward him, and his mouth took her. Fast and strong licks of his tongue.

Her legs opened more. Her hips tilted.

He kept taking.

Her breath shuddered and panted, and she was soon only upright because he held her. As for her orgasm? No way to hold it back. She was coming, and Lark didn't even have the breath to cry out. She was too busy *feeling* the pleasure pour through her.

He rose. Yanked open his pants, freed that big cock, and picked her up.

Her legs locked around him. The orgasm still pounded through her even as he drove into her. Deep, hard thrusts. He lifted her up, then pulled her down against him, and he kept shoving his hips against her.

Over and over.

So good. Better than good. *Fantastic*.

Her arms looped around his neck. Her mouth met his in an open-mouthed kiss even as her sex squeezed him.

No condom. Just him. Just her.

When she came again, he was with her.

"I love you," he told her. "Love. *You*."

***

The bouquet wasn't white. No way in the world would it have been white. She'd thought about not having a bouquet at all, but...

He won't take that from me.

Jase wouldn't destroy something else she loved. Flowers had always been a comfort to her. She would not let him take that comfort away.

But she'd known the bouquet would never, ever be white.

Two weeks had passed since Oliver proposed. Sure, some might say the wedding was too fast. To those people...

I don't care. It's not fast enough for me. Because she would have married Oliver the very night he'd offered the ring to her. Instead, they'd made love until neither of them had been able to move.

"Pretty flowers," Lane murmured.

They were in a small church at the edge of town. Not one of the fast, *Let's-get-married-in-Vegas* places, but a little church she'd visited often over the years.

"Blood red, huh?" His fingers stroked a petal.

He'd been...different since getting out and having his name cleared. Always intense, Lane seemed even more so now. And he'd taken to spending a whole lot of time with Midas and Memphis. Something that should probably worry her.

If she didn't know better, she'd think her brother might be planning to become an Ice Breaker...

Do I know better? She'd revisit that later. She wanted her brother to be safe. To have an easy life now after the pain he'd endured. But...

Easy might not be for him.

Her husband-to-be was already in deep talks with the rest of the Ice Breaker crew. He'd worked out a consulting gig with the FBI. Oliver had lots of dreams. Lots of plans.

So did she.

Her fingers brushed over the flowers. A bouquet of red roses. "Did you know that—pretty much everywhere around the world—a red rose is a symbol of love?" She slowly exhaled. She could hear the music playing. Almost time for her to go out. "But red also means passion." Lark felt plenty of passion when it came to Oliver. "Desire.

Victory." They'd defeated the monster. "And joy." Being with Oliver brought her so much joy.

If they were lucky, they'd know joy for the rest of their lives.

"You don't have to do this, you know." Her brother tucked her hand into the crook of his arm. "We can leave him. Rush out of this place and never look back. I'd take you out. In an instant. If this isn't what you want, I'd run with you—"

She pressed a kiss to his cheek. The silk of her gown slithered softly. "I choose him." Simple. "He's the man I'll spend my life with." What it came down to in the end? "I love him with all my heart."

No running. No rushing out. No leaving Oliver at the altar.

Just loving him. Forever.

"Figured you'd say that." He grimaced. "Just had to make the offer. Big brother thing, you know."

The music grew louder. It was time.

An attendant opened the door. Lark faced forward. Her chin lifted. Together, she and Lane began to walk down the short aisle. Red rose petals had been sprinkled onto the floor. The sweet scent of flowers teased her nose.

She passed Memphis. His wife Eliza. A man named Titan Samson who'd come for the wedding—a friend of Oliver's. More Ice Breakers. A woman named Delilah and her husband Archer—they'd come to town on a private jet. Archer had offered Oliver a whole lot of money to work with the Ice Breakers.

Victims never paid for services with the Ice Breakers. Archer Radcliffe had started bankrolling the whole operation. *After* his wife had cleared him of an old murder suspicion.

There were a few other figures in the church, too. Theo Tutweiler. Shannon Steele. Everett Callen.

Colby Ballard.

Colby sat in the front row. He even smiled at her when she passed him.

She smiled back because...maybe he wasn't so bad. Maybe most people weren't. Once you looked past the masks that everyone wore. Sure, you could go around thinking the world was full of monsters. Monsters *were* out there, after all.

But so were heroes. So were good people.

Her stare drifted to Oliver.

He wasn't smiling. Too much longing filled his face.

Her brother paused with her at the end of the aisle.

Oliver just kept drinking her in.

Sighing, his best man slapped a hand on Oliver's shoulder. "You're supposed to go to the woman," Midas whispered. A loud stage-whisper.

Oliver surged toward her.

"You'd better love her forever. Treat her like a queen each day of her life," Lane said to him. Did Lane *sniff? As in...an almost-cry-sniff?*

"I'll love her until I die," Oliver promised.

"Yeah, well, don't go doing that shit anytime soon," Lane mumbled back. "She likes you breathing. She deserves a happy life."

She didn't wait for Lane to let her go. She pulled her hand from his. Reached out for Oliver. Her hand curled with his. No, that wasn't good enough. She yanked him toward her. Kissed him before there were any vows.

"Lark?" he rasped against her lips.

"I choose you," she told him. "For now and forever. You're mine, Oliver Foxx."

He smiled at her. His dark stare seemed to lighten.

"Now let's get married." Her own smile bloomed as the weight that had been over her shoulders for so long finally lifted.

The past wasn't holding her back.

She'd just taken her future by the hand—and kissed him.

THE END

A NOTE FROM THE AUTHOR

Thank you so much for reading Lark and Oliver's story. I hope you enjoyed their tale!

I am such a true crime addict. I have loved writing about the "Ice Breakers" because their books give me a chance to explore so many mysteries. And, yes, more Ice Breakers are coming your way. I have plans for Midas first...and then, later...well, I think Lane deserves a happy ending, don't you?

If you'd like to stay updated on my releases and sales, please join my newsletter list.

https://cynthiaeden.com/newsletter/

Again, thank you for reading BURIED UNDER ICE.

Best,
Cynthia Eden
cynthiaeden.com

ABOUT THE AUTHOR

Cynthia Eden is a *New York Times*, *USA Today*, *Digital Book World*, and *IndieReader* bestselling author of romantic suspense and paranormal romance. She's a prolific author who lives along the Alabama Gulf Coast. In her free time, you'll find her reading romances, watching horror movies, or hunting for adventures. She's a chocolate addict and a major *Supernatural* fan.

For More Information

- *cynthiaeden.com*
- *facebook.com/cynthiaedenfanpage*

HER OTHER WORKS

Ice Breaker Cold Case Romance

- Frozen In Ice (Book 1)
- Falling For The Ice Queen (Book 2)
- Ice Cold Saint (Book 3)
- Touched By Ice (Book 4)
- Trapped In Ice (Book 5)
- Forged From Ice (Book 6)
- Buried Under Ice (Book 7)

Wilde Ways

- Protecting Piper (Book 1)
- Guarding Gwen (Book 2)
- Before Ben (Book 3)
- The Heart You Break (Book 4)
- Fighting For Her (Book 5)
- Ghost Of A Chance (Book 6)
- Crossing The Line (Book 7)
- Counting On Cole (Book 8)
- Chase After Me (Book 9)
- Say I Do (Book 10)
- Roman Will Fall (Book 11)
- The One Who Got Away (Book 12)
- Pretend You Want Me (Book 13)
- Cross My Heart (Book 14)

- The Bodyguard Next Door (Book 15)
- Ex Marks The Perfect Spot (Book 16)
- The Thief Who Loved Me (Book 17)

Wilde Ways: Gone Rogue

- How To Protect A Princess (Book 1)
- How To Heal A Heartbreak (Book 2)
- How To Con A Crime Boss (Book 3)

Trouble For Hire

- No Escape From War (Book 1)
- Don't Play With Odin (Book 2)
- Jinx, You're It (Book 3)
- Remember Ramsey (Book 4)

Death and Moonlight Mystery

- Step Into My Web (Book 1)
- Save Me From The Dark (Book 2)

Phoenix Fury

- Hot Enough To Burn (Book 1)
- Slow Burn (Book 2)
- Burn It Down (Book 3)

Dark Sins

- Don't Trust A Killer (Book 1)
- Don't Love A Liar (Book 2)

Lazarus Rising

- Never Let Go (Book One)
- Keep Me Close (Book Two)
- Stay With Me (Book Three)
- Run To Me (Book Four)
- Lie Close To Me (Book Five)
- Hold On Tight (Book Six)

Bad Things

- The Devil In Disguise (Book 1)
- On The Prowl (Book 2)
- Undead Or Alive (Book 3)
- Broken Angel (Book 4)
- Heart Of Stone (Book 5)
- Tempted By Fate (Book 6)
- Wicked And Wild (Book 7)
- Saint Or Sinner (Book 8)

Bite Series

- Forbidden Bite (Bite Book 1)
- Mating Bite (Bite Book 2)

Blood and Moonlight Series

- Bite The Dust (Book 1)
- Better Off Undead (Book 2)
- Bitter Blood (Book 3)

Mine Series

- Mine To Take (Book 1)
- Mine To Keep (Book 2)
- Mine To Hold (Book 3)
- Mine To Crave (Book 4)
- Mine To Have (Book 5)
- Mine To Protect (Book 6)

Dark Obsession Series

- Watch Me (Book 1)
- Want Me (Book 2)
- Need Me (Book 3)
- Beware Of Me (Book 4)
- Only For Me (Books 1 to 4)

Purgatory Series

- The Wolf Within (Book 1)
- Marked By The Vampire (Book 2)
- Charming The Beast (Book 3)
- Deal with the Devil (Book 4)
- The Beasts Inside (Books 1 to 4)

Bound Series

- Bound By Blood (Book 1)
- Bound In Darkness (Book 2)
- Bound In Sin (Book 3)
- Bound By The Night (Book 4)
- Bound in Death (Book 5)
- Forever Bound (Books 1 to 4)

Stand-Alone Romantic Suspense

- Waiting For Christmas
- Monster Without Mercy
- Kiss Me This Christmas
- It's A Wonderful Werewolf
- Never Cry Werewolf
- Immortal Danger
- Deck The Halls
- Come Back To Me
- Put A Spell On Me
- Never Gonna Happen
- One Hot Holiday
- Slay All Day
- Midnight Bite
- Secret Admirer
- Christmas With A Spy
- Femme Fatale
- Until Death
- Sinful Secrets

- First Taste of Darkness
- A Vampire's Christmas Carol

Printed in the USA
CPSIA information can be obtained
at www.ICGtesting.com
LVHW031526170124
769198LV00016B/880

9 781960 633590